FIRST
BLOOM

ISBN for print: 979-8-9931817-0-7

ISBN for e-book: 979-8-9931817-1-4

Apple Blossom Press.

Cover design by Amy Hammond.

www.AuthorKatieT.com

 Formatted with Vellum

FIRST BLOOM

UNIVERSITY OF FLOREVALE BOOK 1

KATIE TRAUFFER

For those who dare
to bloom

PREFACE

The curly stalk of sweet pea had journeyed all night to find her.

Wrapping its delicate, arching tendrils around creamy limestone slabs, weaving its way through intricate curls of iron railings, traversing windowed doors still closed in the pre-dawn hours, it climbed.

And climbed.

And climbed.

Princess Aurelia, who insisted the sixth floor had the most spectacular city views, rarely had visitors, but this particular sweet pea was determined.

Onward it grew– seeking, latching, reaching– until it came upon the princess's tidy balcony. There it sprouted two shimmering, iridescent blossoms before at last, deservedly, resting.

14 YEARS AGO

Like most Summoners, Aurelia's magic first appeared in childhood. Unlike most Summoners, whose magic emerged gently– an unexpected cup beside the child's bed or a mismatched sock, some little thing they had inadvertently called up– Aurelia's magic burst forth fully formed and terrible.

She'd been sitting at breakfast with her nurse, Francine, and best friends Jadelynn and Marisol, both the daughters of dukes and cradlemates of the young princess. She loved that dining room with its pink striped walls and crystal chandelier that cast rainbows across every surface. Loved the floral patterned rug with blossoms that opened and closed with every step. Sometimes musicians would come and her and Jadelynn and Marisol would jump from flower to flower like lily pads in a pond, giggling and tripping over one another until they collapsed in a heap.

That morning, the girls were planning a faebunny tea party when her father arrived. His presence wasn't out of the ordinary, but the redness around his kind eyes was. Even though she was only six at the time, Aurelia could still remember the crunch of jam covered toast that turned to dirt in her mouth as he spoke.

"Dearest, you know that mama is away on a trip right now?" he began.

"To Caddlyn," her tiny mouth struggled to form the name of their northern neighbor, Calderith.

"Yes, to Calderith, and she was supposed to be home this morning?"

She nodded, wondering why he was here instead of her mother.

"Her ship was, it was delayed dear."

"Is mama here?"

"No, a storm came and," he sighed and rubbed a hand over his face. "Mama is okay but she was hurt, she'll need to rest for a few weeks before she can travel again."

"Can we go see her?"

"No, dear, I'm sorry, we cannot."

"When will she come back?"

"As soon as she can," he reached out to rub soothing circles on her back as tears welled in her eyes.

"Tomorrow?"

"No, dear."

Her little lips wobbled. Mama had already been gone a month and Aurelia missed her terribly, missed the bedtime stories and the walks through their garden. She closed her eyes, burying her face in her hands. She wanted Mama to come back, to be there right then.

Her father and Francine were talking but she didn't hear their words, the world grew quiet around her. A clock ticked, ticked, then stopped.

Then her friends were screaming, her father's strong arms were scooping her up, she was sobbing.

They were running and then flying and then flailing. She

was wet, her eyes flew open, the room was filling with water. Angry, thrashing, violent water. Storm water. She had Summoned Mama's storm.

AURELIA DIDN'T KNOW how long it had taken the palace magic wielders to calm the waters or repair the damage. She was told that Jadelynn and Marisol had been brought back to their ancestral estates to be with their siblings, but even then she understood it was to keep them away from her.

The dining room had been restored, the broken bones healed, but Aurelia's magic loomed heavily over her crown. And as her magic grew, her life shrank.

CHAPTER ONE

The gentle blue minutes before sunrise were Aurelia's favorite time of day. Waking as the first shafts of light crossed the horizon, she slipped on her plush slippers and wrapped a fluffy blanket around her shoulders. She padded across the room and opened the floor length doors that kept out the almost-autumn chill of her balcony.

Eagerly, if not a bit sleepily, she sat in her favorite woven rattan chair and tucked her knees up to her chest to retain all the body heat she could make.

A sneaking tendril of pothos vine greeted her, winding its way onto the table just as the sun crossed the horizon. The plant carefully placed a steaming mug of coffee before her, the scent mingling with the aroma of baking bread and morning dew that blanketed the city at this hour.

Aurelia shook her head and clucked at the offering. "You know you're not supposed to do that," she whispered.

Sighing, she picked up the mug and added, "But thank you all the same."

The little vine, satisfied, trailed over her hand before meandering back to its place inside the kitchen window.

She took a slow, warming sip as she looked out on the quiet city streets. Today was Aurelia's first day at the Royal University of Florevale, a day that had seemed so far away for so long yet was now, suddenly, here. To others, she would appear to be a typical first year student. Although to say any student of the university is typical is, perhaps, a bit misleading. According to the brochures, memoirs, and historical texts Aurelia had read and reread for years, the Royal University of Florevale was renowned not only for its groundbreaking research and magical advancements, but also for its particular collection of students.

As she looked out on the quiet city, a disbelieving sort of awe settled over her. Convincing her parents, the King and Queen of Serremont, to allow her to pursue this path had been no small feat. It didn't matter how prestigious the school's reputation or how safe living in the city of Florevale was, their conversations had circled entirely on whether Aurelia's magic would be concealed. No one truly expected her to make any progress controlling it, even though that was ostensibly the purpose of her life here. Not even Aurelia. The question was entirely whether anyone would uncover the extent of her magic. The wildness of it.

She was just about to open her journal when she noticed two new pea blossoms tucked into a curl of wrought iron railing. She smiled, stood, and walked over to greet the sweet pea who had somehow climbed all this way. With another half hearted shake of her head and a murmur of gratitude, she plucked the stem. Twirling it between her fingers, she promised to weave it into her braid for luck.

Leaning against the balcony, Aurelia tried to remind herself that no matter how today went, how the semester went, just by being in Florevale, she had accomplished what she set out to do. She knew, however, that even among the assortment of students collected by the university's admissions team, she was a novelty.

While her fellow students were pursuing typical courses of magical study and research, the university had assembled a special team to take on the impossible task of disciplining her magic.

Aurelia took one last look at the city before walking inside. She padded across the smooth oakwood herringbone floors to flip open the music box beside her bed. A gentle thrum of lilting melodies filled the room. Her apartment was small but comfortable. Eggshell walls were framed with boxes of trim and inlaid with plaster cast flowers and vines. Her bed chamber was lined on one side with window-doors that flooded the space with sunlight in the day and with sparkling starlight at night.

Standing before the bathroom mirror, Aurelia slathered a sun protectant moisturizer over her square face down to the dip of her collarbones. She smoothed a hint of shimmer over her wide-set eyes and rosy balm across her full lips, then twisted a few pieces of her long toffee curls with the sweet pea blossoms into a braided coronet.

Aurelia checked the contents of her brown leather satchel, packed the night before, one last time before headed down the long, circling stairs. Her silky green skirt, embroidered with vines of pink roses, brushed her calves with each step. The King had begged her to choose a more modern building in the recently refurbished Trellis district. He said she would miss the ease of their enchanted lifts late at night– although in truth he was mostly thinking of his own aging knees.

But she had insisted on the Shrubs. She had fallen in love with its historic parks filled with pebble lined paths and sculpted topiaries, with the laughter of little ones bubbling from the play gardens around every corner, with the bustling cafés lining the streets. For the past year she had gone to bed every night dreaming of the Shrubs, and even the cleverest of modern magical innovations couldn't replace the hopefulness of her imagination.

"GOOD MORNING," Aurelia called, entering the little boulangerie on the corner. The scent of warm bread and fresh coffee swirled around her.

"G'mornin' dear," replied the nellin behind the counter. Nellins were gentle creatures, short with fluffy ears, glimmering whiskers, and perpetually optimistic outlooks. Despite their small size, they were deceptively strong and hardworking, as evidenced by the heaping trays of pastries, fruit filled hand pies, impossibly beautiful tiny-cakes, and perfectly golden loaves of crusty bread that filled the boulangerie anew each morning.

"What's good today?" Aurelia asked, leaving a few coins on the counter as she made her way over to the orange presser to fill up a glass bottle.

"I'll surprise ya, Lia." The nellin bustled about, collecting treasures and placing them swiftly in a paper bag.

Outside the shop, Aurelia checked her map then headed towards the University. As she walked along the quiet, early morning streets, she opened the bag to find a flaky, buttery, fleuret roll filled with warm chocolate along with two small cheese stuffed egg pies. She was still adjusting to her city name, Lia. For a while, she had debated going by her given name– Aurelia– but decided she should have a totally fresh start in Florevale. Her life in the palace had been increasingly private so she didn't think anyone was likely to recognize her face. And even though the last royal portrait of her hadn't been updated since she turned thirteen, she didn't want to take any chances.

Aurelia knew she would have to return to the palace eventually, but her coronation was still years away. Until then, she wanted to live as normal of a life as she could among her people. And normal for Aurelia meant anonymous, not the royal fanfare and regimented protocol of a someday Queen. Much less a Queen like her.

Aside from the residential quaintness of living in the Shrubs, it had the added benefit of being right next to the University. By the time she had finished her breakfast, she was crossing through the ornate golden gates of the school. Aurelia paused, committing the moment to memory, then stepped forward out of her past and into her future.

CHAPTER TWO

The campus sprawled before her. Tidy paths of smooth whitestone cut avenues for bikes while meandering trails of worn cobblestones stretched in every direction. Pillow-soft grass lawns and colorful flower beds dotted the landscape while fountains bubbled, surrounded by surprisingly comfortable pale green aluminum chairs. It was the kind of place where everyone could find a favorite spot all their own. This early in the morning it was mostly quiet, save the songs of birds flitting tree to tree, the padding of sleep-heavy feet across the cobblestone, and the roll of bicycle tires as unfortunate students stuck with early morning classes began their day.

"Aurelia!" an excited voice clamored, shaking her from her observations.

"Oh!" Aurelia gasped, startled, as she turned to find the source of the voice.

A girl about her age with shoulder length pale blonde hair, cerulean eyes, and blooms of freckles like flowers across her cheeks stood behind her. The girl wore a fashionable blazer of cornflower blue and matching pants pressed with a perfect crease. Her hands were curled around a steaming travel cup of what smelled like bergamot tea, fingers adorned with an array of silver and topaz rings.

"I know, it's supposed to be Lia, but I called your name a few times and I don't think you quite heard me. Don't worry, we'll work on it," the girl said with a smile that was the perfect balance of friendliness and eagerness.

"Oh, right! I'm sorry, yes, I'm still adjusting to this new name, and you must be–" Aurelia paused for a moment remembering back to the letters she had exchanged throughout the summer. The University Chancellor had assigned a student to help with Aurelia's transition to university life and her and Hanielle had hit it off right away, bonding over their shared love of chocolate fleuret rolls and an eerily similar taste in books. Their letters had been the highlight of a summer filled with last minute preparations and negotiations. "And you must be Hanielle. It's so wonderful to put a face to the signature."

"Yes, although my friends call me Elle, and now that you're here, you should too." She linked arms with Aurelia and steered them towards one of the northern pathways.

"Elle," Aurelia repeated, feeling a deep sense of familiarity even though they had never officially met. "Thank you for finding me, beautiful as this campus is, I certainly would have taken at least three wrong turns already."

"Oh trust me, I get lost at least once a week, but that's how my favorite adventures start. Now, what have you done in the city so far? I want to hear all about how your move in went."

THE TWO GIRLS chatted comfortably as they walked through courtyards and past ancient yet pristine buildings, eventually reaching their destination. Before them sprawled Aurelia's last chance to tame her magic: The School for Advanced Graces, Enchantments, and Summonings, or the SAGES, for short.

All the other schools at the Royal University of Florevale followed a specific three year plan of study to help students pursue their interests in one particular area, be it humanities or the sciences or business, but not SAGES. Here each program was crafted to fit the needs, goals, and inspirations of its unusual students. Some studied for as few as two or three years, others for decades before petitioning the University Counsel for graduation.

The SAGES campus was made up of a centralized quad enclosed with magnificent cream-colored stone buildings. Covered walkways of floral mosaic tile were lined with stately two story corinthian columns to shelter students as they strolled the perimeter of the grounds. Hedge-lined pebbled paths led to the tiered fountain in the center of the space while little white tables with blue striped umbrellas dotted the perimeter. And while the formality of the academic buildings lent an air of history and prestige to the space, the blooming gardens, fragrant rose bushes, and shady trees added a welcoming, organic feel to the lawns.

Proudly overlooking it all, the glass domed Plyntharian Library sat peacefully to the north. It was bordered on one side by a meandering path woven between ancient trees. On the other side was a stone patio laden with shady tables and a wall of window-doors encased in climbing roses.

Elle and Aurelia walked beneath the stone arches leading to the SAGES quad, turning left to enter through a quiet side door.

"This is the primary administration building for SAGES," Elle explained as she led them purposefully down the sunny hall. "Here we are." They entered a formal sitting room where an ancient elvish man sat behind an equally ancient looking desk. "Good morning Mr. Scritabella, we're here to see the Chancellor."

Mr. Scritabella nodded and gestured for them to continue through the parlor and out to a private courtyard garden.

Aurelia quietly thanked the elf, who nodded before hurrying off to an anti-chamber.

In the courtyard, Elle and Aurelia sat around a small table in delicate white wrought iron chairs under a wide umbrella. Elle smiled reassuringly at her, but before either could say a word, Chancellor Belthinia walked out, arms thrown wide.

"Princess Aurelia, what an honor it is to have you here at last!" Her laugh lined face spread into a generous smile.

"Thank you Chancellor, it's lovely to meet you," Aurelia replied formally. She stood to shake the woman's hand, her anxiety hidden behind a lifetime of royal training.

Years of private instructors, even the kindest most well intentioned teachers, giving up on her had left Aurelia wary of the initial optimism of academics. Some of her tutors lasted as long as a few weeks, most hardly a month, a few realized their grave over-confidence within just a few days, and every one of them left Aurelia further and further assured her magic had no place in the world.

It had always been a challenge to balance the dire need for Aurelia's instruction with the equally dire need to keep the extent of Aurelia's power– and her lack of control over it– a secret. Aurelia's parents believed the only future worse for Serremont than a magic-less ruler would be a ruler whose magic was out of control. So when it became obvious that mastering her power was not possible for the young princess, precautions were taken.

Aurelia toyed with the golden, rune-inscribed ring on her right hand, the blessing that had allowed her to live freely, albeit magiclessly, for most of her life. Fidgeting with the band was a comforting reminder that her powers were contained and couldn't hurt anything or, more importantly, anyone.

"Now, I know you have worked hard for many years to subdue your power, and perhaps after so many unsuccessful tutors, this may be hard for you to believe," Chancellor Belthinia said empathetically, "but I think if you give yourself and your powers just one more chance, you'll find that this place offers you something you've never had before."

"What's that?" Aurelia replied, still fussing with her ring, uninspired by the one-more-chance pitch she had heard many, *many*, times before.

"A future with magic," Chancellor Belthinia grinned like she was saying something utterly new and groundbreaking.

Aurelia pinched her lips together, deciding how best to answer the Chancellor's enthusiasm. She spied a trailing vine of clematis start to twirl its way up her chair.

"I'll be honest with you, Chancellor," Aurelia said, leaning down to pick the delicate purple flower being offered to her. "I'm out of options. I will not let this magic hurt my people, and as you can see, even the strongest bindings do not seem to be enough to curtail it fully. I would rather be known as a queen without magic than as one without conscience. And left to its own devices, this magic, it's, it's just–" she paused, sighing as she admired the pointed starburst petals in her hand and shook her head. "I'm sorry, I don't mean to say I don't have hope that this will work, I'm here because despite failing everything the palace could come up with, I *do* still have hope. But my magic is dangerous and my people will always come first."

"That's understandable and admirable," Chancellor Belthinia nodded, "but I am a busy woman, this school is a full house, you might say. And I would not have extended the invitation to study on campus and personally overseen creation of your entire instructional team, if I didn't have absolute faith that this place and our people could be different."

Belthinia paused, watching as the clematis wove between Aurelia's fingers. "Speaking of your instructional team, in an effort to ensure the greatest chances for success, we have kept your identity and studies strictly in confidence. Too many cooks in the kitchen and all that," she waved her hand in the air.

Aurelia furrowed her brow, trying to understand what Belthinia was saying.

"Our faculty can be quite... competitive. I believe if everyone knew we had a complex case such as yours in our midst, well they would be climbing over one another to be the one to bring your magic to heel."

"Right," Aurelia hesitated, she had trouble imagining anyone actually wanting to teach her, much less clamoring for the chance to do so, but she supposed Belthinia knew her faculty best.

"To that end, knowledge of your work here has been strictly limited to myself, Hanielle, your advisor who will be coming by later this morning, and your workshop teaching associates. Please inform me before expanding this circle to anyone. Teacher, student, and research assistant alike."

Aurelia nodded, she had absolutely no intention of sharing her identity with anyone.

"Now, let's get to the particularities of your course of study." Belthinia set a stack of folios on the table and began arranging them. "Hanielle, why don't you head to class, Aurelia and I have much to discuss, you can meet her at independent Workshop 812 in oh, say," she paused, looking at her watch, "three hours."

"Yes ma'am!" Elle said brightly to the Chancellor. Leaning closer to Aurelia, she whispered, "You'll do magnificently, and I have just the spot to take you to for lunch." Elle clasped her arm with both hands and smiled encouragingly before hurrying out of the courtyard.

Once Elle had gone, Belthinia turned more seriously to Aurelia. "One more thing, Aurelia, the palace has apprised me of some of your more notable incidents of wayward magic."

Aurelia blanched. She had always assumed the palace kept some sort of records but she felt laid bare. What had these reports said about her magic? What had they said about her?

"I thoroughly reviewed the records regarding the Frostlake incident and wanted to assure you we have taken significant precautions."

Aurelia's blood turned to ice, her chest squeezed, leafy clematis vines snared around and around the base of the table. Twenty years of learning to be a princess had taught her how to boil her panic down to a clench of her jaw, but no amount of training could keep the memories from flooding back.

FROSTLAKE WAS a winter city in the icy mountains of Serremont. Five years ago, one of her tutors decided it would be an excellent place to try out simple Summoning again. It was mostly a holiday town, coming to life every winter for festivals filled with steaming hot chocolate and flourishing night time craft markets. In the frosty summers, though, the town was mostly empty save a small group of year round caretakers. Was.

After settling in, they trekked deep into the snowy forests. Her tutor wanted her to attempt to Summon something small, it was how all Summoning magic was taught— start by Summoning something small and close by that you can see, gradually increase the distance and size. He spotted a small rock and instructed Aurelia to Summon it to her hand.

She obliged, slipping off her gloves then slowly twisting her binding ring down her finger. The barren trees rattled but her tutor encouraged her to keep going. Aurelia desperately wished she had listened to the trees.

There was a thundering crack. She slid her binding ring back in place just in case, but it was too late. She hadn't summoned a rock but rather an avalanche of raging snow and tumbling destruction.

Officially, tourists were told it was an unstable snowpack. Buildings were still being reconstructed, festivals would eventually return. But Aurelia would not.

"AURELIA?" Chancellor Belthinia's voice cut through the memory.

"You were saying something about, about–" Aurelia shook her head to clear the snowflakes, "about protections?"

"Yes, I am aware of how unpredictable experiments with your magic have been in the past."

Aurelia sipped on her tea.

"You will find your cottage has been layered with the most innovative wards known to humans or faeries. This is a safe place for you, Aurelia, I personally guarantee it."

She nodded, biting back a response and reminding herself that she wanted to be here, she chose this.

"The programme?" Aurelia asked, eager to change the topic.

"Yes, let's begin with your group classes." Chancellor Belthinia acquiesced, sliding on a pair of thin gold readers and picking up the first stack.

CHAPTER THREE

By the time they were done going through each of the colorful folios, a tall, impeccably dressed older man with dark brown skin, thick glasses, and a thin smattering of wiry grey hair entered the courtyard.

"Ah, Professor Maillie, perfect timing as always," the Chancellor said, standing to greet the man as he approached.

"May I introduce our newest student to The School for Advanced Graces Enchantments and Summonings." She rested one hand lightly on Lia's shoulder. "Lia, this is Professor Maillie. Professor Maillie, Lia."

Professor Maillie clasped her hand with both of his as he said, "Lia, it is an honor, truly an honor."

"Professor Maillie is the foremost expert in Theoretical Summoning Expansions, he has been studying the limitations of Summoning power for, oh, how long has it been now Maillie, sixty five years? Seventy?"

"Let's just say a long time, Chancellor." Maillie chuckled with a conspiratorial wink towards Aurelia.

"Professor Maillie is going to be your advisor this year, perhaps longer depending on the direction your work leads."

"I'm looking forward to working with you." Aurelia tried to infuse her words with an optimism she didn't quite feel. While Professor Maillie had an obvious warmth about him, a single professor lasting a whole year with her magic sounded highly ambitious and she didn't look forward to watching that enthusiasm fade to frustration or, worse, disappointment. Not again.

"Come, let me show you to your lab, I've been setting it up all through the summer and we have many discoveries to make!" Professor Maillie cheered with a vivaciousness surprising in a man of his age.

Aurelia gathered her folders as Maillie and the Chancellor shook hands once again and the pair were off. As they walked, Maillie handed Aurelia what looked to be a hand drawn map of the quad with arrows and scribbled notes all around.

"Now, I took the liberty of making this map for you. Our quad here at SAGES is smaller than the others, but the consequences of wandering into the wrong lab can be quite a bit more troublesome than among the other schools," he said, leading them out to the quad and toward the northeast quarter. "When I was a student here, I once mistook theater twelve for theater twenty-one and walked right into the lab of a senior level Aviary Enchantments masterclass. Ended up with one fully functional sparrow wing for nearly two weeks. Every time I stepped with my left foot it would give a little flutter."

Aurelia nodded along, chuckling despite herself when Professor Maillie did a little hop for emphasis. They reached the corner between the glass domed library and another building. On Maillie's map this building was covered in so many tiny notes and warning signs that Aurelia guessed it was home to the infamous Enchantment theaters.

Maillie led them along a winding pathway that stretched far beyond the main quad, looping back and forth behind the library. It was dotted with dozens of unique workshops, some shaped like houses or cabins, some more novel in design. There were structures as tall as the trees made of glass or wood or even netting while others were little more than entryways to underground burrows with round doors and mossy hills.

"The Enchanters and Gracers prefer to work in community, so they're housed in the Eastward Dumathieu and Westward Troivillen buildings. Us Summoners, however, have to be a bit more careful about confining our experiments."

The occasional student walked around them; Maillie's pace was much closer to a meander than a purposeful stride. Aurelia didn't mind, though, as she wondered what novelties lie within each cottage they passed.

"Classes with your peers are held in the larger buildings, but each student is assigned a smaller workshop for their independent work. Yours is just this way."

The path curved around a bend and Aurelia gasped. Before her stood the most beautiful garden house she had ever seen. Two floors of cream limestone were accented with long robin's egg blue shutters and topped with a gently sloped clay tile roof. Six sets of tall windows lined the front, three on the first floor and three on the second. An assortment of embellished knee high pots filled with blooming rose trees and manicured shrubs welcomed her to the main door. On the second level, a dainty balcony adorned with climbing ivy gated the center set of windows. To the right, a friendly beech tree swayed, casting speckled shadows across the house. The trellised roses to the left took notice of her, new blooms unfurling eagerly as she and Maillie approached.

"Ah," Maillie grinned, seemingly unconcerned by her unintentional display of magic, "it seems the shop, or at least the gardens, have taken a liking to you already."

Aurelia twirled her binding ring, wondering if it was time for the enchantments to be redone already, but quickly relaxed.

It was nearly impossible to be worried in a space this peaceful and inviting.

Just as they crossed the threshold, two faeries stepped forward in tandem. They were taller than Aurelia with the long, willowy limbs and radiant golden skin typical of their kind. Large intricate wings were tucked neatly against their backs, catching the light as they walked. Despite the inherent faerie similarities, though, these two could not be more different. The faerie on the left was nearly vibrating with excitement, the curls of his toffee hair lifting in an invisible breeze, wide amber eyes crinkling at the corners. Meanwhile, the faerie on the right stood with an other-worldly stillness, her light, strawberry blonde hair pinned neatly into an intricate bun and she had a notepad clasped closely in her arms.

"Lia, may I introduce our wonderful teaching associates for Workshop 812, Clem and Fiora." Clapping the male on the shoulder in friendly encouragement, Maillie continued, "Clem here runs our garden labs, everything growing outside around your workshop was nurtured by his hands. He'll oversee all your outdoor education and experimentation."

Clem's eyes sparkled, his feet just barely skimming ground as he stepped forward. "Princess, it is such a joy to finally meet you. We've been preparing all summer and I have so much to show you!"

"Clementine!" the other exclaimed in a burst of icy frustration. "We talked about this!"

"Yes, yes," Clem said, firmly shaking Aurelia's hand, "Lia, it's a joy to meet you, *Lia.*"

"It's lovely to meet you too, Clem," Aurelia replied, delicately extracting her hand. "And that means you must be Fiora," she turned to the pink-haired faerie who was glaring daggers at Clem.

"Yes, and I apologize for my brother, I have reminded him

we must use your school name no less than a hundred times this week alone," she said, a hint of embarrassment cracking the edges of her stiff countenance. She bowed discreetly, her attention still split between Aurelia and watching out for whatever Clem might do next.

"Fiora will instruct you in our indoor labs and theories of advanced summoning. She also maintains the wards protecting this workshop, ensures everything inside is kept in ideal working order, and" Maillie's voice dropped conspiratorially, "she keeps a stash of the city's *best* shortbread cookies. If you know where to look, that is."

Fiora sighed, momentarily forgetting the formality of the moment to glare at Clem once again. "Well if someone would stop eating them all before noon I wouldn't have to hide them."

"Hey, if they're out on the counter how am I supposed to know they're not for me?" Clem asked with exaggerated innocence. Aurelia laughed at the two, their banter putting her at ease, whether intentional or not.

"Clem, why don't we head outside and get to work, Fiora dear, you can take Aurelia on a tour of the house, I know it's a lot of new places and people so we'll plan a tour of the gardens for tomorrow. I would also like Lia to get started on preliminary readings."

"Yes, I pulled the texts you requested from the library, Professor. I'll pack them up for her before lunch."

"Excellent, excellent," Maillie said, turning to walk out the back doors, "Clem, come along, I want to see your progress with those double winter tulips."

"See you later, Lia! Don't worry, Fiora's only a brat to me, she'll take good care of you!" Clem said with a wink then jogged two airy strides to catch up with Maillie.

"Don't pay him any mind," Fiora gritted out. "Now, there's much to catch you up on, let's get started."

Aurelia looked around, adjusting her bag on her shoulder. "Inside? Really? Most of my tutors preferred to find the most desolate locations, places of rock and decay where my magic would do the least damage, or where the damage wouldn't be noticeable at least."

Fiora humphed indignantly. "Well, then I have good news for you, Lia."

"Already?"

"Yes, you see, we've already answered one of my most pressing questions: why all your previous training failed. And it would turn out that it's because," she chuckled, "your teachers were all stubborn fools."

Aurelia was now deeply confused and more than a little taken aback. She had worked for fourteen years, dutifully followed the instruction of every scholar her parents brought in. She had been so alone in her failures again and again, and here was Fiora, two hours into the first day, laughing at her.

Seeing the distraught look on Aurelia's face, Fiora quickly stopped laughing and reached out towards her. "No, oh, no, I'm not laughing at you. I was laughing because isolation is the exact wrong approach, that's everything that would make your magic spin into chaos. You have done nothing wrong Lia, I'm sorry, I wasn't being clear."

"I don't understand," Aurelia said, appreciating the apology but still feeling a renewed need to be cautious.

"Come, forget the tour, there's plenty of time to explore later. I'll make you some tea and we'll talk. Please, give me a chance to explain."

Aurelia nodded hesitantly and followed Fiora through a wide archway into a quaint kitchen. Typically Aurelia would appreciate the elegant coziness of the space, the golden light pouring in through the wide open glass paneled doors, the way the light made the grey and white diamond checkered floor sparkle. She would notice the warm white oak cabinets lining the wall, the oversized white basin sink under the window, a row of herbs growing merrily along the sill. But not today. She took an uneasy seat at the marble countertop, resting her bag on the woven rattan bar chair beside her, and watched as the carved lines of her ring shimmered.

Fiora set a kettle on the stovetop and stood there for a moment, that ethereal faerie stillness settling over her. She took a deep breath and, without turning, asked "Lia, what have you been taught about magic?"

It was a broad question, one Aurelia wasn't sure how to approach. She was taught what everyone was taught, what answer was Fiora looking for?

"Well," she began, "I know there are three types of magic–Enchantments, Graces, and Summonings. My magic is the latter, the Summoning type." She thought back to her favorite tutor, Mrs. Tallywell, how her colorful earrings would tinkle with an erratic wind-chime melody as she twirled from chalkboard to chalkboard, explaining the colorful diagrams drawn on each. She had stayed with Aurelia nearly six months.

"Enchanters use their magic to alter an object, their magic sort of," Aurelia squinted into the past, "covers the object, adjusting its perceived nature."

Fiora rummaged through the cabinets, but paused when Aurelia stopped talking, so she pressed on.

"Graces are the magically gifted, perhaps in music, or woodworking, they have an ability that's far beyond that of a typical person. Their powers are more than skill, though, because if the Grace is strong enough they can influence the emotions and even actions of others who see or experience their work."

Fiora found what she was looking for and began arranging jars of leaves and colorful petals on the counter. Steam started to waft from the kettle behind her as she measured bits from each of the jars into the porcelain straining dish. Aurelia watched, fascinated by the precision of Fiora's long fingers.

"And then there's Summoners, like me." Aurelia bit out the words. "Our powers draw items to us. We don't create new things, we only shift around what already exists. At least, that's how it's supposed to work. My own lessons in summoning have mostly resulted in, well, there's a reason I wear this binding ring. The few times I've tried even the simplest of summonings there have been unexpected consequences." The hiss of the tea kettle reached a crescendo.

Fiora poured the hot water over the leaves, a sweet jasmine scent lifting immediately.

"Lia, I will start giving you answers soon and I think what I have to say might offer you a measure of," Fiora paused, considering her words now, "comfort." She arranged a few small, square, shortbread cookies around the mug, her nimble hands placing it silently before Aurelia.

"But first, have you always had human teachers? Or did the court ever employ other folk? A faerie or elves, perhaps? Dwarves even?"

Aurelia thought back, it was a painful memory she didn't especially care to remember.

"Once," she replied, "an elvish man, old, even for their kind, but he didn't work out. He was," she picked up the cup, savoring its comfort and warmth. "He was scared of me. It was just after my first binding ring. He picked up my hand, examined the ring for a few minutes, then looked into my eyes and was gone."

"I see," said Fiora. "And I'm sorry for how that hurt you. There is much I would like to explain and now the readings Professor Maillie pulled for you make much more sense."

"Aurelia, what I'm going to teach you might be hard to wrap your head around, being raised as you have with the so-called teachers you had. Eat a cookie, it will help." Fiora said this last part so matter of factly, Aurelia couldn't help but laugh a little, the spell of melancholy broken.

"Humans have one perspective on magic, us folk have another. That's what drew me to the University, the humans here are more open minded, more willing to be curious and explore. It's what allows researchers like Clem and myself to make so much progress, to uncover such incredible new truths."

Fiora pulled up a stool to Aurelia's side of the counter and sat.

"Magic is inherently only one entity, one force. The three divisions you mentioned– Summoning, Gracing, Enchanting– they're how you humans understand magic because that's how your kind express power. But magic has no form, no limitations, it's shaped by the unique characteristics of the being who wields it. The magic of the faeries, the magic of a rosecat or a dwarf or a nellin or you, it's all the same on the most fundamental level. It's the expression of the magic that gives it shape and it's the unique makeup of the creature that determines the expression."

"We have centuries of research here at the University to back this up, you'll start reading about it tonight. With magic as powerful as yours, I don't think you'll be able to control it in any way until you have a fundamental understanding of what power truly is."

"I thought you said you had good news" Aurelia muttered, dabbing her mouth politely as cookie crumbs fell from her fingers.

"Yes, the good news is we have the resources, texts, and methodologies to handle your power and to help you. We will not run from you or your ability. It doesn't scare me and it doesn't scare Clem and someday it won't scare you."

Aurelia was surprised that Fiora had seen her so clearly, especially when she had been so brusque just minutes ago. Fiora busied herself putting away the canisters as Aurelia took a last sip of her tea. She was determined not to let the feelings of defeat that had followed her for so long take this time or this place from her. She let her eyes close and took a deep, steadying breath.

That's when she noticed the soft ring of chamomile flowers encircling her wrist. The pot of it on the counter had stretched to reach her with its fine needle-like leaves. She wondered how much of her relief was her own doing and how much might be from the embrace of this sweet young plant.

Fiora followed Aurelia's eyes to the bracelet, "I was wondering when you'd notice the offering."

"They're always so kind to me," Aurelia replied gently, tears welling in her eyes that she quickly blinked away. Feeling strengthened by the plant's gift, she said, "Okay, tell me more."

Just as Fiora was about to continue, Elle burst through the doorway. The chamomile retreated.

"Lia, have you seen this place?" she asked, turning in circles as her eyes flitted around the room. "Oh, hello Fiora, you've done such a lovely job here."

Fiora nodded back with a formal smile and a quiet thank you as Elle continued, "I mean, you're sitting in it so I'm sure you've seen it but, Lia, have you seen it!"

Aurelia laughed, wiping her eyes, the mood instantly brightened with Elle's sunny presence. "Not much yet, we were going to take a tour but had a little change of plans, perhaps we can all go now?"

"Actually," Fiora said, "it's mid day, you two should head to lunch before afternoon classes. Only give me a moment, I'll go fetch those books for you." She was off before Aurelia could reply.

Elle was still gawking at the kitchen, admiring the small paintings and trinkets lining the open shelves. "Don't get me wrong, I love my workshop dearly, but this is just magnificent!"

"I would love to see your workshop, will you show me sometime?" Aurelia asked, walking her plate and mug to the sink. She turned a brass knob to release the hot water for washing and picked up a dried round of scrubbing loofah.

Elle leaned against the counter beside her, tipping her head back and closing her eyes as the warm light of the sun streamed in through the open window. A light floral scented breeze rustled the sheer linen half curtains framing the opening.

"Of course, of course." Her voice was softer, caught in the moment. "Designing my workshop was a highlight of my first year here. It's one of the first year traditions for SAGES Summoners. There's special cases, like you, of course. But for most of us, we start with a base plot and work on it throughout the year, making adjustments and improvements with every new skill we master. The Enchanters and Graces think we just call up finished products easy peasy, but they don't realize how nuanced Summoning can be."

"Hmm, what do you mean?" Aurelia thought of her own cataclysm of magic, just trying to hold it steady was impossible enough, she couldn't imagine building something with it.

"Oh, you'll learn all about it in Practical Summoning this semester." Aurelia's stomach bottomed out, would she have to perform magic in front of others? In public?

Seeing Aurelia's eyes go wide, Elle quickly continued, "Don't worry, it's a theory only class. We're taught the methodology but then sent to our own workshops to test it out. Wouldn't want a room full of Summoners flying in pallets of wood and nails all at once!"

Aurelia gave a half hearted chuckle and wrung out her clenched hands. Maybe she did need to have a little more faith in the plans the school had made for her.

Just then Fiora appeared, statuesque in the doorway, two books in her hands. "Here we are, your first readings. Professor

Maillie would like you to finish both texts by the end of the week, be sure to take notes and bring back questions. We have much to discuss tomorrow." She handed over the books, giving Aurelia a ghost of a smile before bowing slightly and retreating back up the stairs.

CHAPTER FOUR

E lle led Aurelia back through the windy pathways towards the main quad of the SAGES.

"There's no shortage of amazing cafés in Florevale, but my favorite of all is actually right here on our campus. It's tucked away on the other side of the library." Elle gushed as they walked around the glass domed library towards a sunny blue-stone patio. Four enormous white scalloped umbrellas stood over rectangular wooden tables. Each was surrounded with six of the rattan chairs so common throughout the city. This partic-ular batch was cream toned mixed with a cheery rose color that perfectly matched the bushy climbing roses lounging over the wide open doorway.

"This is lovely," Aurelia breathed as Elle led them inside. Before them stood a long white bartop covered in an array of trays and cloches. Flakey pastries, a rainbow of vegetable packed sandwiches, and gigantic chocolate laden cookies stretched the length of the counter. Behind them, glossy blush tiles lined the back wall and a second work counter housed a bevy of coffee machines, tea canisters, and a kaleidoscope of glass syrup bottles.

"If you think it's a welcoming sight now, just you wait. When it's one in the morning and you've been reading the same two sentences for the last twenty minutes, this café and their almond vanilla lattes are an actual lifesaver. I think I heard angels singing every time I walked in during finals last year."

"Okay but tell me more about these almond vanilla lattes," Aurelia begged as they stood in line to order. The line was short but gave her enough time to survey the space. Against the side walls, deep booths sat with thick, striped cushions and glass-topped work tables. Cozy couches and deep arm chairs in the center of the room alternated with two and four person tables in a haphazard yet charming collection. It was the kind of space that had been arranged and rearranged a hundred times to fit whatever need arose.

"What'll it be today, Elle?" a deep voice asked, breaking through Aurelia's observations. A moment of panic washed over her. She had been so busy taking in the space she hadn't even looked at the menu.

Elle noted her indecision. "Two iced almond vanilla lattes, one of those melted brie and arugula sandwiches, the one with the avocado, and a mozzarella tomato sandwich, and a plate of those little sandwich cookies too. Thanks Adrian!"

Elle looked to Aurelia with a smile, "Hope you don't mind, I ordered my favorites and we can share them, my treat since it's your first day."

"Who's your friend?" Adrian said as he rang them up, his grey blue eyes meeting Aurelia's for a moment through black rimmed glasses. He was at least a head taller than both the girls, wearing a black button-up shirt rolled to the elbows that showed off his muscled forearms. Dark, loose curls of hair hung over his forehead as he punched a few keys on the register.

"This is Lia, it's her first day at SAGES. She's studying under Professor Maillie."

"Maillie, he's a funny one, brilliant though. You must be doing something special, Lia, it's nice to meet you." He reached over the counter to shake Lia's hand. Her eyes darted from his hand engulfing hers to the curl of his lips then back to his eyes. His gaze was waiting for her.

"Nice to meet you too," she said, heat rising to her cheeks as she drew her hand back. "And nothing special just yet, I think it will be a lot of reading for a while."

Elle looked between them before patting Aurelia's arm. "Lia, you wait here for the food, I'll go scope out a table for us outside."

Adrian buzzed around behind the counter as he replied, "Well, Apple Blossom is the perfect spot for that. We're open twenty four hours a day, seven days a week. Not me personally, I mean, but the café." He scooped their order onto mismatched porcelain plates and measured out syrups into glass cups with practiced motions.

"That's great to know! Are you a student here too?" Lia asked, following his tall form along the counter as she watched the easy way he pulled everything together.

"Mhmm, I've been studying stoichiomancy with Professor Olyeider for the last two years."

"Stoich, storry, stoil," she struggled to make her mouth say the unfamiliar word, bringing further pink to her cheeks.

Adrian laughed, his full lips lifting into an easy smile, "Stoichiomancy, I know, it's a mouth full. In a nutshell it's a magically enhanced study of elements but I'm specifically trying to discover the limits of how sophisticated a Summoner's magic can be on a microscopic level."

"That sounds incredibly complex," Aurelia replied, taking the finished drinks he offered and trying to figure out how to carry them and the plates.

"Here, let me." Adrian came around the bar with the sandwiches and cookies easily balanced on his arm. He opened the door, letting Aurelia walk through to the patio before following.

"Over here!" Elle called. She waved to them from behind enormous black sunglasses, perched at one of the tables like a cat in the sun.

They set the plates and drinks down, Aurelia all too aware of Adrian's presence next to her.

"Aww, thanks Adrian. Sorry Lia, I should have realized it was a lot to carry."

"No sweat, Elle, see you later, Lia." Adrian said, running a hand through his hair and grinning before turning.

Aurelia watched as he loped back inside before noticing Elle smirking at her.

"What's that look for?" Aurelia asked innocently.

"Oh, nothing, nothing at all." Elle crooned with a mischievous glint. Passing over one of the sandwich halves she said, "Now, try this."

Aurelia unsuccessfully tried not to blush as she took a bite. Words utterly failed her. The melty cheese, the creamy avocado, the tangy arugula, and that warm, nutty bread. It was perfect.

Elle laughed at Aurelia's speechlessness and the two ate in happy, contented silence listening to the joyful chatter and rustling pages of the students around them.

AFTER LUNCH, Elle brought Aurelia back across the quad to her first group class, Summoning in the Natural World. Students lounged on the grass all around as they walked. Some sat on blankets, notebooks cradled in their laps, others laid out, books sitting over their noses to shield their sun-groggy faces.

"I really appreciate all the time you've spent to make me

feel welcome here," Aurelia said. "Not just today, all summer too. This campus would have been so intimidating alone but because of you it already feels familiar."

"I hope you're not saying that to get rid of me, this isn't some 'thanks but I'm good' speech is it?"

"Of course not! But I understand if you have other things you need to do."

"Nonsense, if I wanted to do something else, I would. I love this place and I love welcoming new students into a world that means so much to me. This is a big school in an even bigger city, finding the nooks and spaces that feel like your own makes all the difference. Besides, we're going to be good friends, I have a sense about these things."

"In that case," Aurelia smiled, "want to get lunch together again tomorrow?"

Before she could even voice doubt, or give Elle an out like, 'it's okay if you're busy' or 'it's okay if you have plans with someone else,' Elle threw an arm around Aurelia and said "I was just about to ask you the same thing. Now, off to class you go."

Aurelia's face lifted in her brightest smile all day, the tulips along the path leaning towards her as if her joy was, in fact, the sun. She was so happy about her new friend, who was truly a friend now and not just a tour guide or penpal, that she entirely forgot to be nervous for her first group class. That was, until she gazed up at the building before her and remembered what she was about to do.

The lecture hall was nothing like her own charming lab. A large set of stone steps led up to a glass enclosed antechamber where a host of students milled about. Aurelia, feet dragging, had just reached the top stair when doors opened to the room beyond.

Students streamed in quickly, their steady chatter dropping lower. Aurelia followed silently. The inner chamber was a large square theater with arena style seats on three sides. Students took spots along the ten levels leading down to the bottom where a man stood scanning the room amid a jungle of plants.

Aurelia clenched her fists tight, as if her binding ring would leap from her body, ripping her magic free along with it. She slipped cautiously into the back row.

"Welcome to the University of Florevale, Summoners, I am Professor Tillgartem" the man's gruff voice instantly quieted the room. "As our newest SAGES students, you are, no doubt, eager to begin pursuing your course of study. The future of magic is in this room, and I am sure you all think I'm referring to you when I say that." A few nervous chuckles bounced off the walls, unsure if it was meant as a joke or an admonishment. The flash of Tillgartem's shadowed black eyes made Aurelia certain it was the latter.

"Look around you," he paused to allow them to glance side to side, "the power within these walls is immense."

Aurelia tried to sink lower in her chair, hoping no one would notice the way potted honeysuckle behind the instructor was starting to send out a lazy, curious branch in her direction.

"Everyone in this room is formidable, that's why you're here. Everyone in this room has the potential to revolutionize the study and practice of magic." He paused again, letting his words hang over them before continuing. "And everyone, and I do mean everyone, has a lot to learn and unlearn before being unleashed on the world." Not one hint of friendliness lined the stocky professor's face, and this time, no one laughed.

"Until I'm confident you lot won't summon a horde of hungry weirmutts, or crush yourself under a palette of bricks, and yes, both of those have happened in this very room, magic in this class will be strictly barred."

The professor's edict, and the condescension of his delivery, were met with disquieted murmurs, deep huffs of frustration, and, for just the secret, solitary princess in the back row, a sigh of relief.

"To that end, you may have felt a slight pressure as you walked through the front door, at least I hope you did with the resumes you lot sent in. It was a binding umbrella, go ahead and try to use your powers, I wish you luck against the restraints of Norwish spellmanship."

A few students in the room clearly tried, whether out of a previously unshaken self assurance, or just mild curiosity. Aurelia trained her eyes on that woody arm of honeysuckle, begging it to turn around before anyone else noticed its slow but steady progress.

"Professor Tillgartem?" An airy, high pitched voice called out from the center of the second row. "We came to SAGES to further our Summoning abilities. I assure you, none of us are going to cause a catastrophe in your classroom. Isn't a Norwish Binding Spell a bit extreme?"

"Extreme, you ask? Miss...?"

"Pennylynn, sir, Lady Pennylynn Tublerice of Clouch-ester," she said with a shake of her pristine hazelnut bob.

"Well, Miss Tublerice, seeing as my sweet old honeysuckle here, a particular variety who scarcely climbs a foot each year, has travelled the length of my arm in the last ten minutes, I would say someone in this room is exceptionally powerful. And as it's an utterly inappropriate time for such a Summoning, their magic is clearly not under control." More murmurs broke out around the room as the professor, with a gentleness certainly not reserved for his students, kneeled down to twine the new branch around the trellis with the rest of its arms.

"Clearly, you all should be glad for the binding spell" Tillgartem continued, and then more to himself added, "and clearly I need to go speak with Horace about amplifying the ward." He picked up a stack of paper packets and half-handed, half-dropped them to a student in the first row.

"Now if we're done questioning my methods," he looked Pennylynn squarely in the eye and no one dared to snicker at her misfortune. He picked up one of the packets from his own lectern and continued, "let's review what we'll actually be doing this semester."

CHAPTER FIVE

Tillgartem spent the rest of class talking over the syllabus; Aurelia spent the time trying not to make eye contact with anything living in the auditorium, be it the professor, the plants, or her fellow students. After what he said to Pennylynn, she was confident he'd call her out as the wayward Summoner if he'd known, but she didn't want to take any chances. The seminar was a weekly class so it was supposed to be three hours of lecture time but Tillgartem, whether by mercy or resignation, let them out after just two.

Aurelia bounded out the doors before most of her classmates had even stood from their desks. She hurried down the path, away from the building until the fresh air of the campus at last lowered her thundering pulse. As she walked back towards the quad, she wondered how it could possibly still be her first day. She chose a sunny green chair beside the fountain and propped her feet up on its edge.

A friendly butterfly danced around her hand and she held her palm out for the tiny message it carried. With a graceful swoop, it dropped an impossibly light curl of petalpaper and fluttered away.

Aurelia unrolled the message, the outside was nondescript but inside she recognized her mother's personal rose and crown insignia.

Our Dearest "Lia,"

You are on our hearts today. We hope your first day of classes is beautiful, exciting, and productive. We look forward to hearing about your progress and seeing you when you visit home.

All our love,

XX

Aurelia tucked the note into her bag. She was glad for their encouragement but after the failures of not just one but two high level Norwish binding spells already, she wasn't sure how to reply without letting them down.

Sighing, she tipped her head back to welcome the warmth of the sun on her cheeks. She would simply stay here as long as they let her. This was such a large school, it would have to take at least a year or two before the university ran out of faculty to set against her impossible magic.

As Aurelia let the campus' peacefulness soak into her bones, she pulled out the first of the books Fiora had given her. She tried to read the first page, she truly did. But when the chime of the five o'clock bell lifted her from her sun-soaked reverie, she realized she had not actually turned a single page.

Shaking the sleepiness from her arms in a satisfying stretch, Aurelia consulted her weekly schedule. She had no classes on Tuesday and wasn't due in the workshop until the afternoon so she decided she would try again first thing tomorrow morning. *Well, maybe not first thing*, she thought, letting out a very un-princess-like yawn as she gathered her belongings.

AURELIA'S APARTMENT was a welcome embrace when she at last made it home. She'd spent all summer drawing layouts, selecting furniture, sourcing fabrics, and collecting decor. Her parents had even allowed her to bring some of her favorite art to adorn the walls- soft pastoral paintings with small, emotion laden brush strokes that emphasized the facets of light in the scenes.

Aurelia had chosen to keep the walls a soft cream color but added romantic, floral drapes surrounding the twin pairs of window-doors. A large stone fireplace sat in the middle, topped with an ancient brassy gold mirror. Aurelia had been particularly persnickety about the oversized blue-patterned reading chair and ottoman situated between the matching couch and the terrace doors. She had always loved reading, but this summer it took a backseat to daydreaming. Aurelia had spent more time imagining how she'd read in this chair, doors thrown wide, the sounds of the city wafting up to her, than actually reading itself.

Slipping off her shoes, Aurelia lit the candles scattered around the room and opened the terrace doors. With a satisfied sigh, she sank down into the chair to watch the last trails of purple-pink clouds drift across the twilight sky.

THE NEXT MORNING Aurelia woke before the sun. She got out of bed at the first chirp of her music box, blissfully rested from a night of cozy reading and bathing in her clawfoot soaking tub. Aurelia wasn't always a morning person but she could be when needed and on this day, she was most definitely a morning person.

She brushed her teeth, wound her hair into a twisted knot atop her head, and slipped on sky blue, butter smooth leggings with a perfectly matched cropped tank. Comfortable sandals, a tiny crossbody bag for her keys, a pouch of sun dried dates with salty cashew nuts, and a truly gigantic water bottle completed the look.

As she walked out the front door of her building, she waved to the Nellin already hard at work in the boulangerie across the street and wondered if they slept at all. Aurelia breathed in deeply, the floral, bready scent of the city this early clearing the last of the sleepiness from her limbs. Her destination was a small studio just two blocks away where the cool morning air gave way to glorious, humid warmth.

"Good morning," Aurelia greeted the serene looking woman seated at the counter inside the studio, "I'm Lia, it's my first class and I was hoping there's room?"

"Yes of course dear! Welcome to Peace Lily Studio, we always have room for more here thanks to an old Enchanters trick my partner came up with years ago. Just leave your shoes in the cubby by the door, we have mats and towels against the wall, and down the hall there's a locker room to store your things and freshen up after class. We'll be in Studio One this morning and you'll need two blocks."

Aurelia thanked her, eager to explore the space. She stowed away her shoes and picked up supplies, pausing in the studio to unroll her mat in a spot near the windows before making her way to the changing area to stow her bag.

The locker room was a masterpiece of serenity. Overhead, the entire ceiling was covered in triangular skylights that Aurelia imagined would bathe the room in the most beautiful light. Rows of neat wooden lockers, painted white and encased in simple white trim, sat across from a long marble countertop. A personal mirror perched at each bench seat. Around the corner, private shower stalls of gleaming pale blue porcelain tile were stocked with thick white towels and an assortment of hair and skin products. Aurelia made a mental note to bring a change of clothes with her next time so she could take advantage of the beautiful space.

Distracted by her self-guided tour of the room, Aurelia didn't notice a person walking by behind her until she had nearly run the poor girl over.

"Oh! I'm so sorry, are you okay?" She grabbed onto the girl's muscled arm in an attempt to steady them both. She was around the same height as Aurelia and looked to be close to her age too with a waterfall of shiny chestnut hair, golden skin dotted with sun-kissed freckles, and a kind, heart shaped face.

"You're fine!" the girl laughed, righting herself. "First time?"

"How'd you know?"

"We all get that look the first time we see the locker room here, it's Florevale's best kept secret." The girl leaned in conspiratorially, "Did you find the patchouli sauna yet? It's right behind that row of lockers over there." She pointed down a row Aurelia hadn't seen yet.

"Oh! Thank you! I'll look for it next time, um," Aurelia trailed off and the other girl smiled and extended her hand.

"Darya."

"Darya," Aurelia repeated, "I'm Lia."

"Nice to meet you Lia. Well, I'll see you in there."

After class, Aurelia lingered on her mat in the heat for a while. It felt so good to move her body in the familiar shapes and patterns but she had never taken a class with other people before, let alone a mix of people, faeries, elves, and others. Back at home, she had either practiced herself, or with private instruction, but she loved the way the group today had moved and breathed and sweated all in unison.

The sun had just come up to the merry encouragement of the city's songbirds when Aurelia stepped out to the street. She took an exceptionally long drink of her water bottle, thankful for its gargantuan size. Just as she was about to start walking, Darya stepped out beside her.

"So what'd you think?" Darya asked, pulling a grey sweatshirt over her head, hair still damp from the showers.

The two girls began walking in unison as Aurelia replied, "It was otherworldly, I wish I could do that every day!" She looked over to Darya, recognizing the SAGES insignia stitched across her chest.

"Oh! Do you attend SAGES too? I'm a first year Summoner."

Darya took a long drink of her own water bottle before replying, "Yes! I'm an Enchanter, I've been there for about three years now researching magical ways to manage anxiety. It's tricky because stress manifests differently for everyone and so what lowers stress for some people might actually increase it for others. Someday I want to be able to enchant crystals that, when activated by mindfulness or physical activity or whatever other anti-stress tools we isolate, would then amplify the mind's natural abilities to soothe. I've been working with a team of mindmendors from the main campus. It's slow but exciting work and I think it will really help people some day."

"Wow! That sounds remarkable, I could think of a few times just yesterday I would have loved something like that." Aurelia wondered if she had shared too much with this girl she had only just met.

"Me too! I had to present my summer work in front of the entire Enchanter's track yesterday, it's a first day tradition and I'm not such a fan of speaking in front of large groups."

Aurelia nodded, relieved Darya felt the same, and pointed to the building ahead, "Well, this is me, but it's been lovely walking with you, thank you for making me feel so welcome at class today."

"Oh no way! I live just around the corner with my room-mate," Darya said, pointing in the direction of the University, "I usually try to go to the morning class on Tuesdays and Fridays, we could walk together if you're thinking of going back?"asked

"Thinking of going back? I'm about ready to move into the place!"

"Great! I'll pick you up on my way, ten past the hour?"

"That's perfect, thanks Darya, I'm so glad I met you and didn't completely trample you," Aurelia said with a laugh.

"Me too Lia, me too."

Midway up the stairs, Aurelia's thoughts turned to her father. While she wasn't quite ready to tell him that he was right about a building with lifts, the stairs were testing her resolve. It's not that she wasn't in shape, she reassured herself, but those stairs after a good workout would challenge anyone. When she at last trudged up the final step to her floor, it took all her remaining strength to finagle the keys into the lock and push her door open.

Her bathing chamber was a haven of stone and softness after so much movement and sweat. Centered in the space was her deep soaking tub with little notches in the wall for candles. It was a longer, more narrow space but full of light thanks to the set of window-doors against the wall. It had been Enchanted with a one way privacy screen. The marble sink had a graceful golden swan faucet and there was a little tufted stool tucked underneath beside it. The counter was organized with glass bottles of moisturizers and serums along with little trays for her jewelry. Over the vanity was a gigantic antique mirror that reached nearly to the ceiling.

On this morning, though, Aurelia turned right, away from the windows, towards her gleaming marble crossweave tiled shower. It had three brass jets, one on each wall, and special nooks for her soaps and creams. A few small, humidity-loving ferns and philodendrons shook with palpable excitement when she turned on the steamy water.

After an exceptionally long shower Aurelia was eager to get to school and take another look at Fiora's books. She dressed quickly in a soft blue, floral patterned dress with a square neckline and short, fluttery sleeves. She loved the way this dress was fitted through the waist then flared out in a swishy skirt that moved with her. Even more so, she loved the deep pockets those skirts concealed.

Walking to the kitchen, she found her favorite travel mug sitting on the counter already filled with fragrant coffee and a sprig of jasmine beside it. She looked around the kitchen, spied her potted pothos innocently soaking up some soft morning light and glared at it knowingly. She wasn't actually upset at the motherly plant, but thought it best to not encourage this sort of behavior all the same.

Aurelia threaded the jasmine through a notch in her satchel and headed out the door, stomach rumbling for a hearty breakfast.

"Goodmornin' Lia," the Nellin behind the counter called out as she entered the boulangerie. "Tha you I saw in t' wee hours of t' mornin'?"

"Yes, I was heading to a class at Peace Lily Studio," she replied, eyes goggling at the assortment of still warm pastries.

"Bah, tha 'ne they make a thousand degrees so yer can all melt, was it?" The Nellin loaded a few selections into a paper bag.

"That's the one! Although it's closer to ninety five, not a thousand," Aurelia laughed. "By the way, I've been meaning to ask you..."

"Hmm?" the Nellin froze where she was, giving Aurelia her full attention. That was a curiosity of Nellins, they were so hardworking and yet so unflinchingly polite. No matter how busy they were, they would always stop for good manners.

"Oh, well, you see," Aurelia was suddenly nervous, "well most boulangeries have the baker's name outside the shop, Twylnda's Boulangerie or Baked by Brigthen, or something of the sort. But seeing as your shop here doesn't have any sign at all, well," here Aurelia started talking faster, "I don't actually know your name and I was hoping you could maybe tell me?"

The Nellin laughed, "Oh tha ol' thing! It fell off las' winter 'n I can'ever get m'self to stop baking long nuff t'fix it. I'm Calyntha."

"Calyntha," Lia committed the name to memory. "Thank you. And I'll have...Oh!" Aurelia stopped abruptly as Calyntha handed over the stuffed paper bag.

"Trus' me on this 'un today, these're what you'll be wantin', 5 frits, please."

"Calyntha," Lia replied, handing over the short stack of bronze coins, "I would happily trust you with my stomach any day."

CHAPTER SIX

Saying goodbye, Lia pulled out the chocolate floret roll and started walking. She vowed to save the rest of her breakfast for once she got to campus, but it was a short lived vow.

By the time she crossed under the school's golden gates, her jam and hard cheese baguette was gone. By the time she passed through the arches to the SAGES campus, the dough puffs were nothing but crumbs and fallen sugar nuggets. By the time she settled a small table to the side of the quad, even those bits were gone too.

Calyntha was truly a magical, magical being, Aurelia thought as she unpacked her bag, ready to take a second look at yesterday's reading.

AFTER A VASTLY MORE PRODUCTIVE morning of reading, annotating, and deciphering, Aurelia headed to the café for lunch. Elle wasn't there yet, but as Aurelia slid herself into one of the empty booths, she realized Elle wasn't the only person she was looking for. Clearing her head of the thought, he wasn't here anyway, Aurelia scanned the room, picking up details she hadn't noticed the day before.

Someone had drawn a beautiful chalk mural on a large board over the service counter. It was the length of the entire counter and featured little puns about the city and the school. To one side of the room was a clear doored chill-box stood with a bevy of packaged sandwiches and cups of all sorts of fruits and vegetables. Behind the counter, two students worked in practiced rhythms, one talking to a customer, the other foaming milk at the enchantment-powered espresso machine. Also behind the counter was a white haired valkyrie woman looking at the trays of sandwiches with hawkish eyes. Despite her aged skin, she had a lean muscle that would make anyone think twice before so much as conceiving of a problem.

Aurelia watched, fascinated by the way the woman marked ticks off on her clipboard as if each stroke of her pen was a cleave of her sword. Suddenly, the valkyrie woman turned to the student foaming milk and Aurelia cowered a bit just imagining that attention being turned on her.

"Helloooo, Liaaaaa, you in there?" a voice beside her called with long, exaggerated vowels and snapping fingers.

"Elle!" Aurelia exclaimed jumping out of her seat, "I'm so sorry! I really have to stop zoning out like that."

Elle burst out laughing. "Don't, it's becoming far too entertaining for me!"

"I was just..." Aurelia leaned in close, dropping her voice to a whisper. "Who is that woman behind the counter?" She could have sworn the valkyrie's eyes flicked in her direction.

"Thlynda? She's an absolute legend! Travelled most of the world defending fae liberation movements, she retired here when her daughter got a job teaching over on the Main Campus. She's the café manager." Elle covered her mouth conspiratorially before adding, "She still frightens me too, but you get used to her if you spend enough time here. Now come on," she dropped her bag in the seat across from Aurelia. "Let's go order, I'm starved!"

As they approached the counter, Aurelia spied a colorful sandwich filled to the brim with grilled zucchini, fresh mozzarella, and heaps of pesto. A little sign informed her that it was lathered with a roasted garlic spread and she was utterly sold.

Elle ordered them two iced cinnamon bear lattes. According to a hand drawn note on the counter, it was a new addition to the menu with infused cinnamon, honey, and brown sugar. Aurelia requested the zucchini sandwich while Elle chose the same smashed avocado sandwich as yesterday and a plate of pastel sandwich cookies.

"What can I say, can't beat perfection," Elle shrugged. This time, both girls waited at the counter for their order. Aurelia busily read more of the menu tags, eager to try something new next time as Elle, to Aurelia's immense shock, chatted with Thlynda.

"When am I going to get you to join the staff here?" Thlynda was saying to Elle. "We could use a few new baristas for the Fall season and you seem to live here anyway."

"You ask me that every quarter, Thlynda, but you know I can't. Between the club fieldball team, tour guide duties, assisting the Chancellor, not to mention my actual schoolwork, my calendar's full."

"Yes, yes, but the first moment that calendar opens up, you come here, you hear me?" Thlynda said with what Aurelia thought might pass for a begrudging smile, maybe.

Elle looked like she was about to introduce Aurelia when their order was called. Aurelia dashed for the plates and was halfway back to their booth before Elle could even look back.

Once both girls were seated and their sandwich halves exchanged, Elle said, "You know, she's really not that scary once you start talking to her."

Aurelia cocked an eyebrow, letting the silence answer for her. A heartbeat passed before both girls broke into uncontrollable laughter.

"Okay, okay," Aurelia said, "just give me a few days to warm up to her, you can introduce me next time. And I didn't know you were involved in so many activities, how do you manage it with your research too? And what are you researching anyway? Yesterday was so much about me, I want to learn more about your work here."

"Oh please, Lia, you just want me to do all the talking so you can eat all the cookies." Elle stared pointedly at the quickly emptying plate of cookies. Aurelia may or may not have been reaching for her third at that very moment.

"That's only a little bit true." Aurelia said, popping the cookie in her mouth.

"They're good, but this is Florevale. On Saturday, I'll take you to my favorite cookie shop in the city, it's over in the Meadow district but always worth the trip. We can get a group together and make an afternoon of it." Elle picked up a cookie and her and Aurelia clinked their treats together in agreement.

"You're just the best, you know that?"

"I know! And as for my schedule," Elle pulled the most overstuffed notebook out of her bag that Aurelia had ever seen. It had clearly started life as a journal but Elle had shoved so many pieces of papers, to do lists, colored tabs, and who knows what else between the pages that the poor binding looked ready to burst any second.

"It's my lifeline, everything I need to do and remember and every place I need to be, every person I need to talk to, it's all in here."

"Uhm, right," Aurelia said skeptically around a mouthful of utter deliciousness, "and that book... helps you?"

"I mean it's a little full but, here," Elle moved to open the book when three paper bees started buzzing out from the pages. "Oops!" Elle snapped the book shut. "Forgot I set those alarms. Anyway, you get the idea!"

Bewildered and yet not in the least bit curious to see what else might come flying out of Elle's planner, Aurelia shifted the conversation.

"Did it take you a long time to find your place here? To know what activities you wanted to do and the people you wanted to do them with?"

Elle chewed slowly, savoring or thinking, Aurelia wasn't sure.

"It was a mix." Elle started, "Some things, like field ball, were a no brainer. I've been playing since I was a little, little kid. I wouldn't want to try to make a career of it or anything, but I knew on day one I wanted to join the club team. Other things like the tour guiding and orientation happened over time. My advisor recommended them, she was probably just tired of my constant yapping about how great Florevale is, but she was right, it's a perfect fit."

Aurelia considered this, picking up her iced latte and taking a sip that sent her to another dimension.

"I think this latte could change my life." Aurelia said blissfully. Elle leaned back in the booth, sipping her latte with closed eyes and an appreciative hum.

Moving the cup a hair's breadth from her mouth, Elle replied "shhh, we're having a moment," and waved her hand at Aurelia.

"How do they even come up with these ideas?"

"The baristas. I've gotten to know a lot of the students who work here and they said they just experiment so much when there aren't customers. Trust me, I've been a test subject enough times to know not every idea is a winner but this one, an instant classic, must be one of Adrian's."

"That's right, I heard Thlynda saying something about you being here a lot? What keeps bringing you back when you have the whole city? I mean, aside from the obvious." Aurelia gestured to the drink she still hadn't put down.

"I don't like studying in my apartment, it feels too still, same with my workshop, so I come here at night or between things. I like having other people around."

"I can see that," Aurelia said. "Okay, how about your research, tell me all about it?"

"No, no, my turn. You had Tillgartem yesterday, and survived?"

The girls chatted merrily through lunch, pausing only once to get a second round of the iced cinnamon bear lattes, decaf this time. Before Aurelia knew it, the half past one o'clock bells were ringing and they both had to get to afternoon sessions.

"Same time tomorrow?" Elle asked.

"You know what," Aurelia replied with a last sip of her drink, "I think I'm going to take your lead and dive into something."

Elle looked at her, puzzled.

"Tomorrow, at lunch, I'm going to apply for that barista job here."

"That's my girl!" Elle cheered as her eyes took on a deeply mischievous glint. Aurelia understood a moment too late that this was a look she would have to be exceptionally careful of in the future.

"Remember how you said I could introduce you to Thlynda next time?"

Aurelia gulped and nodded her head warily, not liking where this was going. Elle threaded their arms together and started walking them up to the counter. "Well, I decided that next time is right now."

"Thlynda," she called, waving. The hawkish valkyrie looked up, squinting for the source of the interruption. "I found you a barista!" Elle sealed her doom with such glee, Aurelia thought. And then Thlynda smiled a real smile and she felt truly bad for anyone who had dared step on a battlefield opposite this warrior.

AFTER A VERY BRIEF INTERVIEW, one Aurelia couldn't remember afterwards in the slightest, she was hired. Thlynda instructed her to come back in two days time for training. She wasn't quite sure what exactly had just happened and suspected that even by Thursday, the shock of it might not have worn off.

She'd never had a job before. Being a princess was sort of a job, she supposed, but not like this. She didn't know the first thing about coffee except that she loved to drink it, and she didn't actually need a job but she supposed she could give the money to the university fund, or use it to treat her friends to cookies this weekend.

Aurelia was just walking out of the café across the patio when Adrian appeared, walking towards her. He raised a hand in greeting, calling out, "Hey Lia! Good to see you!"

A split second of panic went through Aurelia as she tried to decide whether to wave, shake his hand, hug him, or run. Unfortunately, or maybe fortunately, with his long legs he reached her before she had the chance to opt for the latter. He wrapped one arm around her in a half hug and that was that.

"Hey Adrian, good to see you too! I was hoping to run into you." A wave of utter dread coursed through her body as she realized she had said that out loud. The trees surrounding the patio wavered like a storm was coming, but they were the least of her problems.

"Oh?" Adrian replied, slipping one hand into his pocket. He wore short sleeves today and Aurelia momentarily lost the battle not to look at his tanned arms, the way his fingers curled around the strap of his backpack.

"Yes," she said, searching for words that would get her out of this, "I just, Elle just, Thlynda," she shook her head and laughed. "Sorry, what I meant to say is that Elle just somehow wrangled me into accepting a barista job and I wanted to see if you had any advice." That felt plausible, Aurelia assured herself.

Adrian laughed, then leaned in closer to her, saying, "Well she hasn't actually fed anyone to her griffin yet."

Adrian's blue cypress and vetiver scent momentarily distracted her from thoughts of Thlynda, but thankfully he kept talking. "You'll do great! When's your training?"

"On Thursday, and then my first working shift is on Friday morning."

"That's great! I'm on Friday mornings, too. I've got you and I'm sure you'll pick it up quickly." He flashed her a smile that Aurelia was positive could give her wings right there and then.

"Thank you! And, umm, how long did it take you to get over your fear of Thlynda?"

"Sorry, can't help you with that one, fear of Thlynda is a life-long ailment I'm afraid." They both laughed and the quarter bell rang.

"Well, I have to get to the lab but thank you. I feel better already, I just need to survive training."

"Don't worry, she keeps her sword locked in the supply cabinet, you'll have time to run if she decides to change her no-beheadings in the café rule. See you 'round."

Aurelia smiled and walked away, definitely not adding an extra swoosh to her skirts as she headed towards the cottages.

CHAPTER SEVEN

Clem was kneeling in the front yard when Aurelia approached, the pointed tips of his shimmering wings tapping out a melody in the grass behind him. An audience of snow-white leopard squirrels and spotted faebunnies watched as he examined each flower lining the edge of the lawn.

He hopped up, noticing her immediately, and wiped his hands on his trousers as he called out, "Good afternoon, Lia."

Lia walked closer, lifting a hand in greeting "Good afternoon, Clem, how are you?"

"Great, great!" He said enthusiastically, then leaned closer to her, half-whispering, "Especially now that I see my sister hasn't scared you off yet!"

Aurelia chuckled nervously, unsure if this was their normal sibling rivalry or if Fiora had told him about the tension yesterday. Maybe it was a bit of both.

Trying to steer the topic away from the previous afternoon, Aurelia asked, "So, what are you working on here?"

"This is one of your outdoor labs, also your front yard. Professor Maillie and I came up with so many ideas we want to test out here with you, I'm just taking some final measurements to make sure everything is in order for next week."

Aurelia wanted to feel even a quarter of the enthusiasm Clem had for these apparent plans but history held her back.

"That's wonderful, I look forward to seeing more, then," she said in her best impersonation of an eager student. Clem had such an infectious joy, it wasn't as hard as she expected to put on a hopeful face.

Clem inhaled excitedly, like he was about to launch into more details, when a voice called from the house, "Clem if you got your grubby dirt all over Lia..."

Clem rolled his eyes, "Wouldn't dream of it dear sister."

Aurelia laughed quietly, even though she knew they got on each others' nerves, she was already beginning to love their sparring matches.

"You better go on inside before that one comes out here and scares off Clovis and Hansel," Clem gestured to the nervous looking fluff balls waiting at high alert beside him, noses quivering.

"Right, well then, I'll see you later!" Aurelia replied with a true smile to the faerie and his creatures.

Fiora was waiting for her inside the house.

"Hello Lia, I thought we could start today with that tour and then perhaps go over a bit more of your history. Tomorrow we'll test your magic so we can assess where best to begin."

So we're diving right in, Aurelia thought as she placed her satchel on the worn wooden table in the center of the room. In that moment, she decided to trust Fiora, not because of anything the faerie had said or done, but because what was the point of all of this if she didn't at least try?

If she had simply wanted to spend time in the city, she could have apprenticed in the city's governmental offices or moved her court here – enough of the aristocracy resided in the city full time anyway. She could have been studying with her tutors in the mornings, sitting in cafés in the afternoons.

But that wasn't the path she chose. She came to the university with all its complexities and all her secrets. Why was she here if some small part of her didn't believe they really could do *something* with her?

"Okay, I'm ready." Aurelia straightened and every plant in the foyer took notice. Each shimmering bud of the elegant, pink-veined butterfly orchid on the center table burst into rich color. The potted lemon trees sunning by the front door flushed with a cascade of white flowers and juicy fruits. Ferns rustled, shimmying out new branches and the climbing Eden roses outside peeked in through the open windows.

Fiora looked around with a botanist's eye, observing each little joy then looked straight at Aurelia, studying her without reservation.

Aurelia, more wonderstruck than scientist, fidgeted with her ring.

"Hmm," Fiora said, and Aurelia was immensely grateful she didn't push. "Let's begin. You know the kitchen, and as you can see, if we were to walk straight through the foyer we would enter the back gardens. The library is to the right but I would like to save that for last. We'll start upstairs with the laboratories."

Fiora led the way. The marble staircase was wide, curling around to accommodate the oversized ceiling heights on the first floor. At the top of the stairs, Fiora showed her a series of heavy wooden doors. Aurelia found herself equally intrigued and confused at the sterile spaces. She had always thought of magic as something that was just there. Yes, people had spent lifetimes studying it, but she had never truly considered just how that work was done. She shuddered to think of what her own magic, wild and uncontrollable, would do to the delicate machinery and rows of glass instruments.

Fiora was still talking, explaining the functions of each room, wings rippling with eager flutters. Aurelia, meanwhile, was distracted by how similar Fiora and Clem were, even if Fiora might shudder at the thought. The two shared the same zeal for their work, that work just happened to be diametrically opposed. Clem's world was untamed, expansive, filled with life and potential where Fiora's was orderly, measurable to the finest grain, just as laden with possibility but in a totally different way.

"You thought of everything," Aurelia said as they started walking across the gallery to the rooms on the library side of the house.

"When someone of Professor Maillie's esteem taps you to design your dream lab, let's just say I had a wish list for a space like this long before you were even born." Fiora had with a dreamy look to her violet eyes that softened the sharpness of her features.

The tour continued, another large lab space along with a series of smaller rooms that passed by Aurelia in a daze.

"Any questions?" Fiora asked with uncharacteristic brightness as she closed the final door.

Aurelia had many questions, but none she was ready to ask so she shook her head.

"Alright then, let's go to the library." Fiora led her back to the foyer, pointing to a door under the stairs.

"Over there are offices, mine and Clem's, Professor Maillie has his own in the administrative building. You'll mostly work with one of us but Professor Maillie will check in a few times a week to assess our progress, talk about results, and set next steps."

"Speaking of," Fiora said with a sigh as Clem walked in from the front yard.

"Ah, what perfect timing, shall we go for a tour of the gardens?" He had streaks of dirt across his small nose that somehow made his chocolate eyes shimmer even brighter.

"We scheduled the garden tour for later this week. You yourself pushed for that, something about the plumeria trees disrupting the azaleas?" Fiora said, eyeing every speck of soil like it was about to fly across the table to her immaculate lab coat of its own accord.

"Yes, right, but perhaps, just a small peek? I'm sure you've bored her half to death with those labs, I mean, I'm sure Prin, *Lia*, must be overwhelmed with... with important details. A short brain break in the fresh air might do her some good!"

"A *quick* look, Clem," Fiora huffed and Aurelia had to hide her giggle at Clem's overly differential bow.

"Bye sweet sister." Clem said with an overly chipper wave as he led Aurelia to the back patio.

Small white pebbles crunched under their feet as Aurelia and Clem stepped outside. A large wooden table with carved wooden chairs sat in the middle of a raised container garden overflowing with every shade of green. Pathways spread before them, each leading to a uniquely different landscape. It was too much to take in all at once, and Aurelia had a feeling the paths went far further back than truly made sense in the space. Whatever magic Clem had worked back here must have been substantial.

"Clem, this is beautiful, and also enormous, I think every plant and creature that comes into this garden will know they're going to be so well cared for." Clem beamed at the praise, about to thank her, but she continued, "But I have a bit of an odd question and, well, I'm hoping you can answer it for me."

"That's what I'm here for." Clem kneeled down to tend to a vine of cucumbers. "Fire away."

"Well, I noticed yesterday that when I was in the kitchen, there was light coming through the windows from the front and side of the house. Then today, there was light coming in just about every room we toured, and now back here, the shadows of that garden," she pointed to a sunny patch of olive trees and tall lavender bushes, " are going in a different direction than the ones over here." she again pointed, this time to a path lined with rows of fluffy blue hydrangeas. "So I'm wondering, well, how? How is the sun on every side of this place?"

Clem whistled, a high pitched wind chime sort of sound. "That is an excellent question! And unfortunately the answer is not a day one sort of discussion, although I suppose today is day two but still, it is not a day two answer either."

He thought a moment, the seriousness looking out of place on his cherubic face. "I don't suppose Fiora has explained the wards yet?" Lia shook her head no.

"Well, hmm, I guess the easiest way to explain it would be that truly mammoth Enchantments went into the construction of this workshop. We knew we might need light in all of the labs and gardens so we worked with the Enchanters to use those wards to sort of," he paused, making shapes with his long fingers, "bend the light in odd ways."

"So it is real sunlight, not some sort of artificial or magical light?"

"Oh yes! Very much real! Just reflected so precisely so that you'd never know where the true sun was shining except for the time of day."

"That's fascinating, thank you for explaining." Aurelia said, trying to wrap her head around it all.

"That's just the beginning! Wait until next week when we get to start exploring all the gardens. I'm so proud of the work each one of my creature helpers has done and they're eager to meet you!"

"Creature helpers?" Aurelia asked, but just then Fiora pushed the door open.

"Clem! I said short! I already had to reheat the tea once, don't make me do it again."

"Don't put another wrinkle in your wings, we're just about done here. Go on ahead Lia, I'll show you the rest next week."

"I do not have wrinkles in my wings," Fiora seethed and Clem snickered as he walked to the side of the house.

"Please tell me I get to study with both of you sometimes?" Aurelia asked.

"Unfortunately for me, yes," Fiora murmured, "now let's go before he thinks about stealing the cookies I set out for us in the library. I want to hear your thoughts on the readings so far."

A flash of curly hair and a groan from the otherwise proper to a fault Fiora told her that Clem had, in fact, beaten them to the cookies. Aurelia laughed as she found a seat and waited for Fiora and her refreshed plate of treats to return.

CHAPTER EIGHT

After chatting with Fiora in the library, Aurelia hurried home for a dinner meeting with her chief royal advisor. She had no official royal duties while she was in Florevale, but she wanted to stay informed nonetheless.

Josephine was young, for an elf at least, and had worked with her for nearly a decade. She probably knew Aurelia better than anyone and was the closest thing Aurelia had to a real friend.

They cooked a traditional Florevalian dinner of cheese-covered potatoes, slabs of pressed with spice-roasted curds and heaps of herby mustard. It was a quick but reliably delicious meal and perfect for a leisurely night of catching up by candlelight.

When Aurelia could no longer contain her yawns, she gave Josephine letters for each of her parents and sent her on her way with a request to bring a bottle of honey wine for next week's meeting. The dishes, Aurelia decided as she shut the door, would have to wait until morning.

THE NEXT DAY, Aurelia felt like she was truly settling into routines she loved. Wednesday was unique in her schedule since it was the only day she didn't have lab time. Instead, she had two entirely new classes. She rose early, journaling on her balcony as the sun came up, then decided to enjoy her breakfast in the park around the corner with the next installment of her favorite historical fantasy series. Once again, Calyntha packed her a delicious breakfast with two of those delightful chocolate filled Floret rolls.

Full of early morning optimism– and coffee– Aurelia had planned to get ready for class after breakfast. She thought she'd swing by the boulangerie, sit in the gardens, then stop back home to get dressed and pick up her books before going to campus. By the time she had climbed all six sets of stairs to her apartment, she vowed never to make that mistake again.

Aurelia's morning class was one of the graduation requirements for all SAGES students. History of the Orendalian Kingdoms. It was a survey course meant to give students a broad overview of the past two thousand years or so of the entire continent. That included her homeland of Serremont along with Calderith to the north, Bellvanue to the south, Sunsykett to the northeast, Lowden to the west, and Norwish to the far northwest.

Aurelia was the most excited for this class. She had been learning about Orendalian history most of her life, but, for the first time, she would be around everyday people from those kingdoms. She'd have a chance to learn about these places from real sources, not the sickly sweet facade of trade deals or through the sycophantic lens of nobility.

Professor Luciaas shared Aurelia's excitement and then some. After a lifetime of studying, researching, and teaching, he still needed to paw a few genuine tears off his weathered cheeks as he extolled the role a firm historical understanding played in wielding magic. Maybe it all would have been a bit much, but Luciaas' enthusiasm was so genuine, his storytelling so captivating, that Aurelia spied a few students swiping at their own faces. And, Aurelia thought, she had never met someone who made the practical use of a nose-high knobbled walking stick look so... right.

Lunch with Elle was lovely but brief since Aurelia's classes were packed closer together today. Elle, the saint she was, had already ordered them lunch when Aurelia swooped into Apple Blossom. Elle's booth was covered in books and notebooks, tacky notes and diagrams, so much so that the girls didn't even bother to clean up and just held their plates in their hands. Aurelia joked that she was glad Elle's notetaking was so chaotic or she'd be worried about getting crumbs on her work. Elle, in mock affront, said it all looked perfectly organized to her.

Aurelia's afternoon class was her last new class and the only one that hadn't been a first year requirement. It was a course on the main campus through the literature department about the poetry of the Etherialis movement. It was one of her favorite time periods in art, one where artists of every genre –from painting to writing to musicians– started to explore the interconnectedness of truth and purposeful living within the natural world.

Professor Emory didn't have the same charisma of Professor Luciaas, or gruff confidence of Professor Tillegratem, but Aurelia appreciated the friendly, lyrical way she spoke all the same.

After classes, Aurelia found her way home. She cooked her

favorite cheesy pasta for dinner, which she ate on the balcony as she watched the sunset, conveniently pushing all thoughts of tomorrow aside. Pots washed and satchel packed, she changed into her favorite silky-soft sleep set and curled up on her big chair for a night of candlelit reading amid the city sounds.

THURSDAY SNUCK up on Aurelia like a boulder. Thlynda day. Aurelia's kitchen pothos, perhaps picking up on her nervous energy, brewed her tea instead of the usual morning coffee. She thought to herself about how that little plant knew her too well as she sipped the soothing chamomile brew.

Thlynda had mentioned to wear pants and closed-toed shoes for the cafe, so Aurelia slipped on her favorite silk lined trousers. She paired those with a loose, blush-colored blouse embroidered with tiny raspberries and straps that tied on her shoulders.

Somehow, whether by magic or simply her powers of observation, Calyntha knew to pack an extra chocolate filled Fleuret roll for a mid-morning snack. She was quickly becoming Aurelia's favorite being in the city.

Her time in Tillegatem's class did absolutely nothing to help unwind the anxious knot in her stomach. After two hours of complicated magical theories, interrupted by only the most perfunctory of student interactions, Aurelia's nerves were reaching a new high.

It wasn't just that Thlynda was intimidating, she was, of course, but Aurelia had dealt with plenty of intimidating people at court. It wasn't her military background either, again, Aurelia had experience with commanders and warriors and had never been so easily cowed.

Sitting on a bench among the tree-covered cottage pathways, Aurelia stared thoughtfully into her second fleuret roll. Maybe it knew why.

She supposed this anxiety was at having a job at all, which was silly to even think because she had a job from the moment she was born. She was a princess. But maybe that was just it. She had always had her role, it was a part of her, she couldn't fail at it any more than she could stop breathing. *That's not entirely true.* She could be a terrible princess, she supposed, her lineage was certainly filled with prime examples of truly horrendous royals. But she loved her people, that had to make her at least about average.

This job, though, the ways she could fail at this were spectacular and humiliating. And it was all on her, she didn't have the steadying weight of a crown behind her, propping her up. Here she was just Lia.

"That must be some fleuret roll," a familiar voice said from above, jolting Aurelia out of her sugar-fueled meditation.

"Oh! No, I mean, yes, it is, it's great but... I was just a bit lost in thought." Aurelia laughed nervously.

Adrian swung his backpack off his shoulders, sitting beside her on the bench and stretching his long legs out in front of him. He wore chocolate brown slacks with a thin cherry leather belt and a cream short sleeve knitted button down. The top two buttons were undone revealing two thin gold chains around his neck and a sliver of smooth skin. She could have sworn she saw a flash of curling black ink peeking past the edge but didn't want to be caught staring to find out.

"Here, want a bite?" Aurelia asked, immediately kicking herself for offering this near-stranger a bite of her food. That certainly wasn't a normal thing to do, was it? Then again, he had sat with her, so maybe it was?

"I'll never turn down a fleuret roll." Adrian replied, pushing hair off his face and smiling warmly at her.

Aurelia tore off a piece of the roll, silently lamenting the loss of such a perfectly chocolatey bite. Her regret immediately fizzled as her fingers brushed Adrian's in the exchange.

"So, what has this contemplative crescent been saying to you?" Adrian asked, turning towards her as he rested a bent elbow on the back of the bench.

"Well, it's my first shift and, this is embarrassing, but I've never actually had a job before so I'm, I'm just a little nervous, it's not a big deal, really."

"Let's see, do you like coffee?"

"Do I breathe?" Aurelia wiped a bit of chocolate from her lip.

"Do you make your own coffee?"

Aurelia's mind flashed to her pothos and decided he definitely wasn't ready for that. "Uhh, sometimes." *Great job,* Aurelia thought to herself, *truly, the most eloquent princess in Serremont.*

"Okay, what kind of coffee do you like? Did you like the almond vanilla latte you got the other day?"

Aurelia was surprised he remembered but it was probably a popular drink. "Delish, although not quite as good as the cinnamon bear I had after that."

"You tried the cinnamon bear?" Adrian asked with sudden enthusiasm.

"It might just be the best coffee I've ever had!"

"Well thank you, it was one of my special projects, took forever to get right. It's unique because of the way we process the cinnamon. So cinnamon is actually made of tree bark which sounds weird but isn't actually any weirder than, say, tea leaves."

"Anyway, it wouldn't be a very good tree if its bark dissolved in water." Adrian laughed, his expression and hands growing animated as he spoke. "So I wanted to find a way to infuse the cinnamon flavor without the gritty un-dissolved texture. Long story short, instead of sprinkling it on top, I designed a way to combine the cinnamon and coffee beans without compromising on the quality of the espresso. And, sorry, we were talking about you, and your first day." Adrian rubbed his neck, her eyes tracked the motion then quickly looked away.

"No, actually, I think that really did help. Maybe not the bark part specifically but the talking. I just need to get out of my own head about it."

"Precisely! That's exactly what I was going for. Definitely." Adrian nodded with a golden smile.

"Thanks," Aurelia said and meant it. "I should probably get over to Apple Blossom, don't want to start my first day by being late." Aurelia made an exaggerated oh-no sort of expression as they both stood.

"Don't even joke about being late," Adrian's face was suddenly serious as he leaned heart-stopingly close to whisper, "I think she's actually killed for less."

"You're joking, right?" Aurelia teetered.

"Mmm, totally. Totally joking," Adrian replied in a way that did not at all assure Aurelia he was only joking.

"Uh, right, I'll see you later, then" she slung her bag over her shoulder.

"See you later, hopefully," he said with a wink, walking backwards a few steps as he waved goodbye.

She waved back and hurried off, riding the buzz of their banter all the way to the café's doors.

THE CAFE WAS quiet when Aurelia arrived. A catchy song played quietly over the music box, a few students bobbed their heads along as they underlined and annotated their books. A curly-haired girl, shorter than Aurelia with narrow shoulders and a bevy of earrings, stood in front of the counter. She was running her hands over the crinkly packages of cookies and making check marks on a clipboard. Meanwhile, a boy with shaggy blonde hair and piercing blue eyes laughed with a customer at the register. All the windows were thrown open and a lilac scented breeze meandered through the room.

Aurelia gazed around, jolting as she realized Thlynda stood before her. She really needed to start being more aware of her surroundings.

"Miss Lia. Glad you're here, let's get started." Thlynda said, giving Aurelia a brazen once over. "Those shoes are fine for today, but tomorrow let's have something that covers your whole foot."

Aurelia looked down at the light brown Mary Jane's she wore, confused.

Thlynda rolled her eyes. "It's a *safety* hazard, Lia, imagine if scalding water landed on your foot. You know, I had a girl wearing tights in shoes like that, the tights melted right into her skin. Had to go to the emergency magical center for skin grafts, the burns were so severe. Tomorrow, let's have some proper shoes."

"Yes, yes ma'am," Lia said nervously and wondered just how hot water needed to be to cause that kind of damage. She didn't dare ask.

"Come around behind the bar here," Thlynda commanded, not waiting for Lia to follow as she pulled an orange binder out from beside the cash register. "Here's where you sign in and out for your shift. Make sure this is the first thing you do every time, got it?"

"Yes, ma'am," Lia said, eying the other charts and papers taped up inside the counter. A color coded schedule, house rules, important people and a stack of unused petalpaper on a small shelf .

Thlynda moved to the back counter, gesturing to the lines of syrups. "On the counter here, I've taped down every recipe so you just need to follow the list. If a customer orders an almond vanilla latte, you find the name and then follow these instructions exactly. Don't go changing anything, I've made these recipes exactly right. The syrups are all labeled, don't move them around. I once had a boy think he was helping me by putting them in alphabetical order. Took nearly an hour to fix it all. These are in order the way they are on the ordering sheet. I have a system and a reason for everything in this café, understand?"

Lia nodded vigorously, wondering what happened to the boy after that encounter.

"Now, here's the espresso machine, have you ever used one of these?"

Aurelia was certain she had told Thlynda she didn't have any coffee making experience but was still scared as she answered, "No, sorry, I, I haven't."

"Alright, we'll have to train you on it then," Thlynda said with an inconvenienced humph.

"On the service counter we have our trays of baked goods and food, we take inventory twice a day, once in the morning and once at night. You see Bette over there?" She motioned with a jerk of her head to the curly haired girl. "That's what she's doing. I'll still have to check her work, of course, but if you're on an inventory shift and there's a quiet time in the café like there is now you should do this. It's all on the clipboard. I trust you can follow the instructions."

Aurelia didn't have time to respond before Thlynda

marched on. "Under the counter here are our cold boxes, in them you'll find milk. Just like with the syrups, don't move them. If you're restocking, make sure you pull the old ones forward and put new ones in the back."

Aurelia nodded. "Yes ma'am, old ones in the front, new in the back."

"I really shouldn't have to explain this but you wouldn't believe what I've had students do in the past. Some people have no common sense, none at all, so now I explain everything so there's no excuses."

Aurelia held a moment of silence for those students, thankful for the mistakes they made, their sacrifice before this goddess of blood and efficiency.

"Now, over here are the blenders to make smoothies and milkshakes. You see along the bar here," Thlynda motioned to sheets of shiny paper taped around the machines. "These are the recipe cards. Just like the coffee; I've written it all exactly how you should make it. Put ingredients in the blend jars in the exact order I wrote, I wrote it that way for a reason."

"In order, got it."

"And if you ever have a question when you're making a drink, let me know immediately so I can update the cards. I want no room for error. Last year I had a girl, she was from Sunsykett and they must not have bananas there because see this recipe here? The chocolate monkey shake? See how it says to peel a banana? Well that's because this girl was putting the whole banana into the blender cups, peel included."

Aurelia wasn't sure if she was supposed to laugh or not, she went for a nervous chuckle instead.

"So now I wrote, see, peel-the-banana first then the other ingredients. No one even said anything, I just happened to watch her make it one day and asked what she thought she was doing. Still can't believe none of our customers said anything. But it's all here, so if you have a question, ask."

"Yes, ma'am, I'll make sure to ask, anything that comes to mind."

"Good. Now, let me take you back to the store room."

Thlynda told Aurelia about how the shifts worked while they walked, explaining that there were always at least two students on every shift but sometimes three for busier times. The cafe was open all day and night but student shifts only ran from seven in the morning until midnight. Aurelia was expected to have two regular shifts per week but was allowed to pick up additional shifts whenever she wanted. If she ever couldn't make it in for her shift she had to send a petalpaper notice immediately, if she had a conflict coming up it was her responsibility to get her shift covered. They had a staff shift board taped up near the register so she could list any shifts she needed to give away or pick up any she wanted to cover.

Aurelia nodded along, hoping she could remember it all but also certain Thlynda had it written down, highlighted, and underlined somewhere.

"Here's the storeroom, you won't need to come back here much but I want you to know where it is." Thlynda unlocked a door revealing a world of syrup bottles, stacks on stacks of paper cups and lids, pallets of napkins and other supplies Aurelia couldn't begin to name. Her eyes flitted from shelf to shelf, wondering where Thlynda's sword was lurking.

"Now, let's go back to the front." As they walked, Thlynda continued her instructions. "Pastry and sandwich deliveries come every morning, if you're on an early shift you'll have to unpack and organize them."

They arrived back at the main room of the cafe as Thlynda turned her knife-edge gaze on Aurelia and said more than asked, "Any questions?"

Aurelia hesitated but pulled herself together enough to say, "Well, uhm, when do I learn to make the drinks and prepare the food?"

"Bette," she called, "I'll finish the inventory, you're going to teach our new hire Lia how to make coffees. Start with the drip coffee and work your way up. She's never made coffee before so be sure to cover every step, got it?"

"Of course!" Bette said with an enviable air of confidence. "I'll take good care of her, Thlynda."

Thlynda nodded. "Right. Lia, remember, ask me if you have any questions and you'll do just fine here. I spend most of the day in the first booth over there working on the books and schedules."

"Thank you, ma'am, I will." Thlynda hadn't explained the food yet but Aurelia would much rather ask Bette, and she had a feeling Thlynda would point her back to the other girl regardless.

Satisfied, Thlynda turned and strode over to the plates of cookies to confirm Bette's work.

Aurelia let out a relieved sigh and Bette laughed, a deeper, huskier sort of sound than Aurelia would have expected. "Relax, Lia, the worst is over. No, I shouldn't say that, the first time you mess up in front of Thlynda, that's the worst, but don't worry. We all go through it and we all still have our heads! Except for Gretley but that was a weird case."

Aurelia's eyes nearly shot out of her head as she stammered, "wha...wha.. Gretl... who?"

"I'm joking, I'm joking," Bette snorted, "I couldn't help it! Seriously, don't worry, this is the best job on campus."

"Oh, okay" Aurelia gave a hesitant grin, relieved but only somewhat convinced.

"Alright, let's get you going on these coffees, we'll start with the big girls." Bette gestured to the line of self serve thermoses at the far end of the counter. "First, we need to check if any are empty."

BETTE WAS A WONDERFUL TEACHER, Aurelia thought as she excitedly poured her first perfectly frothed milk into a blue floral to-go cup. Nevermind the nine attempts that came before it, nevermind that Aurelia had stopped counting when she hit nine. Bette hadn't given up on her and had gently, if not a bit teasingly, spotted her many mistakes and advised her each time.

They had been fortunate, it was a quiet afternoon with just a few actual customers here and there. Thlynda had been called away on some sort of emergency with the university kitchen and hadn't returned. Bette warned her there was usually a 3:00 rush. Aurelia tried not to panic at the thought but Bette reassured her that she should just observe for now. And yet, the time had rolled around and no students arrived. She was glad of it, both the quiet and Thlynda's absence.

There was so much for Aurelia to learn, so many recipes to remember, so many knobs on the register, so many little procedures and notes from Thlynda to watch out for. But by the end of her shift, she'd made a perfectly frothed latte, brewed three big pots of self-serve coffee, blended two milkshakes, and had even chatted with a few customers. She wasn't quite ready to deal with the behemoth of the register and all its contraptions and couldn't even imagine trying to prepare food too, but she had made progress.

She was feeling just a bit proud of herself until a group of noisy students walked in, their voices rising in excitement as the story they were telling bounced from one to the other.

"Twelve feet tall!"

"No one could get through!"

"And then, that valkyrie started trying to chop it down with an axe!"

"Hey Domarii, what's going on?" Bette asked the group as they approached the counters.

"I can't believe you don't know! Couldn't you see it in here?!"

"See what?" Bette asked.

"They really don't know! See! Even the petalpapers couldn't get through!" another responded.

"Will someone shut up and just tell me? What are you talking about?" Bette repeated in frustration, her small frame giving way to surprising authority.

"Okay, so you know those climbing roses in the pots outside the cafe? The ones that go up the trellis over the door?" Domarii asked.

Aurelia drifted over to Bette's side, not liking where this was going.

"They went rogue!" A cacophony of explanation poured out from the group, Bette looked from one to the next, following the story better than Aurelia who could barely hear anything over the rush of her heartbeat. She stared down at her binding ring. 'The strongest binding in the known world' they'd promised, ' magic escaping was unfathomable.' She'd been ignoring the little moments. The gifts and brushes, the sweet tendrils and kind gestures. Her magic had tricked her, lulled her into a sense of complacency.

"Okay, do I have this right... Those two *plants*, I repeat, *potted plants*, suddenly grew to, did you say twelve feet tall? No way, and then, what, started, nope, I lost it." Bette sighed.

"Shh, guys, let me explain." One of the boys waved his hands in front of the others and the group at last quieted to let him talk. "The climbing roses, the ones right outside the door, they shot up super tall. Ten feet, twelve feet, precision doesn't matter when a semi-sentient *rose bush* is swinging thorny branches like a great sword to keep everyone back from the doors. No one could get through. Every time we tried to send a message inside to see what was going on they swatted it away. No one could get within fifteen feet of the doors!"

Aurelia looked at the clock, she had stopped listening after thorny great sword. Thank the sun it was five minutes past her shift end.

"I'm going to head out," she said, pouring every ounce of stability into her voice that she could. Bette waved, still engrossed in the story that Aurelia couldn't get away from fast enough.

She was nearly to the door when Bette called out, "Lia hold up!"

Aurelia thought she might actually die right there and then. She turned, words evading her.

Bette jogged across the room and gave her a hug. "You did so great today! Just wanted to let you know, I'm glad to have you on the team, hopefully we catch more shifts together! Shifts that don't end in whatever all this turns out to be." She laughed gesturing to her friends who had now started acting out the scene with bananas and pencils as swords.

"Oh, uh, thanks, you were so helpful, I have to run but, yeah, me too." And then Aurelia bolted.

Outside, the ground was strewn with leaves and roses, twiggy branches covered in raging thorns were being picked up by a garden crew. Students were standing in little groups chatting, the same words ringing out over and over.

Out of control, crazy, magic, hurt.

Aurelia walked as fast as she could, not wanting to look up, knowing somehow this was all her fault. Her and her magic and her nerves. She had done this and what if those bushes had harmed someone? And what about the bushes themselves? This made no sense, this wasn't Summoning. She wanted to run to Fiora and ask what could possibly be so broken in her to cause all this. But right now the campus couldn't talk about anything else and since she couldn't do anything to help, she just wanted the security of her little apartment and her shut windows and her bed.

CHAPTER NINE

Aurelia had all but run back to her apartment, all but flown up the stairs, only to collapse in a heap on her blanket. She didn't bother to take off her shoes and she definitely didn't bother to notice the petalpaper already fluttering outside her bedroom window.

She walked heavily into her bathing chamber, turned on the shower, and stripped out of her sweaty, coffee-stained clothes. Next time she'd know better than to wear cream colored anything. *Would there be a next time, though?*

Steam filled the room as Aurelia shook lavender and sandalwood oils into her diffuser. She stood under the hot water, not yet ready to think about what happened, just breathing in the humid air and soothing scents. It was okay to not think about it yet, she decided. So she took her time, pulled out her favorite ocean salt body scrub and slathered her hair in a rice water mask. When she at last emerged, her skin glistened and her fingertips were reduced to shriveled grapes.

Aurelia pulled on her fluffiest sweater set. She lit every candle she could see between her bathing chamber and the kitchen and flipped open the music box to let out its gentle, soothing tune.

At last, she let the petalpaper in, placing it unopened on the kitchen counter. She knew who it was from, but she wasn't ready to bear their opinions and fears until she had settled her own.

Even though she wasn't hungry, she knew skipping dinner would only make the rest of the night harder. She heated up a jar of white bean, tiny pasta, and tomato soup, grateful the palace kitchens had stocked her apartment with preserved versions of her favorite comfort meals. 'For the unexpected days,' the ancient head chefs, Maerys and Wendlynn, had said with vice-like hugs. Aurelia dumped an alarming amount of salty parmesan cheese in and walked out to her balcony to decide if she was leaving the city tonight.

The warm comfort of the soup brought her back from the ledge. She wasn't leaving the city.

The laughter and joyful chatter of the café diners far below brought her further back to herself. She wasn't leaving the university, either.

And then, just as she was settling herself to open the petal-paper, a flash of something dark hurtled into one of her potted dahlias, sending it crashing.

Aurelia yelped in alarm then tip-toed over to see what had happened. Underneath the shards of pottery and white tangles of roots lay a motionless mass of fur with iridescent wings.

"Oh! Oh no!" Aurelia cried out, gently brushing dirt from the small creature, unsure of what to do next. It was an animal, she was sure of that much, but unlike any she had seen before.

"Please be alive, please be alive," she said, heart pounding, as she carefully scooped the creature up, cradling its tiny body within her hands.

Its pelt was astonishingly soft with striped shades of tan,

brown, and grey on its back and head but its belly and the tips of its paws were a white so pure it must have been blinding in the sun. Emerging from its back were two bronzy wings, membranous with bony fingers and tipped with razor sharp claws. Strangely, though, it appeared to have no tail and Aurelia wondered how it could balance well enough to fly.

She could feel shallow breaths on her hand as she carried the little fluff ball back to her table and laid it down gently. The poor thing must have knocked itself out cold on impact. She ran a finger up the bridge of its pink nose, discovering tiny knobs on its forehead that hadn't yet grown into full horns.

Aurelia had never seen a creature quite like this before. Its face and body resembled that of a cat but... a cat with wings? That wasn't right. Likewise, she knew of many creatures with leathery wings like these but none covered in fur, much less fur softer than the finest silk.

She ducked inside, fetching a small saucer and filling it with milk. *Cats like milk, right? Perhaps flying cat-like creatures might like it too?* She picked up a woven basket from one of her shelves, hastily dumping it out and laying a few dish cloths inside.

Should she send a petalpaper to the Royal Physician? Or perhaps the Royal Kennelmaster? She would know more about animals and at the very least it was some sort of animal. But what would she say? A creature she'd never seen or heard of before crash landed on her balcony? Aurelia hurried outside with her supplies but found the creature sitting up tall, licking one of its claw tipped paws as if nothing had happened.

She padded over to it slowly, using her most soothing tone to coax the creature into letting her get close. "Hi little one, I'm Aurelia. It's okay, it's okay."

It spared one glance for her as she approached then went right back to licking its paws as if she was no more interesting than a falling leaf. She placed the bowl and makeshift bed on the floor in front of it and considered trying to check it for injuries. One look at the hooked claws it was meticulously cleaning and she thought better of it.

Ducking back inside, Aurelia tried to spy on the creature through the window but it paid no attention to her offerings. She sat at her desk, chair turned to keep an eye on it, and began to write a letter to the royal librarian. She described it, drawing a crude sketch as best she could to highlight the cat-like ears and talon tipped wings, and asked if he had ever heard of its kind before. She also wrote to the Royal Kennelmaster, figuring the wizened old caretaker might have enough experience with animals to tell her any signs to look out for.

At last, she turned her attention to the still rolled petalpaper, the one she knew was from her parents. With a look out the window to the creature– who was apparently satisfied with the state of its claws and had moved onto vigorously licking its belly– she unrolled it.

Dearest,

Word has reached us of a disturbance at the school. We trust you are well as the reports made no mention of out of place nobility.

We are certain we do not need to remind you of the importance of your responsible management of all matters, magical and otherwise. That said, we implore you, whatever caution you have been using thus far, increase it.

All our love and trust.
-XX

She glanced up, checking on the creature again with a

long exhale. It had moved from smoothing its belly to vigorously cleaning its ears. The note had been about what she anticipated, no better, no worse. They weren't wrong, and in truth what she had been telling herself was far more unkind than they had ever been, but that didn't make it any easier to read.

The creature arched its back in a luxurious stretch, letting out a little yelping sound that made Aurelia smile. She reached her own arms up, taking a cue from the tiny beast and headed to bed.

In the morning the bowl was empty, the box overturned, and the creature was gone.

Darya and Aurelia sat side by side in the blissful warmth of Peace Lily Studio's sauna after class the next morning.

"I never would've thought a sauna could feel so good after a hot class like that" Aurelia said dreamily. Her tired muscles melted amid the dry patchouli-scented air. She felt like a puddle– like the emotional ups and downs yesterday, combined with the sweltering heat and non-stop flow of today's class, had finally melted her mind and body into one big splotch of Aurelia soup.

"Right? I was skeptical at first too, but now I totally get it." Darya replied as she lazily watched a bead of sweat trickle down her arm.

"Okay, so tell me more about this creature last night? You were starting to tell me on the way over but I must have been half asleep, did you say a bird cat?"

"Not a bird cat, but some sort of cat-like creature for sure with wings like, like a, like a bat? It was so soft and fluffy but then it's claws, terrifying. And the talons on the tips of its wings looked sharp too."

"Are you sure it wasn't just a normal kitten with something stuck on it? I feel like I would know if flying cats were a thing."

"No way, I live on the sixth floor, how would it even get up there? It was definitely the body of a kitten and it definitely had wings and it definitely was flying until it crashed into my café au lait's."

"Your café au whats?"

"Café au lait, it's a type of dahlia, they're one of my favorites. Well, they were one of my favorites," she amended, remembering the smashed pot and white roots.

A bell rang and both girls groaned then laughed at their synchronicity.

"Want to grab breakfast after this?" Darya asked as they walked towards the shower stalls.

"I wish but I can't, I have my first actual shift over at Apple Blossom Café this morning."

"Apple Blossom! My roommate practically lives there! What time does your shift end? I'll swing by on my way to class."

"I'm on from nine until noon but don't get your hopes too high just yet. I mean, if you want self-serve coffee, I'm absolutely your girl but my frothing skills are still, uh, a work in progress" Aurelia cautioned with a self conscious chuckle while picking up one of the magnificently fluffy towels.

"I love a self-serve coffee, sounds perfect."

AURELIA ARRIVED at Apple Blossom just five minutes before her shift. It would have been earlier but she spent about fifteen minutes sitting by the fountain in the center of the SAGES quad, staring at the library, willing her eyes to look at the café on its side. Would there still be debris littering the ground? Were the tables and those adorable striped umbrellas damaged from the thorny branches? How could she go to work when she couldn't even look at the front door?

Eventually Aurelia steadied herself and glanced up. There was no trace of the battle. She blew out a relieved sigh but then two students walked by, one recounting the tale and the other lamenting that they had missed it. The heart she had just calmed started thudding again. She took a few more calming breaths, watching as a trio of songbirds swooped and glided across the bright blue sky. Their songs wove together, rising and falling with the curves of their path, steadying Aurelia's pulse with each warbling note.

The café was quiet when she entered. She walked up to the counter, saying good morning to Thlynda in the first booth. Thlynda gave her outfit a once over.

Today Aurelia had chosen a light wash pair of straight leg denim pants with tendrils of vines stitched along the hips and crisp white sport-shoes. She paired it with a loose blue and white striped linen button down, one side tucked in at her waist. She tamed her hair into a low ponytail with a blue scarf but a few shorter pieces around her face managed to escape.

Thlynda nodded. "Better, but don't expect those shoes to be clean by the end of your shift."

"Oh, ah, okay," Aurelia stammered, putting her bag in a cubby behind the counter and trying to get her bearings. Adrian and another boy were behind the counter. The boy anxiously watched at the clock while Adrian was making a drink at the espresso machine. Half the couches and booths were taken but there was no line at the register; music played softly and a few students chatted over their coffee and pastries. It all felt normal, as if yesterday hadn't happened at all. Aurelia didn't know if that made her feel better or worse.

The boy at the register smiled and said, "glad you're here! It's been a morning. The nine AM rush came early and I have so much to do in the library. Uh," he looked around, "self-serve pots could use a check but morning inventory's done, see ya!" He was out the door before Aurelia could even respond and she wasn't entirely sure what to do next.

"Hey Lia! Happy first shift!" Adrian called, walking over from where he had just put a perfectly steamed latte on the counter. Today he was dressed in wide leg tan trousers with a relaxed fit. He had tucked in a loose light blue tee shirt that offset his grey-blue eyes and his onyx hair was swept back into a loosely wavy style. It was altogether a devastating look, but Aurelia quickly admonished herself for the thought.

"Hi Adrian, uhm, what do I do?" Aurelia clasped her hands in front of her to keep them from flapping about nervously.

"No better way to learn than by doing. How about we start with making you a drink. What do you like?" Adrian's smile was contagious as he walked backwards towards the espresso machine.

"Uh, shouldn't I ring myself up first?"

"First rule of Apple Blossom, while you're working you get whatever drinks you want."

"Oh, well, then, how about your favorite drink?"

Adrian grimaced. "Uh, you might not want to do that. I kind of have a reputation for liking strange flavors." He ran a hand through his hair. "I usually go for either straight black coffee or milkshakes."

Aurelia eyed the half melted slush under the counter and laughed. "It's nine in the morning! How are you drinking a milkshake already?"

"It has coffee in it!" Adrian objected in self defense. "Look, for me, coffee is a means to an end. It's a way to stay awake, so if I'm drinking straight coffee I don't want to enjoy it too much. That's why I take it black. But if I'm just having a drink for the flavor then of course I'm going to have the most delicious thing I can make. And what's ice cream anyway except frozen sugar milk?"

Aurelia tried to think of a good response but was saved by a customer approaching the register.

"You ring, I'll brew," Adrian said.

"Right, okay, what can we get you?" Aurelia asked the student.

"Double espresso and a fleuret roll, please," the girl said with a yawn. Aurelia stared at the knobs in front of her as if they were made of living flame.

"Third from the right, top row," Adrian called.

"I've got it, I've got it," Aurelia countered. She most certainly did not have it but she didn't want him to know that.

"Three fifty-five" she said after an eternity. The girl absent-mindedly handed over some coins and then Adrian was somehow right beside her, passing over the drink and plate.

"Alright now, your drink Lia, don't think I forgot." Adrian bumped her shoulder as he walked toward the espresso machine. "You look like you're in the mood for a," he paused, looking her up and down, cocking his head to the side. "A hazelnut mocha, iced or hot?"

"Iced, definitely iced," Aurelia did not need a reason to sweat more than she already was.

"Okay so the trick to a hazelnut mocha is melting the choco-late sauce with the heat of the espresso, come on, you're going to make it." Adrian grabbed a little metal pitcher and slid it over to her.

"Alright, you need 3 pumps of the mocha sauce and a two

second count of hazelnut," he watched as she picked up the cup and followed his instructions.

"Mhmm, good, let's get the shot ready." Aurelia flushed at his praise but tried to focus on the task. He leaned against the wall next to the espresso machine, monitoring her as she pulled the shot.

"Now, swirl it around to mix the chocolate and espresso. Perfect." He ducked down to the cold box to get out the milk and handed it to her.

A customer walked up to the register, "I've got this one, Lia, think you can take it from here?" Their eyes met and she nodded her head.

He was lightning quick, she was just attaching a lid to the cup when he slid back down the line next to her.

"You helped them already? How are you so fast!" She poked a straw into her cup.

"Lots of practice. You'll get there in no time, though. Now, how's your drink?"

She took a tentative sip and let out a contented sigh.

"That good, huh?" Adrian quirked an eyebrow. She felt her cheeks flush.

"Every drink here just keeps getting better and better!" She explained, trying to justify her reaction.

"Don't they have cafés back home? Where is home for you, anyway?"

Aurelia panicked for a moment, they had coffee in the Palace but nothing like a café, and she definitely did not want to explain that to Adrian— or anyone for that matter.

"Uh, I'm from Serremont but a ways outside the city. We have coffee but not all these, these special flavors and syrups, it's more simple drinks. Where are you from?" She wanted to point the conversation back towards him and as far away from her own upbringing as possible.

"Calderith, from the capital Waldon."

"Waldon, that's on the coast, right?" Aurelia mused, leaning back against the counter and taking another sip of her drink.

Adrian started washing steamer pots at the sink. "Mhmm, my family's lived there for generations."

"Do you ever go back and visit? I've never been but I heard it's lovely in the spring, full of climbing wisteria and cherry blossoms on every street."

"Not so much," Adrian dried his hands and came to lean next to Aurelia, crossing his arms in a way she truly couldn't ignore. "I mean the flowers, yes, but not so much with the visiting."

"My family," he paused, reaching a long arm down to grab his mostly melted drink. "It's not that they're not supportive of me being here, well, actually, no, they're not. They still love me and are supportive of me, just not really Florevale. I was supposed to be taking over the family business, I'm the oldest in my family and my parents trained me my whole life to run the company after them."

"So how did you end up here instead? Did you not want to run it?"

Adrian glanced at her, she pretended not to notice. "The thing is, people in Calderith don't have magic the way they do here in Serremont. We have magic, just not a lot of it. My Summoning abilities came in when I was fourteen, we didn't even think I had magic before that."

"Because it usually presents by age ten," Aurelia added.

"Right, so when I turned ten and had no abilities, my parents thought we were all set on the whole succession thing. They really intensified my training. I started sitting in on meetings, planning routes. It's a shipping company, more of a shipping empire really. And they've worked hard, they've been ready to pass it on for a while now. We agreed I would take over when I turned twenty five."

Three customers walked up, Aurelia went to ring them up while Adrian made their drinks. She managed to complete her task before he finished, but just barely.

"So then what happened?" Aurelia asked as soon as they were done, she couldn't just leave his story hanging there.

Adrian went around to check the self-serve pots. "Well it turned out I had a lot of magic, more than anyone in my family had ever demonstrated, and I knew I needed to pursue magical studies. It was too much power to leave untrained and I wanted to do something meaningful with it."

Aurelia nearly choked on how deeply she could relate, how closely his story mirrored her own struggles. "Mhmm," was all she could get out.

"Giving up my role in the company to come here half broke my mom's heart at first, but I think she understood. Even though they didn't want me to leave, they loved me enough to let me pursue my magic. Besides, I have seven younger siblings, they had a few spares."

Aurelia was positive she couldn't have heard him right, he was the oldest of eight kids. It was unheard of in Serremont but before she could ask more, he continued.

"So to finally answer your question with a very long expla- nation" Adrian laughed, "I don't go back and visit because I don't like leaving my work here for long. What's the point of all I gave up and all they gave up if I'm not committed to what I'm doing here, you know? I go for holidays once or twice a year, but never for more than a few days. It's just easier that way."

Aurelia wasn't sure how to respond, he was cheerful about it all, but it also sounded like a hard situation. At the same time, hadn't she been adamant about not going home for so many of the same reasons?

"But, you're right, Waldon's absolutely beautiful in the spring." Adrian was still talking, saving her from needing to figure out a reply. "If you're ever thinking of taking a trip let me know, I'll tell you all my favorite spots."

The moment passed, and Aurelia agreed, "I will absolutely take you up on that." She was about to say more when Darya walked in.

"Lia!" Darya called out, waiving.

"Hey Darya," Aurelia said, "you came!"

"Of course I came, had to see you in action. Hey Adrian!"

Adrian came over, standing beside Aurelia at the register. "Hey Darya, how do you two know each other?"

"We go to Peace Lily Studio together," Darya answered. "Okay, I've been thinking more about your creature, Lia, and I think it must have been some sort of sickly bird, and that's why its feathers were all ruffled making you think it had fur."

"No way, it was way too soft to be feathers, definitely fur. And what about the whiskers? Birds don't have whiskers?" Aurelia replied so seriously that both she and Darya burst out laughing.

"Are you sure?" Darya asked skeptically when they finally composed themselves. She poked around the muffins, selecting the one with the most chocolate chips.

"Feathers and whiskers?" Adrian asked, looking back and forth between the girls, hands in his pockets, brow furrowed.

"Yes, I'm sure! Muffin and a coffee?" Aurelia asked Darya.

"Mhmm," Darya replied as she unwrapped her muffin and Adrian grabbed a plate for her. "Thanks. We're talking about the creature Aurelia found last night."

Adrian looked at Aurelia questioningly, "Creature?"

She sighed deeply in Darya's direction. "First of all, I'm not crazy and I didn't just dream it up. I have the smashed pots to prove it." She turned to Adrian, "Last night I was sitting on my balcony when something crash-landed into one of my dahlias. I thought it was hurt so I picked the thing up, it was so small," she held her hands together to show the size, "and looked just like a kitten with white paws and a pink little nose but it had these beautiful bat wings with sharp talons, at least they looked sharp. What was even stranger, though, was that it had no tail."

Darya made a doubting face, and Adrian's furrow deepened. "I'm not crazy!" Aurelia exclaimed.

Darya scoffed but Adrian snapped his fingers as if he had been in a trance and was now suddenly free. "A dragonette!"

"A what?" Darya and Aurelia said in unison.

"I can hardly believe I'm saying this but I bet what you saw was a dragonette. They're exceedingly rare and impossible to catch. A lot of people don't even think they're real because there's only a handful of accounts of them in captivity and even those are mostly myths. I've, of course, never seen one, but I've read just about everything that's been written on them. They have the bodies of a cat but the wings of a dragon, mature dragonettes are said to breathe fire but I've never heard of one without a tail. I wonder if something happened to yours."

Darya and Aurelia just stared at Adrian, trying to process this new information about dragonettes and Adrian himself.

"What! I like dragons," Adrian muttered in self defense and started wiping down the counter. Aurelia watched over the rim of her latte how the tendons in Adrian's arms shifted with each pass.

"Well now I have so many more questions," Darya teased, taking a sip of her own coffee. "Like, are they dangerous? What do they eat? How big do they get? Are we one hundred percent sure this was actually a dragonette and not a disfigured bird? And if it was a dragonette why didn't it have a tail?"

Aurelia's head spun. She *had* heard of dragonettes but Adrian's cleaning had distracted her from making the connection between those fearsome creatures and her bumbling visitor. They were a creature out of legend, said to have once been companions of Serremont's ancient royalty and noble houses. The last of her ancestors rumored to have kept one had to have been a thousand years ago. It was a tumultuous time in their history, though, so most royal historians believed the creatures were more figurative. The stories could have been embellished and portraits containing them were fantasies.

"Yes, they're extremely dangerous. They mostly eat smaller creatures like mice, birds, and fish. Fully grown, they're not much larger than a typical street cat but their flames can easily engulf a large house and are hot enough to melt any substance. Tiny creatures, big blaze. And no, we're definitely not sure it was a dragonette, but if it was, what happened to its tail is a great question." Adrian fired off answers to each of Darya's questions in rapid succession, his eyes taking on a dreamy far off look.

"As I remember the legends, there's only been a few instances of dragonettes befriending humans, and they were all rulers or nobles of Serremont or, I think, there were a few in Norwish and Bellvanue too. Continental kingdoms with high concentrations of magic." Adrian said, turning appraisingly to Aurelia. She tried desperately to swallow her panic. Adrian apparently had an unusually deep knowledge of magical creatures, and she was definitely not prepared to explain why a dragonette would be seeking her out.

"Whether it's a mythical creature or not, I don't think it was looking for me so much as a place to land. And whatever is going on with its tail must have affected its flight. It was so little I wonder if it had ever even flown before last night."

"Hmm, that makes sense," Adrian agreed, nodding as he pushed a dark curl out of his face. "Do you think it will come back?" he asked, a hopeful glint to his voice.

"You seem to be the expert, Adrian," Lia replied with a nervous laugh. "But I did leave milk out for it and the milk was gone in the morning so... maybe?" She was confident Adrian was right about its species and that it would be back. Maybe she could blame the appearances on feeding it, that had to seem more plausible than her secretly being royalty.

"Well if you see it again, send a petalpaper immediately. I want to see this not-bird baby dragon creature." Darya commanded.

A joyful shriek burst through the door and Elle came flying up to the counter. She grabbed Darya in a crumb filled hug. "Darya! In Apple Blossom! I never thought I'd see the day!"

"Elle!" Darya laughed around her mouthful of muffin, "I just saw you an hour ago at home. Lia, this is Elle, my roommate."

"Wait," Elle pulled back, "you two know each other?"

"Peace Lily," Darya said around a mouth full of muffin, wiping her mouth with the napkin Adrian quietly handed her. He shook his head at the ruckus and turned to help a customer who was looking at the menu.

"How do you know Lia?" Darya asked Elle, looking back and forth between them.

"She's the new student I was showing around earlier this week, the one I said you needed to meet because she's wonderful," Elle cooed, nudging Darya's shoulder. "I was going to introduce you tomorrow on our trip to the Meadow."

"I probably should have figured out that my Lia was your Lia," Darya replied.

Aurelia turned deep pink and wasn't sure what to say. She'd never had casual friends at the palace. Everyone was friendly to her, of course, but these girls were becoming actual friends with her, seemingly because they wanted to, not because they had to.

"Lia," a sharp voice came from behind Elle and Darya, "if

you're done chatting with your friends, I believe there are coffee canisters to be refilled?" Aurelia cringed at Thlynda's admonishing tone.

Even though her and Adrian had just checked the coffee pots, she apologized immediately. "Yes, Thlynda, I'm sorry, of course."

Elle and Darya both silently mouthed "Sorry" to her and went to stand in line together.

Aurelia was still checking the coffees when Darya called out goodbye and said she'd see Lia the next day. Elle, meanwhile, cozied herself in a booth and began unloading her piles of books and papers, petal papers and buzzer bees flitting around her hands.

Adrian and Aurelia stood ready near the register. "That was quite a reveal," he said. Aurelia wondered if he meant the dragonette or Darya; but the dragonette would just lead them back to dangerous territory and she didn't want to go there.

"Mhm, I didn't realize they knew each other, I guess I should have figured it out, I knew they both attended SAGES."

"It's a big school, although here in the café we know just about everyone. I think my roommate is actually going on Elle's field trip to the Meadows."

"Oh? Are you coming too?" she asked, a note hopefully.

"Can't, sadly, the Meadows are always a great time, but I have to spend most of the afternoon in the lab."

"Maybe next time," she offered brightly. "How do you know Elle? And Darya?"

"Through my roommate Hunter. He co-chairs the new student orientation over on the main campus with Elle so they spent basically the whole summer together. Plus she nearly lives in Apple Blossom, I'm surprised Darya sees her at all. And then Darya I know from a magical instruments seminar we both took last year. It's a cross-discipline requirement anytime you're building new magical tech, you'll probably have to take it at some point."

"Oh, that makes sense, and I can see why Elle is here so much, it's pretty wonderful."

"It's a home away from home for a lot of us." Adrian looked at the clock, "Well, my shift is up but I hope I see you around soon, Lia," he said with a golden smile that took Aurelia's breath away.

"You too Adrian, thanks for making this first shift easy for me."

"Nah, you did great, you'll be flipping cups in no time." He winked at her then grabbed his backpack in one smooth motion. After a quick wave goodbye to Thlynda he sailed out the door.

Elle cleared her throat, catching Aurelia's attention from where she had, apparently, been staring. Aurelia flushed as Elle raised her eyebrows and glanced back to where Adrian had walked out a moment before.

"No," Aurelia, wide eyed, implored. "No," she shook her head again. Elle replied with a knowing "Mhmm," to which Aurelia groaned, "What can I make you, Elle?"

"How are your vanilla almond latte skills?" Elle asked.

"Hot or iced?" Aurelia beamed, knowing she was going to love it here.

CHAPTER TEN

E very step Aurelia took towards her workshop that afternoon was a battle. On the one hand, she so desperately wanted to talk to Fiora and Clem about the rogue rose incident but, at the same time, she also didn't want to face whatever conclusions they might draw.

This morning had been so wonderful, Aurelia didn't want the afternoon to claim her newfound peace. Sitting on a bench just outside her workshop, she closed her eyes, soaking in the grounding sensations of the garden campus around her. Overhead, a trio of robins chirped merrily to one another while a jasmine plant, growing along the fence behind her, sent a trail of sweet smelling flowers around her shoulder in an embrace. The sun glowed warm on her skin while all around a cooling breeze stirred the bushes of pink petaled roses.

Calmed, she opened her eyes and was startled to find a confused looking Clem and impatient looking Fiora standing directly before her. Four wings shimmered over their heads, light dancing through their opaque panels. *Moment over,* she supposed.

"So you heard." Aurelia said, squinting towards the sky.

"Oh we heard." Fiora snorted, tapping one long fingernail against the clipboard clutched in her arms.

"Let's take this inside the house?" Clem suggested. Fiora's razor sharp gaze flicked to him and Aurelia got the distinct impression that Clem suggesting to move indoors was more than a bit unusual.

As they entered the house, Fiora led them into the library. It was a stunning, two story room that, on any other day, Aurelia would have loved to meander through. Even now, sinking into a plush armchair across from Fiora and Clem, she couldn't help but imagine how cozy the space would be on a cold winter afternoon with the fire blazing, studying under the painted ceiling covered in roses and leafy branches.

Perhaps she'd curl up on the oversized, pillow-covered loveseat under the arched windows that took up the entire far wall of the space. Or maybe she'd climb the spiral staircase to the narrow second floor balcony and hole up in one of the tiny nooks.

Aurelia hoped she would still be here for those snowy days. It was a thought that took her by surprise– that she hoped she would still be here come winter. Despite all her fears over her rising powers, over more incidents like the café, over the success or failure of the work she'd do with Fiora and Clem, she hoped. That was new, and she wasn't ready to let the spark of it go.

"I think we better start off with an explanation of what happened yesterday." Fiora began.

Aurelia opened her mouth to try to explain but with a subtle shake of Clem's head, she stopped herself.

"Your magic has built up to a dangerous peak, and we cannot put off siphoning any longer. I thought we had more time than this, but clearly, that ineffective ring on your finger is doing a better job than I had estimated."

Aurelia was confused, she had never heard of siphoning before, but she let Fiora continue.

"First, I want you to know that while what happened yesterday wasn't your fault, well, no. It was, but only to the extent that it was your magic that caused the event."

Aurelia had known it was her magic, but hearing it confirmed from Fiora still felt like a blow. The frilly, blush-toned ranunculus set in vases around the room turned their ruffled faces towards her, as if they were checking in on her.

"Nevertheless, you should have come to us, directly to us, so that we could work on a solution. We are supposed to be helping you, Lia, but we can't do that if you don't trust us—"

Clem interrupted, "Fiora, you're not wrong but think about it from Aurelia's–" he corrected himself, "Lia's– perspective for a moment. She's had countless tutors over the last, what, fifteen years, and has made less than no progress. It's actually only gotten worse. Why would she think we'd do anything but judge her for the incident? Look," he turned to Aurelia, who was using every ounce of her royal upbringing to keep her expression neutral. She was not only confused and embarrassed but now also frustrated and just a bit insulted. Clem was right but it was hard to hear, especially in such an earnest defense. Even so, she owed it to herself to hear them both out.

"I understand why you didn't come to us yesterday," Clem continued, "we haven't earned your trust yet. But if you can really listen to what we're going to teach you I know you'll come to see that we *can* help you."

Aurelia didn't reply but chewed over the words, she wasn't sure what to do with the emotions threatening to trample her fragile hope, but she nodded for the faeries to continue.

"Lia, you are an immensely powerful Summoner," Fiora said, standing to pace about the room as she attempted a less confrontational tone, "but that is not all you are. We're going to get into the root of your magic and these outbursts soon, but first, we have to make your magic safer. I want you to think of your magic as a watering hose. Typically, a magic wielder sustains a certain level of," she paused, thinking.

"Magical water pressure," Clem piped in, leaning forward in his chair. His wings perked up at the talk of metaphorical gardening.

"Right," Fiora agreed, "yes, magical water pressure. And that ring you wear, the one I suspect you've been wearing most of your life, is like a kink in the hose." Fiora made a twisting motion with her hand, trying to demonstrate the concept.

"That kink works for a while, probably for years, to cut off the flow of magic." She perched in her seat again, "But as time goes on and you accumulate more magic, that pressure is going to build and build. And soon, little drops of magic will start leaking through because something has to give, either the hose or the tie."

Aurelia nodded along, spinning the ring on her finger and thinking about how scared she was the first time magic seeped through. Even though the little strawberry vine had been so friendly, presenting her with a perfectly plump little fruit, she knew enough about the strength of binding rings to be terrified of herself, of what she had done.

"We can't teach you to control your magic until we safely release that built up pressure," Clem explained, putting his warm, calloused hand on her arm reassuringly.

"But I've taken the ring off before," Aurelia said, trying to fit the pieces together.

"Yes, in the far north winterlands, right?" Fiora asked.

Aurelia nodded, looking out the window rather than meeting Fiora's stare, "So that I wouldn't hurt anyone."

Aurelia remembered all the times she had shut herself away to protect the other children of the court. Times when her childhood friends had gotten little cuts or bruises while playing, the adults always thought it was typical childhood games, but Aurelia and her parents had known the truth. An overexcited rose bush lashing out thorns here, an old tree lifting a root in greeting there. The little moments that taught Aurelia her own childish fun wasn't worth the risk, that she was the only one who could keep everyone safe.

"The problem with that way of thinking ," Clem took over explaining with a let-me-handle-it look at Fiora, "is that your magic needs somewhere to go. When you release it from the binding ring, it needs to be used and absorbed back into the world. Your magic, all magic really, comes from the life of the world. When you release it, if it doesn't have a specific purpose, it becomes dangerous."

This was not at all how magic had been explained to her at all. Her tutors had always said that magic came from within a person, that it was just how you were made. The way some people ran quickly and others slowly, and while anyone could train to run faster, there were limitations to how fast a person could learn to run and how hard it would be to learn that swiftness. Magic was a combination of training, effort, and natural inclination, but it all stemmed from a place inside you. Magic wasn't around you being drawn upon, it was in you being released and you had what you had.

Aurelia looked between the two faeries, trying to decide how to voice her confusion. At last, she settled on simply, "Why isn't that what's taught at court?"

"Because human hearts are hard to change." Clem lamented, softer than before.

"Our ancestors have always had magic, long before the passageways from the faerie realms opened. Even though your kind received magic from our people, the separation of humans and faeries in the Celestial Wars stole so much knowledge of magic from your people."

Aurelia fixed her eyes on a row of gilded history tomes beside the fireplace, some she recognized from the vast collection at the palace, others she did not. She had so many rising questions for Fiora and Clem, and even more for the keeper of the royal libraries. But before she could voice them, Fiora chimed in.

"We will talk more about this in the coming months, but for now, we have to get back to the more pressing matters at hand." Fiora eyed Clem and he sat back with a sigh, clearly wanting to talk more about the Celestial Wars and history of humans and faeries.

"If yesterday was any indication, and based on what I know of that ring you wear, your power could very well level this city if not handled properly. Luckily for you, and all the citizens of Florevale, I have a plan and I am an excellent planner. Come with me."

Fiora stood abruptly, picking up a nondescript wooden box the size of a few stacked books. Aurelia and Clem followed behind obediently as she walked to the back gardens.

"Clem has been preparing siphoning gardens for you all summer, these are spaces where your pent up magic can be safely reabsorbed into the world."

Outside, Clem took the lead. He brought them to a grove of low hanging oak trees where clusters of silvery moss swayed in the breeze. Dappled sunlight shimmered across the path, filtering through winding branches thicker than Aurelia herself. She had never seen these trees in person before, only read about them in descriptions of Lownden's marshy lowlands. No birds sung from these branches, though, and an odd stillness pervaded the glen.

"I designed this siphoning garden to be capable of

handling your initial bursts of raw power," Clem said with pride, "you don't even want to know how many favors I had to call in to get these particular trees here. They've been established as vacuums of a sort, empty vessels, so when your power is released, these trees will drink that magic into themselves and absorb it safely. Don't worry, it won't hurt the trees."

Aurelia hesitated. "So what do I do with them? I mean, are you suggesting I just take off my ring?"

"No!" Both Fiora and Clem yelped in unison. Clem grabbed her hands as if she was going to rip the binding ring off right there.

"No," Clem said again more calmly while Fiora took loud, huffing breaths, muttering something about the hastiness of humans.

Clem motioned for Fiora to open the box. Inside were five rows of gleaming gold rings almost exactly like the one Aurelia wore. Each was carved with a unique swirl of Norwish runes that glinted in the light.

"Fiora and I hope, and believe, that someday you'll be able to control your magic entirely without the aid of binding rings, but for now, we need to slowly release the pressure."

Clem began picking through the rings, selecting three and examining the runes with an enlarging glass. Unsatisfied, he put two back and picked up others. "Once we've safely drained off all the excess build up, we'll be able to measure your magic's natural flow level and the depth of your reservoir."

"So all that excess magic will be contained in these trees?" Aurelia asked skeptically.

"Goodness no," Fiora said, having regained her calm. "See how the path leads through the glade? Clem created these siphoning gardens so that as you exhaust each one we can move on to the next."

Aurelia looked suspiciously at the white pebble path. "How far back does this go? Aren't there other workshops nearby?"

"Fiora cast special wards that would expand the space as much as needed without ever getting closer to the surrounding workshops." Fiora rolled her eyes at the praise. It reminded Aurelia of the Enchantment at Peace Lily but did that mean Fiora was an Enchanter? Aurelia had simply assumed the faeries were Summoners since she had never heard of a Graced faerie or a faerie Enchanted object. But now that she thought about it, she'd never actually learned anything about faeries' magic except that they had it.

She considered the magic Clem was describing. To create a ward able to contain all the power magic like hers would throw at it, to be able to sustain such lush, living gardens like the ones surrounding them, this wasn't just an expansion of physical space, it was an expansion of magical boundaries. She let the question go, these wards were far beyond what she could understand today.

Aurelia looked at the faeries in awe, wondering just where Fiora and Clem had come from and how they had ended up here with her.

"I'm trying to follow, I really am, this is a very new way of seeing magic for me." Aurelia said, "does this mean after today I'll just," she furrowed her brow, "be fixed? No more magic spilling out everywhere?"

The faeries looked at each other nervously. "Not exactly," Clem hesitated after a heart thundering pause and Aurelia wondered what had passed between the two.

"Your magic will certainly be less dangerous after today," Fiora assured her, cocking her head thoughtfully to the side, "but siphoning is a slow and careful process. We don't know precisely how long it will take. We'll get started today but this could be a long journey ahead of you, Lia, you should prepare yourself."

That sounded great to Aurelia who was in no hurry to leave Florevale anytime soon.

"Well, a little progress is better than none, I suppose. Tell me what to do."

"We're going to start with a one percent reduction in binding strength," Clem said, slipping his final selection of five rings onto her left hand before stepping back. Aurelia couldn't help noticing how Clem positioned himself protectively just a hair in front of Fiora and wondered if his sister had noticed it too.

"Okay now, Lia," Clem said, "go ahead and take off the binding ring."

Aurelia stared down at her hands for a long moment. Then another. The only sounds in the radiant clearing were the trio's discordant breaths and her own erratic pulse.

This wasn't a new process for Aurelia. Every time they renewed the enchantments on her rings she had to go through a procedure similar to this. New rings on before the old rings came off, usually in some remote, barren setting where her flaring, angry magic could take out its temper in that fleeting instant of vulnerability.

She looked again to the beautiful oak trees, hoping she wasn't about to undo their centuries of glorious life in a moment of magical chaos. With one more hesitant glance at the faeries – Clem nodding encouragement, Fiora's face scrunched up in concentration – Aurelia slowly started to pull off her ring.

Before the ring had fully come off her finger she felt her magic roaring to the surface. Her little magical leaks might have resulted in friendly sweet peas and cheerful greetings from petite rosebuds, but her true magic was a roiling ocean gathering itself into a frothing, surging wave that promised to devour everything in its path.

Power coursed through her body, sending her to her knees where she panicked and shoved the ring back into place.

Utter silence.

Clem knelt before her, fitting three more rings onto her fingers. "Let's start with a quarter of a percent reduction."

She could tell he was trying to smile but all the color had drained from his face and she knew he could sense the danger lurking beneath her skin.

Aurelia nodded, words had not returned. She stayed there, kneeling on the ground, eyes shut, waiting until she was steady enough to try again. Clem and Fiora gave her space and time, held so still that the only movement in the grove was the occasional rustle of wind in their hair.

At last, Aurelia gathered herself, opened her eyes, and tried again.

Again her magic swelled, sending tingling needles down her arms and across her back. But this time, it didn't overtake her. She was still breathing. Slowly, she took off the ring. The loss of it was a physical blow as she clasped her hands over her wild heart.

The trees around her shook in an unnatural gale. Golden veins of raw magic shot up the gnarled trunks as new branches erupted violently from the tangled arms of the oaks. The clearing grew dark as swells of oblong green leaves grew in thickly crowded clusters, blotting out the sun. The illuminated threads of her power cast a strange glow over the clearing. Aurelia would have thought it was beautiful, like a summer night lit by swaying lanterns, if not for the terror of the darkness all around. Ripples of magic undulated through the blazing streams, slowly sinking into the mossy bark.

And then it was over.

Aurelia took a ragged breath as Clem leapt in joy, letting out a loud whoop, his fluttering wings lifting him off the ground. He flitted from branch to branch, examining the damage she had caused. The trees were covered in a lattice of black scars, marred wherever her magic had touched them.

Fiora nodded approvingly, her pencil scratching line after line of notes. "Good, let's continue."

Aurelia's trembling spirit flagged. That was just a quarter of a percent, and how far did they have to go? A quarter of a percent of the *excess* magic, the magic she couldn't naturally contain within herself. And how quickly would her magic just refill what she had let out? Would it be back to one hundred percent tomorrow? In an hour? In a minute?

She looked up at Fiora, "I have so many questions." Her voice was little more than a rasping whisper.

Fiora's lips formed a thin line. "I expected you would. Professor Maillie will be joining us on Monday to review today's results and set a schedule for moving forward. Let's continue. The more data Clem and I collect now the better he'll be able to answer your questions then."

Aurelia didn't love that answer but made her way to her feet regardless. Her limbs were heavy, like she'd just run the entire perimeter of Florevale with a heavy bag of books on her back. She gave Fiora a small shrug, the closest she could physically come to saying okay.

"Clem!" Fiora called, "are we ready for the second round? You can come back for more of these measurements later."

Clem flew down, eagerly circling the two. "Yes, yes, on to the next!"

At least someone was enjoying this, Aurelia thought, although she didn't fully understand why. And at the moment, with barely enough energy to walk to the next clearing, asking him about it– much less actually listening to his answers– was fully beyond her reach.

CHAPTER ELEVEN

B y the time they paused for the day, Aurelia had cleared just over half a percent.

After the initial release, Clem decided to be even more gentle, taking off mere fractions of a percent of power with each ring transfer. He said something about wanting to study the effects of various sized magical releases on the flora and fauna of the meadows. Something about refreshing and renewing the clearings better as time went on; making them more efficient at absorbing her magic.

He might have said more but Aurelia's whole being had fizzled into just three essential tasks: breath, walk, switch rings.

AURELIA COULDN'T REMEMBER the trek back to her apartment afterwards. She couldn't remember climbing the stairs, she couldn't remember opening her windows or lying on the couch or falling asleep without so much as taking off her shoes.

She woke a few hours later to moonlight mixed with the soft glow of the city falling through the balcony doors. It was just enough light to outline the barest of shapes in the room. And she wasn't alone.

A SMALL WINGED creature perched motionless on the table before the couch. Somewhere in Aurelia's thoughts, she knew this was concerning, she should be afraid. Yet her sleep addled and magic weary mind was so slow to wake that she could only muster the barest sense of confusion. She stared at the creature, trying to make sense of what she was seeing, trying to remember where she even was.

As Aurelia's eyes adjusted to the darkness, the shadows took the shape of her couch and chair and books. With a yelp she jumped up away from the creature and fumbled to light a candle.

In all the ruckus, the creature simply sat, head tilted in feline concentration, wings tucked in tight to its back. Aurelia rubbed her bleary eyes.

She struggled for what to do. The Royal Librarian had written back yesterday saying he would send a bevy of books on dragonettes with Josephine this week. The Royal Kennelmaster had also written back saying young cats, once weaned from their mothers, typically ate small creatures like mice, bugs, or worms, whatever they could catch really. Whether that translated to a dragonette kit, she had no idea.

Aurelia knew this kitten was old enough to eat meat since she could see, in spectacularly terrifying detail, its tiny dagger-teeth gnawing at some invisible enemy nestled deep in its claws.

She stood to pace, lighting more candles and trying to decide what to do.

"Do you have a name?" she asked the dragonette who yawned and rolled onto its side for continued bathing. Her side– his side? Aurelia didn't know and she was absolutely not about to try to check. This creature had far too many pointy bits to be poking around at it.

Aurelia went to the kitchen to fetch some milk for the creature and put a pot of water on for her own dinner. While the water heated, she gingerly slid the bowl of milk across the table towards the little thing. The creature sniffed the bowl then looked at Aurelia, pupils narrowing to concentrated slits.

Aurelia dropped small, hollow noodles into the pot and sat a steamer pan over the water with fresh florets of broccoli. She watched as the dragonette dipped an experimental paw into the milk and licked it off a few times, like it couldn't make up its mind if it liked the taste or not.

When her noodles were done, she drained out most of the pasta water and tossed everything with a few knobs of butter and grated parmesan overtop.

She mixed the dish vigorously, filling the kitchen with the comforting scent of cheesy pasta. She spied the fresh truffles she had picked up at the market earlier in the week and shaved them generously on top of the plate. Too exhausted to wait for it to cool, Aurelia took a bite and groaned in satisfaction. After such a roller coaster of a day, the first familiar bite of buttery, creamy, truffly pasta was exactly what she needed.

Dinner ready, she set a glass of sparkling lemon water, a pitcher of pink peonies, and two short candles on her small dining table. Just as she turned to get her bowl from the kitchen, a flurry of uncoordinated wing beats flashed above her. The dragonette landed on the counter, knocking the plate of truffle shavings to the ground in a clatter of broken ceramic and mushroom crumbs.

She hurtled to the kitchen, afraid the dragonette had crash landed like last time and might be hurt. Instead she found the mischievous creature purring loudly among the wreckage, its little pink tongue darting out again and again to lap up truffle bits.

Aurelia didn't know whether to laugh or cry at this point. She sank to the floor, pulled her knees up to her chest, and leaned back against the cabinet as she watched the jubilant, clumsy little thing. Reaching up, she grabbed her own plate – thankfully undisturbed in the kerfuffle – and said "cheers" to the dragonette before taking a few bites of her slightly colder but still delicious pasta.

"I'm going to call you Truffi," she said to the dragonette, experimentally reaching one hand out to see if it would let her scratch its soft white chin. Her tutors probably would have admonished her for touching a creature, especially a powerful, magical creature, while it was eating, but it didn't seem to mind. Instead, the creature paused, tilting its head to give her better access.

"Truffi," she repeated, inspecting the dragonette, "are you a Truffi?" Threads of iridescent light ran down the length of its wings, Aurelia wasn't sure if she was imagining it or if the creature could understand her, but she decided to take that as approval. "Truffi it is," she hummed, and the two ate in contented silence until every morsel of food was gone.

Aurelia cleaned up, both her dinner and Truffi's mess, then took a long, steamy shower. When she emerged, drying her long hair in an soft cloth, Truffi was gone. Aurelia wasn't sure where the dragonette went off to, but she smiled, confidant Truffi would be back soon.

CHAPTER TWELVE

Although Aurelia woke early on Saturday, she lingered in bed long past sunrise. She watched as the first rays of light filtered across her fluffy white comforter, as the shadows around the corners of her sleeping chamber gently faded to light. She wasn't sure what to expect from her magic after the first day of siphoning, but when her motherly kitchen plant wriggled its way to her bedside, a steaming mug of coffee cradled in its leafy vines, Aurelia knew she still had a long way to go.

She sat up in bed, sipped her coffee, and picked up her latest read from its spot on her nightstand. Eventually, though, Aurelia's stomach had enough of the lounging and demanded she get food. She glanced at the clock, trying to decide what to do now. She was meeting with Elle at noon but it was still early and, for the first time in her twenty years of life, Aurelia could do whatever she pleased.

She dressed, brushed her teeth, and twisted half her hair up with a mother of pearl clip.

On the way out the door, she grabbed her book and a short stack of petalpapers to send a few notes over breakfast.

Six quick flights of stairs later, she stepped onto the sidewalk and took a deep breath of the crisp late summer air. Across the street, a pair of elves were arranging blue and white rattan chairs around tiny outdoor tables pressed up one next to another as if to say 'we're all friends here.'

Aurelia darted across the road and asked for a table for one. The younger of the two elves, a boy with short cut pin straight white hair and pointed ears decorated with baubles, said she could sit wherever and handed her a menu.

Aurelia chose a seat facing out, eager to watch the sleepy city wake up. She ordered their classic breakfast– a plate of creamy scrambled eggs with fresh herbs, a fleuret roll, and a cappuccino. Her stomach rumbled with gratitude at the first bite.

"Mornin' Lia" a voice called from the street. Lia looked up to see two fuzzy legs walking beneath a precariously balanced stack of covered trays.

"Good morning, Calyntha, do you need a hand with those?" Aurelia replied, sure that the stack of trays was taller than the nellin herself.

"Nah, but thank ya," the voice huffed. "This here but a lil stack, ya shoulda seen th' towers Pa could 'arry back in th'day, now thos're a sight."

"I thought this floret roll tasted familiar, I should have known it was yours." Aurelia mused as the elven servers rushed to unload the trays. They didn't seem to share Calyntha's confidence in her tower. Aurelia watched, fascinated, and wondered if Calyntha's Pa was the one who taught her to bake so beautifully.

"Oh for sure, most of tha café's n'such on this street come ta me for breads n'pastries n'tha' like. Easier for them ta not 'ave ta make em and easier for me 'cause I can make 'em all together."

"And great for everyone else because we get to enjoy your delicious bakes wherever we are." Aurelia added.

"You're a sweet 'un, Lia, well, I best be gettin' back, 'ave a good mornin'." Calyntha waved and hurried across the street to retrieve her next delivery.

BACK AT HER APARTMENT, Aurelia changed to meet up with Elle. For their outing to the Meadows, she swapped out her pants, comfortable as they were, for a pair of high waisted light wash denim shorts with a thin leather belt and chunky sport shoes. She plucked a sprig of fluttering cosmos from her balcony and pinned it into her half up hairstyle.

Aurelia bound down the stairs and around the corner to the little garden where they all planned to meet. Of course, Elle was already there. She was clearly not ready for summer to end in her light blue crop top with its high neck and thin straps and a sporty high waisted white skirt.

Beside her, Darya adjusted the strap of her medium wash denim overalls, the rolled cuff of the shorts showing off her golden Bellvanuan skin. The girls waved as Aurelia entered the garden, each embracing her in a warm hug.

"This is so sweet," Darya said, lifting a hand to gingerly touch the flowers in Aurelia's hair.

"Thank you! Here," Aurelia plucked one from out her twist and tucked it into the pocket of Darya's coveralls, "now we can match."

"I love it!"

"What no flowers for me?" a cool voice drawled behind Aurelia.

Elle squealed and jumped to hug the new arrival. "Lia, this is Hunter, Hunter, this is your new best friend, Lia."

"Hunter," Aurelia repeated, reaching out to shake the tall, dirty blonde haired newcomer's hand. He pulled her into a bear of a hug.

"So *you're* the mysterious Lia I've been hearing about," he said. Lia eyed Elle, not wanting to know what she'd been saying about her. Elle had entirely too high of an opinion of Aurelia.

"Adrian mentioned there was a new girl at the café." Aurelia's heart skipped a beat at the mention of Adrian's name, she had assumed it was just Elle but had Adrian been talking about her too?

"Hi sweetie." He hugged Darya next then slipped on a pair of gigantic black sunglasses.

"Oh! You must be his roommate! Adrian said that you and Elle co-chair the new student orientation?" Aurelia asked as the group started walking.

"Sure do! I dated her older brother back in Lownden years ago. We made a disastrous couple but I got to keep this little sunshine in the breakup so," he paused, looking over at Elle lovingly, "it was all worth it!"

They all laughed as Elle sighed, "I warned you two it was a terrible idea."

"Yes hun, and that's why we had to give it a try." Elle rolled her eyes and gave his arm a playful shove.

"So, where are we off to first?" Aurelia asked.

"Treasure hunting" Elle beamed, starry eyed and on a mission.

TREASURE HUNTING, as it turned out, meant a bustling, wide open market square filled with tables, tents, and endless racks of everything imaginable.

Florevale's classic six floor buildings rose on every side of the square, trailing ivy and bushes of star jasmine hung leisurely from the wrought iron doors and higher up balconies.

Blooming crab apple trees filled the cobbled streets with shady greenery while corner cafés bustled with satisfied shoppers.

Elle had clearly come for the vintage clothes and made a bee-line to the largest of all the tents. It was run by a curmudgeonly older woman, impeccably dressed in a gauzy blouse with high waisted dark denim, whose eagle eyed gaze softened as soon as she spotted Elle.

"She'll be there all morning, come on, let's go see if we can find a lost Master," Darya linked her arm through Aurelia's and pulled her towards a table across the market.

Darya led her to a smattering of tents covered wall to wall with hanging artworks. Gold-painted frames— some pristine, others cracked and frayed until they were scarcely wood chips— encased everything from sunny watercolor pastorals to moody chiaroscuro oil portraits. Diptychs and painted boxes littered the tables mixed with stacks of canvases and scrolls.

"How does a person find anything in here?" Aurelia asked, more than a bit overwhelmed at the selection.

"The key," Darya assured her, "is to not look for anything in particular. That way you'll always find what you want."

"Uhm," Aurelia furrowed her brow, "I'm still confused."

"Clear your head, try not to think too much, just see what catches your eye. Have you never been to a vintage market before?"

Aurelia most certainly hadn't, but she knew that would be

hard to explain without letting out the whole 'I'm a Princess and always have a retinue of guards' thing.

"Not one this..." Aurelia paused, looking around at the cacophony of shoppers negotiating deals and passing finds back and forth, "...energetic." That felt safe, and Darya didn't pry as Hunter walked up to browse with them.

"True, this is the busiest market in Florevale. There are others nearly every day of the week but this is the longest running and always has the best pieces."

"I once found an authentic early Reyonaldo sketch, the sale paid my rent for two whole years." Hunter gushed, joining their conversation.

"The man finds one half formed napkin sketch and will never let us live it down." Darya said, rolling her eyes.

"What can I say, I have an eye for authenticity." Hunter proudly tipped his sunglasses down for emphasis.

Aurelia laughed but wished she could show Hunter the mural in the palace that Reyonaldo himself had painted three hundred years ago. It framed the carved stone fireplace in her private library, full of swirling snow gusts and winter-cloaked trees. It made for the most beautiful contrast to a roaring fire in the winter and when she gazed at it, she could almost for a moment believe she was actually looking out on the frosty forests of northern Calderith.

The trio wandered the art market, rifling through stacks of paintings, wandering the stalls set and styled so beautifully they seemed like works of art all their own. Darya purchased a notebook full of handmade drawing paper bound in tan leather with gold embossing. Hunter, meanwhile, haggled a golden haired faerie to include two framed paintings of the Serremont Riviera for free after picking up a four hundred year old set of chenouri salad plates covered in fluttering butterfly motifs. Aurelia was mesmerized by their flickering wings – and that was saying a lot considering the palace's vast Enchanted china collections.

Aurelia herself hesitated to purchase anything. She was surrounded with so much beauty, but didn't know what to do with it all. As princess, she had truly limitless funds, so it wouldn't be right to haggle with these vendors who worked hard to procure such unique prizes. Watching Darya and Hunter, though, she didn't know how to explain that to them and she couldn't shake the guilt of how welcoming they had been compared with how secretive she was.

After a highly successful morning at the market, particularly for Elle whose finds were en route by direct courier back to her apartment (she couldn't possibly carry the beautifully wrapped packages around all afternoon), the little group decided it was time for lunch.

The Meadows, like most of Florevale, was laden with sidewalk cafés and charming little restaurants on every street. They followed their noses to a particularly popular eatery. The homey scent of sauteed garlic and melting cheese like an invisible string leading them to a jovial pastaria.

Its walls were worn turquoise, speckled with golden sunlight that streamed through the glass ceiling. Greenery climbed across wooden trellises and enormous trees in even more enormous clay pots made diners feel more like they had stepped into a beautiful garden patio than a two room café.

"Our specialty is burrata, balls of milky cheese that are firm out the outside with a gooey center," their server, a chic dark haired girl around their age said as she set a decanter of water on the table. "My favorite is the heirloom tomato burrata salad, it's dressed with cold pressed olive oil and fresh basil. But you can't go wrong with today's homemade pasta, it's tossed with butter, egg, pecorino cheese, crispy guanciale, and slices of burrata. Or if you're in the mood for pizza, our signature burrata prosciutto pie is a classic, it's drizzled with fresh pesto and just a bit of chili oil."

The four of them looked around the table before Hunter spoke up, "Yes. All of that, yes please. We'll take all of it." The group laughed and agreed, ordering a pitcher of fizzy orange sweet wine to share.

"I love this place," Darya breathed as they divided up the plates. "It tastes so much like home."

"If this is what home tastes like," Hunter said, "then I vote we all spend the winter holiday at Darya's."

"I don't think my little town could handle you *and* Elle at the same time."

"No problem, leave Elle at home and bring me to the food." The group laughed some more, Elle giving Hunter's shoulder a shove.

"You act like we don't feed you back in Lownden which couldn't be farther from the truth." She started ticking off her fingers, "there's Big Mill, South of Market, Calliope's Biscuits, Gracie's Porch."

"Alright, alright, you win, the food back home is pretty great but I mean, look at this cheese pull." Hunter said, stretching a piece of pizza up as high as his arm could reach.

By the time all four of them at last put down their forks in defeat– or victory, Aurelia wasn't sure which– they nearly had to roll each other onto the street. After the pasta and the pizza and the cheese, someone's grandma had strolled out of the kitchen wielding an enormous bowl of cake layered with coffee cream and chocolate, scooping heaping mountains of the mixture onto plates at every table.

They decided to take a walk along the Floriéne river waterfront that bordered the Meadow and Shrubs districts. Street musicians stationed every few blocks filled the air with a jazzy mix of saxophone, cello, and thrumming guitar.

Elle walked arm in arm with Aurelia, Darya and Hunter close behind. "So, how are you liking Florevale, Lia?" Elle asked.

"I think I could be happy here forever," Aurelia replied, eyes wandering from groups of friends laughing on benches to couples hand in hand crossing the ornate bridges that spanned the river.

"You're in love that quickly?"

"How could I not be? The people, the food, the gardens, it's beyond everything I had imagined, and I had imagined so much."

"Could you just... stay? Rule from here?"

Aurelia looked back warily to see if Hunter and Darya were listening, frantically planning how she'd explain Elle's question.

"Don't worry, once you get those two started on the design of the city bridges they'll never stop." Elle reassured her. And it was true, Hunter and Darya were locked in a heated debate with phrases like 'stone veneered parapet' and 'sixth century granite voussoirs' flying about.

"I guess I never really gave much thought to that. The palace has been in Jardeisailles for so long, but there is a royal residence in the city. I suppose I could technically come back but... it wouldn't be the same."

"Well I, for one, am glad you're here for as long as we can keep you."

"And what about you? Don't you want to go home to Lownden someday?" Even though Elle was right about the others, she didn't want to think about ruling Serremont any more than absolutely necessary. Enough of her life had been about that future, this part of her life she wanted to keep for herself.

"Maybe. I still have so many years ahead of me with my research, though, it's hard to imagine a future beyond Florevale." Aurelia could sense Elle didn't want to talk much about the future either, they had that much in common, so she changed topics.

"So, where are we off to now?"

"Now, my dear," Hunter said, looping his arm through her free side, "it's time for a time honored Florevale tradition."

She raised an eyebrow at him.

"You can't truly call yourself a Florevalian until you've shared a bottle of honey wine while watching the sun set over the Foriéne, and I have just the spot."

CHAPTER THIRTEEN

Professor Maillie was waiting for Aurelia when she entered the workshop on Monday morning. The weekend had been so full of laughter and exploration and friendship unlike any she'd ever known before. She was determined to do whatever needed to be done to stay in Florevale as long as possible.

"Ah, Lia, right on time," Maillie said as she set her bag down on the table. "Come, let's talk in the kitchen. Fiora, dear, do you have any of those little sandwich cookies tucked away in here?"

Fiora called down from the second floor that she would be right there as Clem emerged from the backyard, his wings crusted in a layer of pinkish dirt that sparkled brilliantly whenever it caught the light.

Aurelia leaned over to Clem as he started to follow them to the kitchen and whispered, "You might want to clean up before Fiora gets down here."

"Clem!" An annoyed voice called out from the second floor and Aurelia cringed.

Clem paled. "I'll meet you in there," he groused as he half-walked, half-flew back outside.

"Faerie hearing," Maillie chuckled, seating himself at the table and motioning for Aurelia to sit across from him.

"Should we wait for them before we start?" Aurelia asked.

"No need to wait for that one," Fiora huffed as she sailed through the door. "He knows better than to come into the workshop with pink lotus dust, he'll be cleaning that off for the next hour."

"It's next to impossible to fully clean off, beautiful how it sparkles but a true monster to get rid of," Maillie explained quietly, leaning forward as if it was a secret between just himself and Aurelia.

"Fiora and Clem caught me up on all your progress last week." Maillie said as Fiora placed three mugs of tea before them. "To start, I'd like to hear your take on all of it, Lia. How did you feel Friday with your first siphoning? Did you notice anything different over the weekend? Anything at all?"

Aurelia thought about it as she sipped her tea then promptly added another scoop of sugar. Maillie and Fiora sat in amiable silence, giving her the space to assemble her thoughts.

What could she say, really? The siphoning had been scary, painful, exhausting. So much magic had poured through her and yet if anything it felt like there was even more magic than before, only now it was twice as insistent on being set free.

She wanted to give Maillie some sort of hopeful report, something positive, but she didn't get the sense he wanted her platitudes. And she knew Fiora would see right through her. So she said the most truthful thing she could, while still preserving a seedling of hope.

"It feels like I have a very long road ahead of me," Aurelia began.

Fiora's pen flew across the page as she wrote down every word.

"We didn't build all this for a little one or two semester

project!" Professor Maillie laughed. "Of course it will take time. You've spent your whole life building up a veritable ocean of magic, to release it in anything short of an apocalypse is going to be an arduous process. But we will rise to the tide!"

"Based on our measurements of power expended and bindings exhausted," Fiora added, "we're hopeful we may be able to start training your magic within the next year, but establishing your true baseline is going to take," Fiora paused, flipping through pages of notes and complicated looking calculations, "well, lets just say it can be done, it will be done, but putting timelines on it would only be discouraging. Not to mention the work it will take Clem to create enough receiving gardens. Aurelia, you should plan to be here with us for a great long while."

Aurelia knew she should be intimidated, Fiora didn't even want to tell her how long the siphoning would take, and Maillie had called her magic apocalyptic. After a lifetime of living with the enormity of her magic, hiding just how immense it was from everyone around her, she should be anxious. But all she felt was relief.

She loved Florevale, she loved this school, she loved the people she was getting to know, the burgeoning friendships, the freedom and belonging a princess could never truly have. And now they were telling her to settle in, they were telling her they thought this would work and that she would get to stay. The small potted miniature roses in the center of the table burst into riotous bloom as that little seed of hope within Aurelia sprouted roots, cocooning her heart. She was only a little afraid to let it.

"Now, let's talk next steps." Maillie said, eying the pot warily as more buds and blooms mounted on top of one another.

"You'll work with Fiora and Clem for the next few weeks to siphon off magic each day. They'll report your progress to me and you and I will sit down every two weeks to chat through your work and assess how the siphoning is affecting your break-throughs. I do need to warn you, Lia," Maillie was suddenly more serious than Aurelia had ever seen, "your magic may feel more intense over these next few months. Even though we are relieving the pressure, we're also stirring the pot, so to speak."

"Your magic had been laying mostly dormant, the waters still, but now we are disrupting it, creating eddies and flows that make your reserve more volatile. You may experience more breakthroughs, and those breakthroughs may be more intense. I don't want you to be afraid, but you will need to be cautious."

Aurelia was always cautious but she nodded her head, chewing over the words as she spun her binding ring.

Clem walked in, bits of shimmering pink dust still falling from his wings as he reached over Fiora to grab a cookie from the plate before her.

"Clem, I thought you were going to clean that off!" Fiora yelped, leaning away from his wings and brushing at a fleck that had fallen on her arm.

"I did!" he chirped like a proud child. "But you know it's impossible to get every speck, I think it looks rather nice anyway." His wings made a flickering motion which cast bits of dancing light around the room.

"She's just grumpy because the last time we went to the Spring Fae Equinox–"

"Clem finish that sentence and I promise pink lotus dust will be the least of your problems." Fiora growled, cutting him off with a menace that made Aurelia shudder.

Clem put up his hands in mock innocence and took a seat next to Aurelia. She tried to hide her laughter behind a sip of her tea but was unsuccessful.

"Let's focus, shall we?" Fiora said. Clem mimicked her motions and Aurelia couldn't hold her laughter in any longer.

Fiora rolled her eyes and snatched up a cookie, muttering in a faerie dialect Aurelia had never heard while Maillie brought order back to the table.

"As we were saying, you'll be attending classes and siphoning most days, once a month we'll do a more formal assessment to determine when your magic has reached a safe level to begin instruction. Now, I have to get off to my next meeting, Fiora, walk me out dear while these two get to work."

The group stood, setting their plates in a neat stack next to the sink, but Maillie turned back.

"Oh, and Lia, I want you to start keeping a journal. Please log every time you have a breakthrough and any details about it you can remember. We may need to make adjustments if they become too powerful."

"Okay, Professor," Aurelia said, groaning inwardly. She preferred to ignore the breakthroughs most of the time, preferred to pretend they were someone else's intentional doing. Truth be told, she had worked very hard over the years to not notice breakthroughs and now she'd have to spend nearly her whole day jotting down notes. This was not a task she looked forward to, but the concern in Maillie's eyes made her wary enough that she would try her best to do as he asked.

CHAPTER FOURTEEN

Elle and Aurelia met up for a picnic dinner on the SAGES quad that afternoon. The weather was still summer warm but there was a crispness to the air that promised Fall was not far behind.

As usual, Elle beat her to the spot and was already spreading a light blue blanket with the school's insignia across the grass. Aurelia waved, and Elle jumped up to meet her.

"Please don't tell me you carried this blanket around with you all day!" Aurelia said, hugging her friend. It felt so wonderful to say that, even just to herself, her friend.

"Bah, no," Elle laughed, "I stashed it under the counter in Apple Blossom this morning."

"I can't believe Thlynda lets you do that, she doesn't even let me keep my bag under there when I'm working!" Aurelia sat, arranging her skirts around her.

"Thlynda and I go way back," Elle cooed. "Oh! And here, I brought us some chilled honey mint tea." Elle took a glass bottle out of her bag along with two little cups she had clearly borrowed from Apple Blossom.

Aurelia eyed Elle as she pulled containers out of her own

bag, "I don't think she'd be such a fan if she knew you were taking the glassware."

"I'll return them before she even notices!"

Aurelia snorted. "That valkyrie sees everything, it was nice knowing you!"

"I'll be just fine, you'll see. Now I'm starving, what did you bring?"

Aurelia opened the little paper boxes to give Elle a tour of her haul. "We've got some fresh bread and a round of honeyed goat's milk cheese here and then over in this one is a grain salad with lemon and asparagus and candied nuts. Oh, and then here are spiced chickpea patties with an herby yogurt dip."

"Ugh, where do I even begin!" Elle sang, eyes wide as she looked at the array. "And what's in this box?"

"That's a surprise for later!" Aurelia said, trying to be responsible even though she wanted nothing more than to dive into the three layer caramel cream cake she had spied in Calyntha's window that morning. She'd doubled back to the bakery over lunch and it took every ounce of decorum in her body to not devour it immediately.

"Ooh, I love surprises, especially when those surprises involve dessert." Elle reached a fork toward the box that Aurelia batted away with her own.

"Speaking of desserts, I think there's a treat heading this way for you." Elle grinned, eyes catching on something behind them.

Aurelia turned to see a very sweaty and very, very shirtless Adrian jogging along the path towards them. She felt her face flush as Elle raised an arm, calling out a greeting.

Adrian raised a hand and jogged over to them.

"Hey Elle, hey Lia, this looks fun!" he panted, checking his watch and pulling a pouch of some neon green concoction out of a small bag slung around his back.

Aurelia didn't mean to stare but she couldn't look away as a bead of sweat ran across his smooth chest. She took the moment he tipped his head back to drink to take in the patchwork of shapes and symbols crossing the left side of his body. Intermingled depictions of ancient sculptures, scrolled writing, and others she'd need a much better look at to identify formed a patchwork running from his collarbone down the hard planes of his abdomen to his hips and disappearing past his waistband.

"Hey Adrian," she choked out, surprised she could even form words.

"Tell Hunter he better respond to my last petalpaper tonight or I'm going to send Darya after him."

Adrian laughed and pushed sweat soaked curls of hair out of his face.

"I'll be sure to pass on the message." He moved to go but stumbled, foot caught in a looped strand of ivy that had crawled across the lawn. He shook his foot free then called "See you Friday, Lia!"

Aurelia could have sworn he tensed his already defined muscles just a little more as he turned, but maybe it was just her imagination.

"See you." she stammered back.

After a long moment she looked over to see Elle smirking like a rosecat after a fresh hunt.

"What?" Aurelia asked innocently even though she knew exactly what that look meant.

"Oh nothing," Elle hummed, handing over the bottle of tea. "You just look a tad thirsty, thought you might want a drink." She wiggled her eyebrows suggestively and the two of them were lost in a fit of giggles.

It took a few tries and they were both crying by the end, but eventually they composed themselves enough to start digging into the food.

"Really, though, Lia," Elle said, scooping a round of cheese onto a piece of crusty bread, "Adrian's cute and you're gorgeous, you're both kind and smart and talented, you'd make such a good pair. Not to mention apparently your magic wants him to stick around, why don't you go for it?"

"Well, first of all, thanks, and so are you, and how do we even know that was my magic? It could have been anyone" Aurelia protested, "but I guess..." She took another bite to stall for time. Why not go for it?

There were, in fact, about a million reasons to not go for it. They started with her being a princess, continued with her being a princess, and ending with an extra large scoop of her being a princess, all of which she told Elle in those exact words.

"Yes, yes, but beyond that," Elle needled her, "do you really not plan to date at all in your entire time in Florevale? Wait, have you ever dated anyone?"

"Yes, I mean, no, well," Aurelia hedged, "sort of?"

"How can you not know?"

"It's not that easy! If I were to officially date someone, that would be considered courting and it would be a whole big affair."

"It's not like I could ever just go to dinner with someone, get to know them casually. If I was being courted, it would be political. My parents would need to be consulted, the future of the realm would need to be considered, and everything would have to be monitored very strictly."

"But you said sort of?"

"Well, I've had a few..." she tried to think of a better way to explain it. Coming up empty, she leaned in and whispered, "trysts."

"Trysts!" Elle nearly shouted.

"Shhh!" Aurelia threw a piece of bread at her. "What would you call it? It's not real dating but, I mean, I've snuck out, met up with the cute son of a duke in the garden, I mean, not like that, just kissing, okay!"

Elle guffawed and Aurelia turned scarlet red. This was not something she'd ever talked about with anyone, ever.

"Okay, okay," Elle soothed, putting Aurelia out of her misery. "I get it, but while you're here, you're just Lia. Not Princess Aurelia. And just Lia is allowed to date. She's especially allowed to date her hot co-barista who was definitely showing off for you just now."

"And how do you know he wasn't showing off for you?" Aurelia asked, trying to hide the slight shade of jealousy that was climbing up her throat. "I mean, you've known him much longer, and he's always so friendly to you."

"He's so friendly to everyone because he's a nice guy. But no, it definitely wasn't for me. He's been caught in the middle of way too many of me and Hunter's blow ups to ever consider dating. Trust me, he's seen some pretty ugly things, anything even remotely romantic withered and died after last winter. And also, we're friends, and we both know it."

Aurelia took a thoughtful bite of her food, this whole topic was something she probably should have thought about before coming to Florevale because Elle was right. Regular person Lia was allowed to date and it might be fun to get to know someone, get to experience that kind of relationship before she gave her life to her crown.

Aurelia meant to tell Elle she was right when she noticed a swath of violet creeping phlox had entirely surrounded their picnic, buds opening in undulating waves.

"Wow, what is this?" Elle asked, reaching out to run her hand over the blooms in wonder.

"This would be my first major project under Professor Maillie, he and the faeries are helping me siphon off my excess magic."

"You're doing this?" The sense of awe in her voice only intensified.

"Sort of? It's my magic but it's not me doing it." She explained the Norwish rings, how her magic had built up all these years, how it's been breaking through the bindings she wore even more since coming to Florevale.

"This is incredible," Elle breathed as the patches started to settle.

"Breakthroughs seem to happen more when I'm emotional. When I'm scared or stressed or nervous."

"So anytime I want some flowers for my apartment I should just stick you and Adrian together."

"Hah, hah, funny funny."

"No, seriously though, your magic is so beautiful."

Aurelia didn't have a response to that. Her magic was most definitely not beautiful but she didn't want to interrupt their happy evening with lonely, terrifying, definitely *not* beautiful memories of her childhood.

They sat a while longer, looking out over the gold-washed quad as the sun began to set. The sky filled with streaks of lavender and bright pink as students slowed down to watch. Aurelia briefly wondered if the color had anything to do with her too, but dismissed the thought. She had never heard of a Summoner's magic controlling the skies. Then again, running a hand over the fluffy phlox, she had never heard of a Summoner's magic doing most of what hers had been doing recently either.

On the way home, Aurelia stopped by a bookshop to pick up the notebook Maillie had mentioned. It was a cute little shop she'd been meaning to explore for days. They would be closing soon, but she figured she still had a few minutes to take a peek around.

The shop was named Bunny's Book Borrow and it was immediately obvious why. In the center of the shop was an enormous tree, a real, living tree, circled with wooden stairs leading to the second and third floors. Carved into the trunk of the tree were haphazardly placed alcoves– some with worn reading chairs and towers of books, others covered in framed art. Twinkling lights hung from the tree's branches, illuminating the shop in a warm glow.

"Can I help you find something?" a Nellin with peachy fur asked from the base of the tree where he stood behind a worn wooden counter.

"Oh, yes, I'm looking for a journal. Something small that I can easily carry around yet big enough to hold, well, what I think will be quite a large volume of information."

"A dreamer, are we? Well I have just the thing." Aurelia didn't want to correct him; what was going in this journal was more of a nightmare, though.

He grabbed a walking stick and set off down the stairs. Aurelia followed him under the tree to where more shelves and book covered tables mingled among the tree's magnificent roots.

"Miss? Uh, miss?"

Aurelia startled, she had been too lost wondering whether the tree or the shop had come first to notice the creature waving her over to a particular section.

"Oh, I'm sorry, yes," Aurelia hurried over to where the nellin stood.

"I think any one of these might suit your particular needs. Small enough to be carried in a pocket but I think you'll find you never seem to run out of pages."

Aurelia looked where he was pointing. The books were

about the size of her palm, slim, each bound with a beautifully engraved leather cover.

"These are perfect, thank you."

"Yes, yes, let me know if you need help finding anything else. We close in ten minutes."

The nellin hobbled away back up the stairs as Aurelia turned about, not ready to leave. She roamed the tables, soon realizing this lower area seemed to be more of a novelty section.

Beyond journals and pens of every hue, there were art supplies, candles, coffee mugs, even a wall of teas and small batch honeys in all sorts of flavors. Aurelia counted the bills in her wallet, her first week's pay from the café, and decided to treat herself to a vanilla and brown sugar candle that smelled like a cookie.

She would light it as she started writing today's entries. Maybe the warmth and comfort of it would make the task a little less hard, maybe she could pretend she really was writing down dreams. She thought that, in a sense, she was writing down one dream at least– the dream of finding peace in the chaos of her power.

CHAPTER FIFTEEN

"Looks like you're getting the hang of things pretty fast, Lia," Adrian said after handing over the last customer's latte. Aurelia was wiping down the back counter, fighting with a particularly sticky spot of dried caramel.

Today was her second café shift with Adrian. After their encounter at the picnic, Aurelia was equal parts excited to talk to him and scared of what might come out of her mouth. Thankfully, from the moment she arrived, the café was overrun with the longest line she had ever seen. Aside from calling out orders, they didn't have a chance to say much for the entire first hour she was there.

She laughed. "More like a trial by fire."

"The Friday rush will do that to you. Hey, I've been working on a new drink, want to try it?"

"Sure!"

"I'm calling it the spiced apple crumble latté, still playing with the recipe, though."

He pulled out a tray from under the counter filled with little ramekins of various spices, some she recognized, some she didn't. There were measuring spoons, pipettes, and a strange looking scale with a multitude of little colored beads.

Aurelia was about to offer to help when Thlynda approached the bar.

"When you're finished socializing, Lia, the coffee pots need to be checked."

Aurelia flushed. "Yes ma'am," she replied, eyes downcast as she hurried over to check the jugs.

By the time she was done, Adrian had finished with his brewing and had three small cups lined up for her, each covered in a steaming layer of perfectly frothed milk.

"Okay, so I have the recipe narrowed down to these three variations, let me know what you think of each." Adrian pulled out a little note pad from his pocket and stared at her.

She lifted the first cup to her lips. It smelled cinnamon-y and nutty and buttery.

"Mmmm," Aurelia murmured, closing her eyes to savor the complexity.

"Thoughts?" Adrian asked, watching her intently.

"Beautiful," she breathed, then hastily added, "the flavors, I mean, it's beautifully balanced. Cinnamon and nutmeg and a hint of," she took another sip, "cloves, I think, and the buttery-ness of the crumble comes through."

"But?" Adrian prompted.

"Well, I can't really taste the apple. It's great overall, though!"

"That's what I was afraid of." He scribbled a bevy of notes. "Okay, sample number two."

She lifted the second cup to her mouth, this one looked different. Rather than a creamy white, the foam was a rich reddish brown.

"Now I get the apple, and... is there caramel in the foam?"

"Yes! What do you think?"

"Ten out of ten," she downed the rest of the cup. "But..."

"But?" he questioned again.

"Well, if it was a caramel apple latte it would be divine, but I'm not really getting the crumble aspect."

"Hmm, okay, hold on, let me adjust number three."

A customer walked up and Aurelia took their order. She loved how comfortable she was starting to feel behind the counter, how confident. She couldn't believe that only eight days ago she had never made a coffee in her life.

"Here we go." Adrian was standing right behind her, so close they were almost toe to toe. He held two steaming cups, both topped with that caramel foam she'd loved.

"Cheers," she said, gently clinking their little cups together. She took a sip and let out a nearly indecent groan.

"Adrian," she looked up as she said his name and his eyes flashed with something she couldn't quite place.

"You hate it," he joked, a dimple forming on his cheek as he smiled back at her. "Here, I'll just take it."

"Ah ah ah," she purred, covering the little cup with her other hand and turning away, "touch this cup and die."

Thlynda's eyes shot up, presumably at the mention of violence, then quickly returned to her papers. Aurelia could have sworn there was disappointment in the press of her lips.

"This might be the best thing I've ever put in my mouth," she groaned and might have been embarrassed if she wasn't too busy being in sheer coffee heaven.

"Elle, Elle come over here," Aurelia called to Elle who was sitting in her favorite booth surrounded by her usual heaps of folders, books, and scribbled notes on shards of petalpaper.

"Ugh, thank you for rescuing me," she said as she walked up to the bar.

"Try this," Aurelia said, handing her cup over. "Adrian's

testing new recipes, tell me this isn't the best thing you've ever had."

Elle downed the cup. "Okay, I need a full sized one of these immediately."

"Thanks, Elle, it's not ready yet, though."

"I don't care, make me one now." She paused, then added "Please."

"Make it two!" Aurelia called over her shoulder, not realizing until that moment how close Adrian stood behind her.

He chuckled but obliged.

"So, we still on for dinner tomorrow?" Elle asked.

"Yes, but I was thinking maybe instead of going out, you and Darya could come over to my place and I could cook for you?"

"Ooh, I love that idea! Our cooking skills are mostly limited to sandwiches and eggs but if you're cooking I'm there."

"Here you go." Adrian plunked two steaming mugs before them.

"Hey, Adrian, you and Hunter should come too," Elle said with a sly wink at Aurelia.

"Come where?" Adrian asked, looking between the two girls as Aurelia tried to hide her flaming cheeks.

"Lia's place, tomorrow night, she's having a little dinner party."

"It's not really a party, just dinner, honey wine, casual." Aurelia shrugged. Was she more terrified of him saying yes or no?

"And I know you're usually busy on the weekends with lab work," Aurelia continued before taking a long sip of her drink for emotional support. Her eyes closed and she sighed, momentarily distracted by the mix of flavors.

"Sounds like fun, I think the lab can miss me for one night." He bumped Aurelia's shoulder with his own.

"Great!" Aurelia squeaked, her voice an octave higher than normal. "Here, I'll give you my address."

She pulled out a scrap of paper. "Dinner's at seven but it's open, come by anytime."

"Well, my work here is done and my notes are calling. See you later," Elle waved, slinking back to her seat with a satisfied smirk at Aurelia. Aurelia, for her part, pretended not to hear that first part.

Adrian turned to her. "So, two weeks in Florevale and hosting your very first dinner party? Impressive stuff, Lia."

"It's really not a big deal," she tried to laugh it off. "I like to cook but I like to feed people even more."

"Do you do most of the cooking at home? Where is home anyway?"

Aurelia thought about Maerys and Wendlynn. She'd essentially grown up at their skirts, sneaking away from her nurse to help them stir and roll and chop every chance she got. She couldn't exactly tell Adrian that, though.

"Oh, I'm from a village outside the city." *That was technically true.*

"And, sort of. My family..." she trailed off. Why hadn't she thought up a better back story before this moment? Why hadn't she expected anyone to want to get to know her, to be her friend? She spent so much time thinking about the city and the markets and the gardens, why hadn't she prepared for this?

"Sorry," she admitted, "I'm, well, I just don't love talking about home so much. Coming here wasn't easy and if I'm being totally honest, my family doesn't really love having me in Florevale either. Especially alone in Florevale."

"It's okay, I understand, really," he ventured and she knew he was referring to his own family.

"But for what it's worth, Lia," he leaned back against the

counter next to her, their shoulders a hairswith apart, "you're not alone here."

He smiled at her openly then walked up to the register to help a customer who was browsing the cookie tray.

Lia was sure she wasn't breathing. She looked out to see if Elle had witnessed that. The sneaky girl raised her glass in a cheersing motion and Aurelia knew she had.

Truthfully, though, Adrian was right. Aurelia looked around the room, the people she recognized, her friends and her regular customers, the potted string of hearts on the windowsill that marched ever closer to the service counter with each passing day. She wasn't alone. But the comfort of that realization was quickly interrupted by the reminder that if this room knew who she really was, she would be.

WHEN AURELIA at last shuffled out of her lab later that afternoon, she barely had the energy to lift her feet. The siphoning wasn't getting any easier and her magic was taking more and more gardens to soak up the power with each new release. It was almost as if it was angry to be forced out, like it wanted to stay bottled up within her forever. Which made no sense with the pages and pages of breakouts she had documented already.

If it wasn't for Clem's constant encouragement and Fiora's careful measurements, she wasn't sure she'd believe she had made any progress at all.

Aurelia took a meandering route home, one full of random turns and hidden passageways. She knew she was within just a few minutes of home and yet there was so much she hadn't yet explored.

She walked down a quiet side street then under an arch and discovered one of the most beautiful rose gardens she'd ever seen. Little dogs ran merrily around the square, benches lining each of the wide pebbled paths. People and faeries lounged on blankets in the little grassy corners and around it all dozens of varieties of roses danced in the breeze.

A quiet café sat on one corner of the square, tiny tables pressed one against the next. A young woman bustled from table to table, passing out large goblets of a fizzy orange drink and plates piled high with savory pies and leafy salads.

Aurelia chose a table in the center and scooted herself around to sit facing the garden. The woman greeted her as she slipped a circular paper mat printed with climbing ivy and jasmine vines before her along with a short glass of water and a painted menu booklet. Its cover read Square Grand-Glisse Café with a simple illustration of trellised roses, inside were rows of Serremont wines and a variety of traditional dishes.

Despite living in Serremont her whole life, Aurelia had never eaten much of the local staples. What was served in the palace was always so complicated and fussed over. Not that it wasn't good, it was always delicious, but she felt a closeness with her people living here and eating these recipes that had been passed down for centuries.

As she looked over the menu, a petalpaper fluttered down. One look at the seal and she knew it was from her parents. She opened it quickly, scanned the contents, and was relieved to find that Professor Maillie had been keeping them updated on her progress. He had apparently called her work thus far "profoundly encouraging," a praise no one had ever ascribed to her magic. She snorted and was about to write out her response when a voice interrupted.

"Welcome, what'll it be?" the serving woman stood before her.

"What do you recommend?" Aurelia queried, tucking the paper into her bag. She always ordered whatever her servers suggested and it hadn't led her wrong yet.

"The three onion soup is particularly good today, it's stewed with wines from the southern region and topped with crusty bread and salty Gruyère cheese."

"That sounds divine, I'll take a bowl of that, please, and one of those cheery orangey drinks."

"A spritz and a soup, a bit of an odd combo but both house favorites." The server took the menu and turned her attention to the next table.

Aurelia sat back, a knot of tension relaxed as she observed the garden. She took a deep breath of the cooling night air, a flurry of roses unfurling in time with her exhale. Groaning, she pulled out her journal and logged the entry.

As she wrote, she thought about how frustrating these encounters were. She actually loved gardens, she loved being in gardens, caring for gardens, planning and planting gardens. She loved flowers and trees and surrounding herself with beautiful living things.

But these overflows of magic, they took all the enthusiasm she used to feel and turned it into dread. When did a beautiful rose in bloom become a problem she had to deal with instead of a pleasure she got to experience? There were so many reasons for her to learn to control her magic– the safety of her people, the security of her crown, the good she could do with it– and for once it dawned on Aurelia that her own joy was worth being on that list too.

CHAPTER SIXTEEN

The next day Aurelia was up and out the door before the sun rose. While Florevale might have been a sleepy city in the early morning, the legendary Florevalian Produce Market was not.

Aurelia picked up one of the community bikes on the street, tied her hair back in a silky ribbon and was off. Her long, super soft, stretchy leggings were perfect for a morning of errands, especially paired with her favorite oversized milled cotton tee and a woven bag stuffed with more woven bags for collecting all her finds. She had dressed for comfort and getting things done, not for style, but she couldn't imagine anyone was up this time of day on a Saturday unless they were just as busy and task minded as she was.

The market was split into five distinct loops, each lined with tents shouldered one next to another. In the middle of each loop was a circular fountain surrounded by chairs shoppers could use to rest, organize their purchases, have a bite to eat, or simply observe the comings and goings of the place. In the heart of it all, a trio of musicians played a light tune under the cover of the raised gazebo. Their songs were magically amplified to be the perfect unobtrusive volume no matter where in the market you went.

Aurelia parked her bike and waited in line at the coffee cart beside the gazebo, trying to decide where to start. She knew she wanted to do the flower loop last so they wouldn't get crushed under everything else, and the homegoods loop— filled with artisan made candles, pottery, and glassware— was also a lower priority depending on how much space she had remaining in her bags. That left the produce loop, the dairy farm loop, and the preserves loop. She decided to start with produce and let what she found inspire her recipes, then she would know what other items she needed.

Blueberry white chocolate latté in hand, Aurelia set out. Everywhere she looked were piles upon piles of gorgeous fruits and vegetables, fat asparagus standing in trays of water, pyramids of glossy eggplant and speckled zucchini, baskets of fragrant onions and bushels of leafy herbs. Vendors called out from either side, offering wedges of succulent mandarins and slices of juicy peaches.

Aurelia found it all more than a little intimidating, especially the way everyone seemed to know exactly what they were doing. She wandered for a bit, feeling like maybe she should go back to her local corner market, the produce there was great too, she reasoned.

She was just about to talk herself into turning home when she spied a vine of plump heirloom tomatoes sprouting little leaves and yellow flowers in a basket beside her. Whether it was because the tomatoes looked so perfectly firm and rich or simply to hide her breakthrough episode, she turned and made her first purchase.

She remembered a tomato and goat cheese tart she'd once had at the palace and, after last night's soup, imagined how sweet caramelized onions would be the perfect accompaniment.

Within minutes her bag was full of ingredients, as if once she decided on the first recipe, all the others fell into place.

Beyond the tart, she would serve crispy rosemary miniature potatoes, a tart lemony salad with roasted beets and sliced figs, and boiled eggs topped with tangy homemade mayonnaise.

She stopped by the dairy to pick up her eggs and a few wedges of cheese, selecting both creamy and salty pieces for snacking, and a log of goat's milk cheese for her tart. At the butter stall, the seller insisted she try a peppery radish topped with freshly churned butter and flakey salt and it was so good she then had to double back for a bunch of radishes to serve too.

Something had broken free in her and as much as she wanted to spend all morning with this newfound confidence, the bags were quickly digging notches into her shoulders. She would have to run back out later for bread and a dessert from Calyntha, but did make a quick detour to the homegoods loop for a few beeswax taper candles to set the table.

Aurelia precariously loaded up her bags in the two wicker baskets hanging astride the back tire of her bike– endlessly thankful she had selected a carrier bike even if it was a bit more wobbly– and slowly started to make her way home.

Within just a few blocks, the din of the market died away and she was returned to the quiet peace of the dew damp streets. Each garden patch and blooming park she passed called to her, but she kept her eyes focused steadily ahead, knowing one over-zealous vine could ensnare her tire and send her and all her precious cargo flying across the stones. She begged her power to stay nestled within her and, for once, it complied, allowing her to return safely to her building without inter-ruption.

Before Aurelia could start cooking, she needed to clean her apartment. It wasn't so much that Aurelia was a messy person, as far as princesses go she was actually quite tidy, but she had never truly had to take care of her own space before. Sweeping, scrubbing, laundering, it was all new for her and, if she was honest, she wasn't especially good at it.

When her apartment at last felt presentable again, Aurelia took the quickest shower of her life and vowed to never take the spotlessness of the palace for granted again. She dressed in a tan, calf length slip dress with thin straps that wouldn't get in her way while cooking.

Somehow it was already afternoon by the time she turned her attention to the kitchen. She set a pot of lavender mint tea to steep on her sunny balcony and lit a rosemary scented candle on her counter.

She tied her frilly patchwork apron around her waist and sorted the ingredients by dish. She would start with the tart, she decided, and got to work mixing and pressing out the dough while the onions caramelized low and slow on the stove. After spreading a thin layer of basil infused dijon mustard over the crust along with the gooey brown onions, she arranged thick slices of tomato into a single layer and drizzled it with a fragrant olive oil.

It was right as Aurelia was slipping the tart into the oven that she realized she had a problem– she had nowhere to set a table.

Originally she had planned to seat herself, Elle, and Darya at the counter in her kitchen. Now that the guest list had expanded to include Hunter and Adrian, that space, charming as it was, just wouldn't do.

She walked around her apartment, evaluating each corner for where furniture could be pushed together, rearranged, or stored away to somehow create a place where they could all sit together.

Just as Aurelia was convincing herself that standing around the counter would be fine– it wouldn't but she was out of ideas– there was a knock at her door. She frantically checked the time, scared she had somehow lost track of the entire afternoon, but, no, she still had three hours until everyone arrived.

Aurelia opened the door to find Darya garnishing a bottle of bright yellow limoncello. "My grandpa's specialty, I thought your first Florevalian dinner party warranted celebration."

"Hi, thank you!" Aurelia said, her mind lagging behind her body as she ushered Darya inside.

"I know I'm early, but I thought you might want some help," Darya explained, setting her things down and taking off her shoes. She wore an ankle length skirt in a green and yellow print with a ruched waistband and had paired it with a cream-colored strapless top and a bevy of silver rings that offset her tanned skin.

"Ugh, thank goodness," Aurelia sighed in relief.

"Your place is amazing," Darya swooned, her gaze travelling appraisingly around the room. "And I'm not just saying that, you have some pieces in here that are... wow."

Aurelia tried to come up with a cover story, she hadn't thought about what a university student might or might not have.

"Oh, it's just... things we had at home, bits and baubles my grandparents passed down."

Darya was examining a particular piece of art hanging on the wall to the left.

"Is this–" Darya started.

Aurelia cut her off before she could ask if it was an original, it was. She desperately did not want to lie to Darya but knew it would be impossible to explain. Why had she thought this was a good idea?

"I'm glad you're here early, I actually have a problem I could really use your help to figure out."

"Set me to work." Darya said, tying her hair up with a long thin silk scarf.

Glad this strategy was working, and also truly in need of help, Aurelia started to explain the seating dilemma.

"So you see, I don't have a table big enough to fit everyone and even if I did, I wouldn't have anywhere to put it."

"Hmm," Darya walked around, pondering the space. "Have you considered the balcony?"

"I thought about it but I only have my little breakfast table and two chairs."

"Ah, that's not a problem at all." She patted Aurelia on the arm, her skirts swishing as she walked out to get a better look at the space.

Darya started rearranging pots and planters immediately. "You just keep cooking, this is more than enough space, I've got it."

"Uhm," Aurelia hedged, "okay?"

"Really, trust me! You just go on and keep all the good smells coming, I'll surprise you."

Aurelia was not sure about leaving her friend to somehow turn a table for two into a table for five but she really did need to get back to the kitchen. Darya gently pushed her back inside. Even if they didn't have a place to sit, at least they could have good food to eat.

Back in the kitchen, Aurelia turned her attention to the salad. She peeled, chopped, and dressed the beets before sliding them into the hot oven to roast.

She was just starting to assemble the snacking board,

arranging each of the cheeses she had chosen with fruits, nuts, and honey when Darya popped her head in.

"Lia, where are your table settings?" she asked, stealing a blackberry from the board.

"I set everything out on the desk over there," Aurelia replied, pointing to her desk in the corner covered in mismatched floral-printed plates, mother of pearl inlaid utensils, and opalescent wine glasses.

"Perfect, thanks, and don't even think about coming outside until I'm finished."

Aurelia laughed then turned back to her work, her ever helpful kitchen vine handing her tiny spoons for the jams.

"Uh, Lia?"

"Mhmm?" she replied, looking up.

"Did that plant just hand you a spoon?"

Aurelia flushed scarlet and stumbled for words. Eventually, she settled on, "Well, it was actually three spoons." She figured she was in too deep to turn back now.

"And does it do that often?"

"With spoons? No, but sometimes it brings me coffee in the morning."

"Your..." Aurelia could see the wheels in Darya's brain turning as she struggled for words. "Your kitchen plant brings you coffee? That you, it, who brews this coffee?"

"Uhm, the plant does." Aurelia fussed with the cheese board, scared of what she might see on Darya's face. Maybe if she acted like this was a totally normal expression of Summoner magic Darya would believe it. Darya wasn't a Summoner, maybe she wouldn't even know.

"I've never seen a Summoning like that before. Granted I'm an Enchanter so maybe this doesn't seem like news to you, but I've never heard of a Summoner imbuing a living thing, or any thing for that matter, with such agency. The complexity of your magic, that it could respond to the world around it. That's incredible!"

There goes that idea, Aurelia thought, but Darya didn't sound horrified at least.

"I guess. It, uhm, my magic is just a bit different." She gave Darya a sheepish smile and begged her with her eyes to let it go.

"Anyway, I should keep cooking, everyone will be here soon." Aurelia turned back to the stove.

"Right, right, I'll just be setting up outside, no peeking, remember!"

Aurelia let out a long shaky breath as soon as Darya was back on the balcony. She knew this was most definitely not the end of the conversion but hoped, for the night at least, it would be.

As afternoon turned to evening, Darya returned to proclaim the balcony space as her greatest work yet. Eager as she was to see it, Aurelia still had too much cooking to do to stop. She set Darya up with a bowl for peeling eggs while she washed and seasoned the potatoes.

"Thank you for coming early to help," she said as she sprinkled flakey salt over the tray. "I don't know how you knew I was in distress but I could never have had everything ready without you!"

"It's nothing, really! Back at home my Mama and Papa host big dinners every Saturday. They call it family dinner but it's more like community dinner. We spend all morning cooking and preparing and all our neighbors and friends come by throughout the afternoon bringing dishes and wine and pastries. The house slowly fills up until Mama rings the dinner bell and we all sit at one enormous table for hours laughing and eating and sharing."

Darya had a far off look on her face as she spoke, wonder and homesickness mingling in her voice.

"Even though I've been here in Florevale for over a year, I still miss those weekends at home and, ugh, look at me getting all sappy." She wiped her eyes with the back of her hand.

"All I mean to say is, I know how much work goes into gatherings like this and I'm grateful for you taking it on for us."

"Your parents sound wonderful," Aurelia replied, thinking about the state dinners and formal balls her own parents threw, how different and lonely those were compared to Darya's memories.

"They are, although don't for a second think Saturdays were as peaceful as," she motioned to Aurelia's apartment, "all this. Our Saturdays were loud. Lots of yelling across the house. My family prefers to argue more than talk most of the time, but it was always with so much love."

"And," Darya continued, "that's how I knew how to solve your seating problem. Back home, we never knew how many people would show up so Mama created a special Enchantment that allowed a table to stretch to whatever size was needed. It sounds fancy but it's really a simple working. You'll see soon."

Aurelia was amazed. "But I want to see now!"

"Patience! Now, what else can I do?"

"Sit, relax, you've done enough!" Aurelia started to wash dishes and tidy up the kitchen. She went through her mental list, the potatoes were in the oven, the salad was assembled, the eggs were ready to be dressed, what was she missing?

There was a knock at the door just as Aurelia exclaimed, "The radishes! Oh, could you answer the door? I just have one more thing to get ready."

Aurelia dried her hands, the sounds of Elle and Hunter

elbowing their way through the door echoing from the other room.

"Lia!" Elle shrieked as she walked into the kitchen. "Your apartment is unreal!" She plopped a large box of rainbow sandwich cookies onto the counter and added "Picked up some treats for dessert."

Aurelia started to thank her as Hunter let out a bone jarring screech from the other room.

"So glad you're here!" Aurelia said to Elle, cringing. She knew what that yell was. How would she explain why she had an original Old Master worth more than all their tuition combined casually hanging over her desk. Especially when that friend was Hunter who was obsessed with vintage art.

"Elle," she gulped, lowering her voice, "I didn't really think through the, uhm, implications of everyone being here. Some of the decor is from the palace and," she looked at Elle, letting all the fear and worry she felt show.

"Hmm? Oh, *ohhh*," Elle nodded, catching on to Aurelia's problem.

"Wealthy uncle?"

Aurelia shook her head.

"It's... on loan? Uhm... your family is the secret head of a crime organization?"

Aurelia burst out laughing and Elle quickly joined in. By the time Hunter flew into the kitchen, his words tumbling out in a confused jumble of shock and excitement, Aurelia and Elle were sitting on the floor, tears running down their faces. This caught Hunter off guard enough to pause his ranting, but only for a moment, as a stream of how, when, why, and what flew from his mouth.

"Hello to you too, Hunter," Lia said, trying to rein in her giggles.

"Yes, right, hello. But back to the point, what in the world is a Clyvet original doing hanging in your apartment?"

"Uhmm," Aurelia and Elle looked at each other again and burst into another fit of laughter.

Hunter threw his hands up in exasperation and, by some miracle, was distracted enough by the charcuterie board to shift his questions from why do you have priceless art to ooh, what kind of cheese is this.

"Here," Elle said, handing two paper wrapped baguettes to Aurelia, "we picked these up around the corner too, want me to slice them?"

"Oh! That would be perfect, thank you!"

Darya came in and swatted Hunter's hands away from the food. "Enough of that, be useful and carry some of this with me, will you?"

He complained loudly about being hungry but did as Darya instructed. Aurelia, meanwhile, topped the tomato tart with circles of goat cheese and set the oven to its highest temperature to brown the top.

"Knock, knock," a familiar voice called from the entry to the kitchen. Aurelia looked up to find Adrian leaning in the doorway. Tonight he was dressed in high waisted black slacks with a white dress shirt, the sleeves rolled to his elbows and three buttons left open to reveal the top sketches and lines of ink across his chest.

"Ah, hi, you're here." Aurelia said, wiping her hands on her kitchen apron, remembering she was still wearing her kitchen apron. She had meant to take some time to freshen up at least a little bit, but time had gotten away from her. She imagined she must look like a frazzled mess by this point, but there was nothing she could do about it. All her friends were here.

"It smells amazing in here," Adrian praised, walking over to give her a one arm hug. "What can I do to help?"

"Thank you," Aurelia blushed, frozen in place as she looked around. "Uhm, you could butter the radishes?"

Adrian chuckled. "I can't say I've ever buttered a radish before, but sure." He pulled out one of the counter stools and slid the platter of radishes closer.

"Here, just cut a curl of butter and stick it on top," Aurelia said, the familiarity of cooking giving her at least a few of her senses back.

The rest of the group came piling into the kitchen asking for jobs to do. Aurelia handed them each a platter or bowl and hurried them right back out of the tiny room.

Aurelia looked around, murmuring to herself, "Salad, done, tart, done, charcuterie, done, what's left?"

"Oh!" She leaned over the counter towards Adrian to sprinkle the flakey salt over top. His breath hitched, and she looked up to find their faces much closer together than she had realized.

"Sorry," she blurted out. "Just need to season these, they should be good to go outside now." She turned, hiding her flushed cheeks, and pulled on the bow string holding up her apron.

"Right, great, I'll just," Adrian swallowed, standing perfectly straight, "take these out, yup." Aurelia smiled to herself as she hung the apron, she had never seen Adrian flustered before but she liked it. She batted the thought away quickly as it came and headed out to the balcony.

CHAPTER SEVENTEEN

Darya had worked wonders outside, entirely transforming Aurelia's little balcony. Before it was quaint, the tiny table and two chairs, a bevy of planters set on stools and littering the ground. Perfect for a morning coffee for one or maybe two.

But now her petite table had elongated into a rectangle and her two chairs had morphed into five: two on each side and one at the end. Whatever enchantment Darya wove, it was certainly not as simple as she had claimed.

Overhead, Darya strung hanging lights that eagerly waited for the sun to set. On the table, the beeswax taper candles Aurelia had purchased that morning flickered beside short tea candles in little glass jars. Bud vases were filled with three or four stems of mauve, cream, and honey toned blooms. The lavender mint sun tea and a bottle of white wine were set in frosty Enchanted goblets to keep them cool. And interspersed with all of it were the dishes Aurelia had spent the day preparing.

As her friends sat around the table, talking and laughing with one another, Aurelia held back tears. It was all too much, too perfect. She desperately wanted to hold onto nights like this forever but knew with such painful clarity she couldn't– which only made her more afraid of saying the wrong thing and ruining everything.

"Come on, Lia, we can't eat without you!" Hunter cajoled.

"Sit, you've been cooking all day. Plus getting between Hunter and his meal any longer could be a serious risk to your safety." Elle added.

Aurelia laughed, wiping her eyes and hoping no one noticed their shimmer as she took the open seat at the head of the table.

"Darya, this is magnificent," Aurelia said, admiring the beauty of each place setting; the artful way Darya had laid out the table.

"The real magnificence is this view, Lia, it must be the best view in the city." Darya replied.

And she was right, the twilight view was truly something special. Pinks and purples stretched across the sky, golden flecks of light dotting the apartments and streets spanning the horizon. Fluffy clouds bent the last rays of sun into painterly swirls of darkness and light.

"I propose a toast," Adrian said, "to good friends, great views, delicious food, and to Lia for bringing all of it together."

Everyone clinked glasses as a tear slid freely down Aurelia's face. She tried to laugh it off. "Aww, stop, this is too much. You all welcomed me to Florevale so openly and genuinely, I'm just glad you're here."

"No," Adrian insisted with a smile more beautiful than the sunset behind him, "we're glad *you're* here, Lia."

"I think this should be a new start-of-term tradition." Elle said.

"I'll drink to that." Darya agreed.

Aurelia chuckled nervously, and smiled at her friends. "All right, all right, stop now, let's eat."

"You don't have to tell me twice," Hunter proclaimed,

cutting himself a large slice of tart and taking a bite before anyone else had so much as picked up a fork. Elle elbowed him and murmured something about manners. His reply was lost to the satisfied groans around the table as everyone else caught up and started eating.

THE FIVE OF them sat around the table long into the night, their chatter echoing the vibrant streets below. They talked about everything and nothing, life in the city, school, dreams both literal and figurative. There were topics quickly dismissed— when Adrian would go home next, Elle's progress in narrowing down her research, why Aurelia's apartment was fit for a princess. Those were Hunter's exact words and Aurelia took her sweet time draining her wine glass in the hopes that the question would go away before she reached the bottom. It did but the warmth that spread through her limbs stayed.

Eventually the chill of the night shooed the group inside. Aurelia boxed up the sparse leftovers, more crumbs, really, while Elle and Hunter stacked plates in the kitchen. Darya undid her enchantment on the balcony and Adrian helped put all the plants back in their rightful places.

"I don't suppose you have a few spare bedrooms back there for all of us?" Hunter moaned as he brought the last dish in.

Elle rolled her eyes but whatever she said was lost to an impressive yawn.

"Come on, let's get you home," Darya said as they all squeezed into the kitchen.

"I'm going to stay and help Lia clean up," Adrian replied, pushing up his sleeves.

"Oh, no, you don't have to do that, really" Aurelia protested, passing little boxes of food over to each of her friends.

"I insist," he said. "Besides, this is still early for me compared to a typical night in the lab."

"It's true," Hunter yawned, opening the box and popping half a cookie in his mouth. "He doesn't even bother coming home at least twice a week."

"I'm not that bad!" Adrian scoffed. Hunter made a face at Aurelia to say he absolutely is.

"Well, if you're sure, thank you," Aurelia said and started walking the others to the door. Elle was the last one out, suddenly wide awake and waggling her brow suggestively at Aurelia who promptly pushed her out the door with a playful "Go!"

Aurelia closed the door, laughing until the sound of running water in the kitchen reminded her she was well and truly alone. *With Adrian.* In her apartment. What had she done?

Aurelia stood just inside the door for a long moment and tried to talk some sense back into herself. They had worked two shifts in the café together, it's not like they had never spent time together, but this was different. So totally different.

"Lia? Where do you keep your drying rack?" Adrian asked, popping his head out of the kitchen. She had to move.

"Ah, under the sink, to the right," she replied, jumping into motion. "I'll grab it."

She brushed past Adrian as she walked into the kitchen, kneeling down to get the rack.

"Thanks," he grinned, suddenly right behind her as she stood.

"On second thought, how about I wash and you dry." Adrian amended, eyeing the tiny drying rack that was definitely not meant for a dinner party.

"You sure?"

"Absolutely, you sit and dry, you've been cooking all day. Besides, some crumbs and caramelized bits are nothing compared to glassware when I'm running crystallization trials. You've never scrubbed until you've scrubbed a beaker filled with zinc oxide."

Aurelia wasn't entirely sure what he meant by crystallization and had never heard of zinc oxide but knew any attempt to explain would just leave her more confused– especially after Darya's limoncello– so she nodded along. Besides, she liked listening to him talk, liked the way he got more animated with each word.

"You're so passionate about your research," she said.

Adrian chuckled a bit self consciously and Aurelia, realizing she had said that out loud not only in her head, quickly added, "I mean, you spend all day and night, if Hunter is to be believed, working on it and yet every time you talk about it, you light up."

"Well, I have a lot of years to catch up on."

"What do you mean?"

"I spent so much of my life thinking I would be practically running my parents' company by now. I mean, I always liked science, I always found the intersection of magic and science fascinating, but since I didn't have magic until I was older, I never really pursued it. Now that I'm taking this chance, I don't want to waste a single second of it."

Aurelia thought about this as Adrian picked up the next dish and muttered. "That limoncello was stronger than I realized."

"You and me both," Aurelia agreed and the nervous tension that had been building fizzled out into something warm and comfortable.

Aurelia stood, starting to put away her pile of dry dishes and asked, "Can I make you a cup of tea?"

"I'd love a cup, what do you have?"

Aurelia crossed to the coffee station under the window. She gave her kitchen plant a stern look as if to say, *don't even think about helping right now*. It had already acted up in front of Darya, she didn't trust herself to explain away another magical encounter. She reached for a green tin covered in depictions of camellia leaves and flowers. Aurelia hoarded teas, it didn't matter how many varieties she had, if she tried a tea she liked she was always eager to add it to her collection.

She held the box as she turned around, leaning back against the counter as she answered, "Uhm, a lot, I have a lot. What do you like?"

Aurelia couldn't help but watch as Adrian dried his hands on a towel before coming to inspect her assortment. Was it her imagination that he was standing far closer than necessary? Was she holding the box just a bit closer to herself so he'd have to lean in?

"I'm a big fan of black teas, especially ones with cinnamon or nutmeg."

"Black tea, this late at night?"

He smirked, "I've had so much coffee at this point, it takes a scary amount of caffeine to have any effect on me."

Aurelia rifled through the tin, her fingers dancing from satchel to satchel.

"Hmm, how about this one?" She opened the seal, lifting the pouch for him to smell. Adrian leaned down, the crown of his head just inches from her face, so close she could smell the sandalwood of his shampoo.

"That's perfect," he breathed, their eyes catching as he pulled back.

"Great!" Aurelia chirped with far too much enthusiasm, turning to put the kettle on. Adrian ran a hand through his hair, the hair she had now smelled. Why had she smelled his hair?

She was talking to Darya about what exactly was in that limoncello first thing tomorrow.

"How do you take it?" she asked, her back turned, trying for the second time tonight to talk some sense back into herself. You're not looking for a relationship, she thought, you couldn't possibly be in a relationship, you're a princess and he's... *wonderful.* She took a deep breath.

No, he didn't know she was a princess, this had no future and there was only pain if she let them try.

Adrian was drying the last few dishes as the kettle whistled, jostling Aurelia from her thoughts.

"Uhm, sugar?" She realized he had probably already told her, but he didn't point it out.

Instead, he just replied, "Heaps. With a dash of cream if you have it."

They carried their mugs out to the balcony. Darya had left the string lights hanging and Aurelia decided they were too beautiful to take down. Buds of pristine white moonflower unfurled, releasing their sweet lemony scent as Aurelia and Adrian sat at the little table. The clattering city sounds had quieted but in their place, a gentle jazzy melody drifted across the night.

Adrian leaned back while Aurelia pulled a fuzzy knitted shawl around her shoulders. They sat peacefully, sipping the tea and watching the flicker of the city lights. They passed bits of conversation back and forth, stretches of contented silence filling the spaces in between. At last, the tea ran out, and with it, Adrian's reason for staying.

"Thank you for hanging back to clean up," Aurelia said, walking him to the door.

"It was the least I could do. Although next time I'm bringing you a reasonably sized drying rack."

Aurelia laughed and gave him a brief hug goodbye, forcing herself to close the door and not watch him go.

The exhaustion hit swiftly but she made herself stay awake long enough to slip on a set of soft pajamas and wash off what remained of her makeup. Just as she was settling under the blankets, a petal paper drifted through the window she kept cracked open by her bed. The note was from Adrian, his words following her into her dreams.

I never got a chance to tell you…
you looked beautiful tonight, Lia.

CHAPTER EIGHTEEN

Elle was waiting for Aurelia at their usual table on Apple Blossom's patio Monday afternoon. It was a particularly perfect spot for the pair because it had total sun on one side and jasmine scented shade on the other. Elle was blissfully sunning herself like a cat, perched so peacefully Aurelia wondered if she might actually be asleep.

That was, until Elle tipped her enormous black sunglasses down her nose and said "Tell me everything, now."

Aurelia laughed but also looked around to see who else was on the patio. She spent some amount of time nearly every day at Apple Blossom and had quickly realized there was an essential core of people who did the same. She might not know all their names, but she knew which faces belonged to which tables, booths, and couches. And from the smiles, nods, and waves, she knew they knew her too.

She also knew Elle was asking about what happened after they all left, but she was feeling a bit cheeky at the moment.

"Everything, hmm, well this morning's session at the work-shop was utterly draining." She grimaced for a moment at her own unintentional siphoning pun. "And this afternoon I have to face Tillegratem which is never a good time."

"Lia," Elle huffed.

"Oh! You meant about the weekend?"

"Mhmm."

"Let's see, I slept in on Sunday, it was a late night..."

"Uh huh" Elle prodded, now at rapt attention.

"So then I went over to the café down the street, I just did not have the energy to make breakfast. I sat there for a while reading and then-"

"Lia! Do not make me spell this out for you! He is definitely inside and I can definitely talk a *whole lot louder*." She raised her voice with each word for emphasis.

"Alright, alright, just shhhhh," Aurelia cried, laughing at her friend's antics.

"Not much happened."

"Louder, I can be louder!"

"Really! After you three left we finished washing the dishes and then made some tea and sat on the balcony for a while. It was nice."

"Nice? It was nice? That's it?"

"Nice!" Aurelia sighed and Elle waited, knowing she finally had her.

Aurelia collected her thoughts for a moment, taking a few bites of her sandwich. Herb roasted tomato, avocado, salty griddled halloumi cheese.

"This is really good," she said, her mouth still full.

"There is no way those are the manners you were raised with."

She rolled her eyes but swallowed and took a sip of coffee.

"It was nice, he's nice. And sweet. And thoughtful."

"Uhhuh," Elle urged. "And?"

"And good looking in that dark haired high cheekbones kind of way."

"Mhmm."

"And I really like spending time with him, I like how open he is, but that's part of what makes this such a bad idea. He's an open book, and he's so trusting and welcoming, he makes me feel safe but, Elle..." She paused, leaning forward to speak as softly as she possibly could.

"Elle, I'm not... safe. I'm not really Lia, not this girl he thinks I am, and he deserves someone who isn't lying every second they're next to him."

"You *are* Lia,"

"Elle."

"No, hear me out. You are Lia, you're just also Aurelia. No one's saying you have to marry him but he obviously likes you and you obviously like him. You're not pretending to be someone else, you're just being a different side of you."

"Marry!" Aurelia squealed then hastily lowered her voice again. "That's, I mean, put aside the secret identity problem and there's a world of political problems that come along with a princess' dating life, with me, that I just..." She trailed off, shaking her head.

"Alright, you're not ready, but I'm not giving up. Not on you giving yourself a chance to make real connections and not giving up on you and lover boy in there being the cutest thing to come out of Apple Blossom this century."

Aurelia laughed but was more than happy to let this topic drop.

"What sandwich did you get? It looks delish," Aurelia asked, eyeing the colorful rainbow of vegetables on Elle's plate.

"Hey Lia, hey Elle," a deep voice called, passing behind Aurelia. She turned redder than the tomatoes on her plate.

"Hey Adrian!" Elle waved cheerfully.

"Hi!" Aurelia squeaked.

Their eyes met for a moment.

"Have to get to the lab, see you later."

"Bye Adrian," Elle and Aurelia said in unison as he walked away.

Neither of them breathed for a long moment as he disappeared around a corner then they burst into heaving laughter.

"Elle!" Aurelia couldn't even form words.

"He definitely did not hear us!" Elle protested.

"Elle!" Aurelia leaned forward, still trying to gauge how much he might have heard.

"Maybe the part about him being super hot and you wanting to marry him but that's it!"

Aurelia slammed both her hands on the table and seethed, "Hanielle!"

"I'm kidding, I'm kidding, I saw him walk out the door when you asked me about my sandwich, which has rainbow veg, pickled onion, and chickpea spread to answer your question. He didn't hear a thing."

Aurelia grumbled but knew Elle was right. Probably.

AURELIA DIDN'T SPEND much time in the siphoning gardens for the rest of the week. Apparently she had exhausted all the clearings Clem had prepared much faster than either him or Fiora had anticipated and he needed time to reset. Instead, Fiora assigned her a mountain of incredibly dense texts to read and suggested Aurelia use the workshop's library so she would be close by for when questions arose. Not if questions arose, when.

She didn't mind, though. Her library was a work of art in

itself. She was especially fond of the upstairs corner nook. A large, plush sitting chair covered in striped cream and sky blue fabric sat peacefully beneath the two corner windows. It had a matching ottoman and beside it, a little wooden table perfectly suited for Aurelia's ever present mug of tea.

She wasn't exactly sure what most libraries looked like but she didn't think they were typically this cozy. From her seat she could look down on the lower level since the gallery was open to below. Or, on the other side, look out the windows to the front yard and beyond where students milled by, heading to or from their own workshops.

Aurelia sighed, closing the book she was currently fighting her way through and stood for what felt like the thousandth time that morning. She was starting to wonder if, beautiful as this library was, she should just set up camp in Fiora's lab so she didn't have to interrupt the faerie every time she turned a page.

"Fiora?" Aurelia asked, gingerly pressing the lab door open.

"Has it been five minutes already? Fiora replied from behind a large metal contraption on the table. The device had tall metal poles with arms like branches of a tree holding an assortment of glass tubes. A strange purple-hued fire blazed on one side, coils of glass cascading from one tier to the next. Aurelia dreaded the day she was asked to make heads or tails of whatever was going on in this room.

"It's fine, come on over, where are we?" Fiora encouraged, seeing Aurelia's hesitation at the door.

"So yesterday we were going over the history of magic since the joining of the human and fae territories." Aurelia flipped back to a few of her previous notes as she spoke.

"Mhmm," Fiora replied, jotting down a string of numbers in her elegant script.

"And that was somewhat familiar, I knew the broad strokes of it at least, but with today's reading," she thumbed through the hefty tome she had been working on all morning. "I'm having trouble wrapping my head around the more, uhm, theoretical elements."

"Yes of course. Today you're studying the original crossing of human and fae magic and the results of that union."

"Right, but, well, at the palace I was taught that human and fae magics were entirely different. But this says they come from a singular origin. And I know you've told me that before, but I'm having a little trouble making sense of it."

"Let me ask you this, Lia..." Fiora's lips moved but her body held unbelievably still as she monitored the quivering sea green droplet of, something, hanging from the end of a pointed glass nozzle. "Where were you taught human magic comes from?"

"I don't think I was ever taught where exactly magic came from. We were taught that there's the three types of magic– Summoning, Enchanting, and Gracing– but were taught to see magic as an inherent part of a person, something they merely had. Like fingers or green eyes."

"And that right there is the great loss of human scholarship."

"All magic is, at the most fundamental levels the same, one essence. Over the centuries, humans in their search for control have segmented it into the three branches." Fiora picked up speed as she spoke. "This outlook is much easier for humans to understand and so it gained support. Over the centuries, humans forgot that this was a simplified view of the world and now, when humans come into their magic, they label it, call the classifications the natural order of things."

"Enchanters don't try to Summon, Summoners don't try to Grace. Your magic presents in a certain way and that's the path you pursue. It's wrong but it works for most wielders. But you, Lia, are not most wielders."

"So..." Aurelia fidgeted with her binding ring, spinning it

around her finger. "Are you saying Enchanting and Summoning and Gracing, they're arbitrary distinctions?"

"Not necessarily. As I said, that way of thinking works for most wielders. The power of most human magic is limited enough that focusing on one particular skill is appropriate. Most humans are just not powerful enough to work any sort of broad magic. Think of it as both a matter of natural power and skill. Where humans lack power, they can gain strength through skill. Focusing your shorter human lifespans on mastering one outlet of magic allows humans to accomplish greater feats."

"But not me."

"Precisely, you have a power level much more akin to a faerie. That enables your magic to cross boundaries and do things very few humans' magic has ever been capable of before."

"Uhh, right. Are you sure that's not just because of the surplus that's built up over the years of binding?"

"Certain. Your magic was that way from the day it manifested, the surplus is simply what made it dangerous. I know this feels very theoretical now but once we begin training your magic, it will be vital for you to understand. We are going to need to employ faerie methods of training you, not human methods. In fact, your human methods are quite the opposite of what your magic needs."

Aurelia tried to consider this without conjuring up memories of failed classes and exasperated tutors, but to no avail.

Fiora paused her work, taking in Aurelia's hunched shoulders and quiet demeanor. "Why don't you take the afternoon to let this information settle. Go somewhere outside, be in nature."

Aurelia nodded and gathered her books. "Sure, thanks Fiora. I'll see you tomorrow."

It had been three weeks since the start of the term and Aurelia had only ever seen the entrance of the main campus on her way to SAGES, so she decided to do a bit of exploring.

A bit of exploring quickly turned into a lot of exploring, though, and it didn't take long for Aurelia to be utterly and hopelessly lost.

Wherever she had ended up, it was beautiful. The architecture had changed to a more ornate, sculptural style, all stone gargoyles and sweeping turrets.

Unlike the simple rectangle of the SAGES campus, this school was more of an octagonal shape with narrower yet taller buildings. In the center of the giant courtyard sat the largest tree Aurelia had ever seen. It was some sort of flowering willow, long arms brushing the ground in graceful sweeps, crisp white petals swirling through the air until they circled around her.

Aurelia was delighted at first, but as more branches started drifting in her direction she hurried forward under the tree. She realized quickly yet not quickly enough that walking into the tangle of branches was probably not the best place to hide from an onslaught of petals, but it was too late to change course without drawing even more attention to herself.

Underneath, Aurelia was shocked to find a wide clear-glass tunnel encircling the tree. Entering, she found a thriving craft market filled with drawings, paintings, sculptures, and all manner of textiles. She realized this must be the Graces campus to have so many artists gathered in one place.

"Lost, Little Dove?" A deep, velvety voice said from behind her.

She turned quickly to find a god of a man. He was tall and broad, with sun bleached hair and a scruffy beard that accented his angular jaw. He wore a tight black shirt that offset his muscular build and showed off the swirls of inky runes running down his arms.

"Oh, uhm, yes, I think so," Aurelia replied.

The man laughed and extended a hand. "Thris."

She shook his hand, replying, "Lia."

"Lia," he echoed, his bright green eyes unabashedly meeting hers. "Looks like you're not lost anymore."

She chuckled and said, "Are you offering to give me a tour, Thris?"

He looked at his watch with an exaggerated hum of consideration. "I suppose I can spare a few minutes." With a sly smirk he led them down the pathway to the left.

They spent the next half hour meandering from table to table, Thris pointed out different projects and how they related to the traditions and histories of that Grace.

He explained how the school ran this pop up show every Thursday to give art Graced students a chance to showcase their projects and gain community feedback. It was also a chance for students across Graced disciplines to work together and be inspired by one another.

Aurelia and Thris were admiring a particularly beautiful sculpture of a wyvern in flight when a loud bell tolled.

"Alas, it seems my minutes have run out. Perhaps we can continue this later?"

"Oh, oh!" Aurelia's brain was somewhat lagging behind her common sense so it took a moment for her to understand that he was asking her on a date.

"Uhm, sure." She wasn't quite sure what happened next. She'd been asked to balls or royal affairs, events with particular dates and stipulations, but never actually on a regular, ordinary date.

"Tomorrow, seven, Garden Royale."

"Garden Royale," Aurelia repeated, trying not to let on that she had absolutely no idea where that was.

"See you soon, Little Dove," he said, and all her confusion

melted away as he wrapped a thick arm around her shoulder in a goodbye hug.

She was still standing in the same spot a minute later, dumb-founded, wondering what exactly had just happened, how she had somehow agreed to a date just hours after telling Elle she had no intention of dating, and, most of all, what exactly was this Garden Royale?

CHAPTER NINETEEN

Aurelia hustled down the stairs before the sun rose the next morning. Darya was meeting her to walk to Peace Lily as they did every Friday, and Aurelia couldn't wait a moment longer to get her take on Thris.

"Good morning," Darya said, giving her a sleepy hug.

"Hi, hello, let's chat," Aurelia replied, about ready to explode.

"Someone's energized this morning, excited for your shift with Adrian?" Darya nudged Aurelia's shoulder.

"Funny you should say that." This news was about as far from an Adrian update as she could get.

"Oh?" Darya asked, looking significantly more awake than she had a moment ago.

"I have a date tonight."

Darya cheered.

"Not with Adrian."

"Uhm, what? How? What? Who? You and Adrian were making googly eyes at each other all night."

"That's kind of the problem. I do like Adrian, and I like being friends with Adrian. What we had, the five of us, not to be dramatic but that was one of the best nights of my life. I'm not ready to do something that would change all that."

"Okay" Darya dragged out each syllable like it pained her.

"So yesterday afternoon I met this guy Thris." Regardless of the complications with Adrian, she was going on her first ever real date tonight.

"Thris," Darya repeated, rubbing her temples. "Wait, hold on, so, I'm so confused. Why does not complicating things with Adrian translate into going on a date with Thris?"

"Well, Elle was saying how I should be open to meeting people and I think she's right. I've never really dated before and I just want to see what's out there, who's out there."

They were nearly at the door to the studio now.

"Okay, we have so much to unpack here, so much. Consider this next hour a pause because we *will* be talking more about it after class."

Aurelia laughed, Darya's doubts not dampening her enthusiasm one bit. She was going on a date, an easy, uncomplicated, absolutely no stakes date with a gorgeous Norwishian. This was meant to be fun and Aurelia was determined to see it through.

An hour and a half and a blissfully relaxing eucalyptus steam shower later, Darya wasting no time returning to their earlier conversation.

"Okay, so just to be clear. In order to avoid a wonderful relationship with an amazing guy, you're going on a date with a random man you just met named Thrips? Like the bug?"

"Thris, a gorgeous Norwish Graced sculptor who's taking me to the Garden Royale. Oh, and also where is the Garden

Royale? What is the Garden Royale? I didn't have a chance to ask before he had to go to class or something."

"Ugh, hun, alright, I think this is a lesson you're going to have to learn for yourself. But okay, I'll help."

Aurelia squealed and hugged Darya, "I knew you'd come around."

Darya laughed and shook her head, "Okay, okay. I'll come over at half past four and get you ready. But tell this guy if he even looks at you wrong I'm going to shove an Enchanted ladle so far up his—"

"I got it, I got it!" Aurelia interrupted, cutting her hot blooded friend off before she could finish that sentence. "Now tell me, what is this place? Just a garden?"

"Oh, ho, ho, it's not just a garden, it's an experience. During the day it's a horticulturist's dream with nearly one hundred different gardens to walk through, each totally unique. But I've heard that at night it's called the Lover's Trail. Imagine a walking tour of the most romantic garden scenes lit by enchanted candles and string lights. It's a whole thing."

AURELIA ARRIVED at the Garden Royale just as the seventh peel of the bell rang out. She would have been earlier but could not for the life of her find the front entrance to the garden.

She had tried on nearly half her closet for Darya before settling on a romantic floral printed dress with a corseted waist and flowing skirts. It was perfect for twirling among flowers. The thought soured as she hoped the flowers didn't start twirling with her, though.

Thris was waiting for her, leaning casually back against the side of the visitor's center. Even in her hurry, Aurelia couldn't help pausing to appreciate the way his wavy golden hair glowed in the early evening sun.

He wore a fitted emerald green collared shirt with short sleeves that hugged his muscular shoulders like a second skin. It was tucked into trim tan pants paired with a brown leather belt and dark sunglasses. He was adjusting the gleaming gold watch on his wrist as she approached but as soon as he saw her he broke into a cocky smile.

"If it isn't miss Lia," he crooned, wrapping her in a warm hug rich with his amber and cinnamon scent.

"Thris," she replied enthusiastically, adjusting the strap of her small shoulder bag. "Sorry, I meant to be here earlier but I just could not seem to find the way in."

"Nonsense, I'm glad you're here. Shall we?" He gestured with one hand into the garden, the other gently pressing the small of her back.

"Have you never been to the Garden Royale before?" He asked as they walked through the gates.

"Well, no, I had actually never even heard of it until yesterday. I'm new to Florevale, this is my first semester."

"In that case, Little Dove, I'm glad to be your first. This is a magical place in a city already rife with beauty and now, with you here, it's even more beautiful."

Aurelia blushed, she was accustomed to courtly flattery but this was something else entirely.

The garden divided into three paths with wide grassy lawns between each. Thris led her confidently along the path to the right. It was lined with tall poplar trees that scattered golden shadows across the wide path.

"The gardens make a loop. We'll start at the farthest point and then explore our way back before going to dinner."

"Oh there's dinner involved?"

"What do you take me for, a barbarian? Of course there's

dinner, Little Dove." They didn't hold hands but every once in a while their shoulders or knuckles would brush, setting Aurelia's heart racing.

"So, Thris, tell me about sculpture, how did you discover you were Graced with it?"

"It was obvious from a young age. I'm the youngest of three so my parents knew what to expect by the time they got to me. They thought they did at least." He chuckled with a roguish grin.

"In other words you were trouble." She grinned at him.

"Heaps of it. But, the way they tell it, the one thing they could always count on to tame my wildness was a block of clay." He held his hands as if imagining the clay was before him again.

"While my older brothers made simple balls or logs, basic, childish shapes, I would craft exact replicas of buildings and homes in our village. My folks couldn't believe it. I was barely speaking at the time and yet here were these flawless architectural renderings. My Ma still has them lined up over the fireplace."

"That's incredible." Aurelia said, pointedly ignoring how the trees seemed to bow as they passed. "Do you still focus on structural design or have you branched out since then?"

"I specialized in Serremont Renaissance architecture now, I actually landed one of the most prestigious apprenticeships in the field at the Grand Chateau Serremont two summers ago to work on the restoration of the palace's famous double helix staircase."

Aurelia vividly remembered how she and her parents had extended their annual trip to the Summer Chateau that year to accommodate renovations. Renovations that were only necessary because of the Spring Equinox incident when she was sixteen. There had been a boy, the son of a Bellvanuan Lord, a dance, a slip of her binding ring as they raced up down the grand stairs hand in hand. Aurelia shoved the image away, trying to focus on the greater concern— Thris had been at the palace. Even though she hadn't been there at the time, the possibility that he recognized her combined with the unwelcome memory left her queasy.

"And did you happen to see any of the royal family during your time? Attend any receptions in the palace?" *Do you know who I am?*

"Sadly no, I caught Rhode Rhiderian Virus just a week before the internship so I couldn't go. My roommate was first up on the waiting list, though, and said the royal family wasn't there that week anyway. But it was still an honor to land the internship at all an—"

Two giggling faerie girls stepped into the path, momentarily distracting Thris. "Come on," he said abruptly, taking Aurelia's hand and veering them sharply to the left.

"The dahlia garden is just through here and it's the best place to start."

The dahlia garden was exceptional. A square courtyard surrounded by high hedges with three levels down to a lily pond in the center. On each tier were dahlia plants of different colors— a riot of pinks and violets on top tier, yellows and corals on the middle, and whites and creams around the bottom. Each layer was encased in a riverstone retaining wall with stone steps leading from one level to the next.

Thris led Aurelia around the winding tiers, each of them selecting their favorite blooms. Aurelia was partial to the more unique varieties, the ones with honey toned stamens inside the pointed pink or cream petals. Thris agreed, admiring the sculptural, precise nature of the rows of petals.

"This garden changes every season," Thris explained, "because of the way the plants cross with one another. Each is altered and made new by their interactions. Kind of like us, no?"

"So he's a poet and an artist," Aurelia teased and was rewarded with a hearty laugh.

"Who could be among such beauty and not be inspired, Little Dove?" Thris purred in a husky voice, stepping closer to Aurelia and lifting his hand, the back of his finger just grazing her jawline.

Aurelia dared to meet his gaze for a moment, her breath catching until she noticed each of the dahlias leaning closer towards them. She ducked back quickly.

"What's in the next garden? If this is only the start I can't imagine what's coming up."

Thris chuckled and hurried after her, catching her hand and leaing her on through the bushes to the next pavilion.

The rest of the gardens passed by in a whorl of petals and sweet floral breezes. They wandered a maze made entirely of hydrangea, wound around butterfly shaped beds of zinnias, took a wooden bridge across a river of dancing cosmos, and realized just how hungry they were as they meandered through the kitchen garden rife with the scents of rosemary, basil, and tomato. Every time Thris got close, the plants in the garden would creep in, forcing Aurelia to hurry them along to the next section.

At last, the tour concluded at the trellised garden where they walked through a tunnel of prolific miniature roses, the path to either side an ombre amalgamation of dozens of heirloom varieties of oversized garden roses.

"So, Little Dove, ready for stop two?" Thris draped an arm around her shoulder as they walked out of the garden.

"Lead the way," she beamed, eager to leave the watchful garden behind as she leaned into the warmth of his shoulder.

THRIS BROUGHT Aurelia to a nearby street tram heading back to the Shrubs district. After a short ride through the twilight city, they got off at a busy street lined with bustling cafés and bars. Tables sprawled under colorful canopies, storefronts were thrown wide open making the entire row seem like one great space. Skinny trees wound with flickering lights rustled in the gentle evening wind, a jazzy beat carried on their leaves from all around the city.

His hand slid down to her back as he guided her inside a particularly popular restaurant. It had a red and white striped awning lined with warm string lights and underneath were cluttered gold-rimmed tables pressed one against the other. Inside the tables were just as close with two narrow strips left for servers to walk along.

A mosaic tiled bar sat before the right wall, every stool taken, as a willow limbed faerie poured shimmering drinks with dazzling speed.

After a quick word with the host they were led to a table in the center of the room. Thris pulled out Aurelia's chair for her before taking his own seat, back to the bar. The faerie server started to hand Aurelia a menu but Thris got to it first.

"She'll have a purple iris spritz and the roasted feta cavatappi and for me a Norwish ale and the coastal platter with a side of those rosemary fritters. We'll take an order of the pâte crostini and a half dozen oysters to start, too."

The server didn't miss a beat. They plucked the menu from

Thris's hands and replied "Coming right up." before gliding back through the tables.

Aurelia gave Thris a quizzical look. "And what if I don't like roasted feta cavatappi?"

"More for me," he said with a wink.

"Lucky for you, I do in fact love both feta and pasta." Aurelia tried to relax her posture, to lean forward and let loose, but so many years of state dinners held her back rod straight.

"Of course you do, that's why I ordered it for you." They both laughed, fingers just grazing across the table.

"Here we are," the server placed two beautifully plated dishes on the table along with a large foaming glass mug in front of Thris, and a mysterious purple concoction lightly smoking in front of Aurelia. A deep purple flower rested on top while currents of shimmering lavender swirled in the frosted glass.

"Hey, hey!" She was jolted back to her surroundings by the sound of Thris snapping his fingers towards their server.

"Yes, sir?" they said, turning back.

"I said Norwish ale, not whatever this Calderith piss water is."

The server studied the glass for a moment. "I'm sorry, sir, I'll take it back and get a fresh one for you, perhaps there was a mix up."

Amber liquid sloshed over the cup as he pushed it into the server's hand. The faerie grimaced but said nothing as they retreated to get a new drink.

Aurelia was frozen, taken aback by Thris' sudden hostility.

"These faerie workers, all show no attention to detail. Their entire job is to just pour a few bottles, amazing how they manage to get even that wrong. And wings like that in a space this small..." Thris reached for her hand again, still shaking his head.

Warily, she let him, and when he smiled at her, she softened. His sudden shortness had taken her by surprise but they were having such a wonderful night so far, she didn't want to make a big deal out of it.

A different server returned quickly with a nearly identical pitcher. Aurelia couldn't tell the difference, but Thris apparently could. "Now this is a Norwish ale, about time too." He took a long drag from the mug.

"Now, what were we talking about, Dove?" He slathered a dollop of pate onto a slice of crusty toasted bread and passed it across to her.

"You were telling me about your exhibition project?"Aurelia said before taking a sip of her drink. It was fruity and bitter, not like anything she had ever had before. Pretty as it was, she didn't especially want to take another sip.

Thris clocked her distaste. "Don't tell me they boxed up your drink too? I swear this place has lost its touch, hold on." He snapped his fingers again, turning in his seat to locate one of the servers.

"No, it's fine. Really, it's good." The drink, in fact, was not good at all, but she was sure that had more to do with her own taste than anything wrong with how it was made.

"It's not fine," Thris argued, back still toward her as he called out for the server causing a few heads at the bar to turn. Aurelia shrank back into her chair.

"Sir? Is there a problem?" the first server asked, returning.

"Yeah, I'd say there's a problem." Thris' voice was rising. "First you serve me gutter filth, thinking I won't notice you trying to swap out my order for a cheaper ale so you could pawn off a few coin. Then you mix my girl's drink completely wrong. It's disgusting."

"I'm sorry, sir," the faerie said, casting a look back towards the bar for help.

"Sorry, what is sorry. Fix it and I better not see either of these on the tab."

"Of course, sir."

The server hurried away, wings plastered to their back in the slim walkway, to get another of the awful purple mix. Aurelia turned to Thris, heat rising to her cheeks even as she kept her voice low. "Why did you do that?"

He spooned mignonette onto an oyster, slurping it loudly before responding.

"It was a matter of respect. We're students at the university, not some common riff raff, they think they can make a few quick coins serving us one thing and charging us for another."

"I don't think that's what happened."

Thris gave her a condescending smile. "That's because you're too kind, my Little Dove, these creatures take advantage of the goodness in people like you and me."

Aurelia sat back in her chair, pulling her hands back onto her lap and wondered how the date had gone from good to awful so quickly. Thris had seemed like a great guy but suddenly he was rude and loud and mean. She had never dated before, though, and she wondered if perhaps this was what people, men, were like on dates?

A new purple iris appeared in front of Aurelia, she took a sip pretending a completely different drink was before her, not the exact same bitterness she had already disliked. It wasn't the server's fault she preferred a crisp white wine to whatever this was, and she wasn't about to let Thris' temper out on her account.

As Thris regaled her with more details about his project, Aurelia wondered how fast she could get out of the restaurant. Whether this type of behavior was typical or not, it wasn't for her. Thris wasn't for her. Darya and Elle had known, she wasn't sure how, but somehow they'd known. She was going to have to ask them what they had seen that she hadn't.

Aurelia, who had been escaping Thris' story with her own internal musings, was brought back to the present by the sound of Thris scooting his chair back to get a better view of the bar.

"Where is the food already?" Thris' eyes narrowed as he searched.

"It's fine, really, it's only been a few minutes," she sighed, hoping to avoid another outburst. She could only imagine what her etiquette tutor, Julietta, would have said about all this.

"Lia, Dove, I am not going to let this shithole ruin our night."

Aurelia rolled her eyes, resigning herself to sticking out the remainder of the meal. She played with the flower in her glass, twirling it between her fingers and watching as new petals poked out from the underside.

"Hey Lia," a familiar voice said above her.

"Can I help you?" Thris barked before Aurelia could get a word out.

"Oh, hi Adri–" Aurelia started to say.

"What are you, the manager?" He was looking Adrian up and down dismissively. Adrian.

"No?"

"Hey," Aurelia tried again, smiling for the first time since their drinks had arrived.

"In that case, do not talk to my date, bud, alright?" Thris lashed, drowning out her attempt.

"Date, huh?" Adrian asked, something flashing across his face as he looked back and forth between them.

"Yeah, so why don't you back the hell up?"

Aurelia's smile vanished as fast as it had come.

"Thris, stop," Aurelia pleaded, reaching out to try to touch his hand.

"I'm handling this," Thris snapped, moving to shove her hand away but Adrian caught his wrist first.

"Listen, I just came over to say hi to a friend..." Adrian leaned down close to Thris. His voice sunk into a chilling steel, so low Aurelia could feel it more than hear it. "But we're going to have a problem if you ever so much as think of touching her again."

A moment passed between the two, their eyes locked. For all of Thris' size and bravado, his quick anger paled in comparison to the icy calm and commanding certainty of Adrian's glare. Adrian let go of Thris' hand and stood straight, adjusting the rolled cuff of his black linen shirt.

"You know what, this shitty date isn't even worth it." Thris threw his napkin down, rattling the table as he stood. He threw Aurelia a disgusted glare. "You're not even worth it," he spit out before shoving past Adrian towards the street.

CHAPTER TWENTY

The two of them watched Thris go, trying to hold in their laughter as he got caught at table after cramped table, anger only growing as he shuffled through the narrow aisle.

"Can I sit?" Adrian asked.

"Please," Aurelia replied, feeling more relaxed than she had all night.

Adrian sat in Thris' chair, knees just brushing Aurelia's. Silence stretched for a long moment.

"I'm sorry about all that," Adrian blurted, pushing his hair out of his face nervously.

"You're sorry? I'm the one who's sorry. Sorry you had to see that and sorry for Thris' behavior. I don't even understand what just happened." She didn't know if she was more humiliated by Thris' actions or how badly she had misjudged his character.

"You have nothing to be sorry for. And, just so you know, Lia," Adrian said, holding Aurelia's gaze, "you're always worth it." Her cheeks flamed in the shadows as he continued, "Now, what are we drinking?"

"Anything but this," Aurelia laughed, pushing away the purple iris.

The faerie server appeared. "I have your food, do you still want it?"

"I'll never say no to a plate out of Brasserie Chelley's kitchen." Adrian replied.

"I'm so sorry," Aurelia said to the faerie as they set the plates down.

"It happens more than you'd think. And it's not the first issue we've had with that guy, hopefully it will be the last, though." They offered her a sympathetic grimace and slipped away.

There was a lot to process in the faerie's words. How often had Thris come here? Why was he allowed to treat people that way? Was this because the server was faerie or was it simply Thris not having a decent bone in his body?

"Hey," Adrian interrupted Aurelia's thoughts. "Where'd you go?"

Aurelia chuckled nervously. "Back to about ten minutes ago, wondering how I ended up sitting across from someone like that."

"Fair, but I think you should stay here with me and this food. Say what you want about that cretin but at least he has good taste in restaurants."

Aurelia realized Adrian hadn't taken a bite of his food despite his high praise for it. She looked down at her own pasta, just now noticing how delicious it smelled. The sweetness of the roasted tomato, the nuttiness of the toasted pinolis, the slight brininess of the melty feta, it all wafted up to her nose, inviting her to forget Thris and his angry mouth and his cocky smile. It was an invitation she happily accepted.

"You're right, actually, my night has significantly improved in the last ten minutes. I'd much rather be here." Aurelia smiled at Adrian. "And seriously, thank you, I don't know how you knew I wanted out of that date but I'm glad you stepped in."

"If you could have seen your face, you would have known too."

"Really? I thought I was doing a good job at pretending!"

"Not to anyone who's paying attention. Now seriously, take a bite or I'm going to have to eat it all. It's a crime in Florevale to let one of Chelley's dishes get cold."

Aurelia dug her fork in, letting out a very unladylike groan as she tasted the pasta.

"Right?" Adrian asked, waving his fork at her.

"I can't believe you let me talk so long with food like this in front of me, what kind of friend are you?"

Adrian laughed, dimples softening the angular planes of his face. "Terrible, the worst."

"Truly," Aurelia said between bites. She took another sip of her drink, hoping it would be better now that she had some food in her stomach. It wasn't.

"Purple iris?" Adrian seemed to already know the answer. "No wonder you were so miserable. The drinks here really are great, just... not that one."

"Oh thank goodness, I didn't think I could go on pretending to enjoy it for one more second."

"Let's make a promise, you and me." There was an earnestness to his voice that threatened to tear her apart.

"A promise?" She lowered her eyes, suddenly mesmerized by her glass.

"No more pretending. If we want something or don't want something, like something or don't like something, we'll be straight with each other. Promise?" he asked.

"Promise," she lied.

"Now, let's get you something better. What are you in the mood for?"

"Hmm, something cold, sweet, maybe fruity?"

"I know just the thing."

"I'm not sure I can handle any more surprises tonight."

"How about just one more?"

She sighed dramatically. "One."

Adrian's smile lit up the room as he called over the server and asked for the bill.

"Adrian, no, I can't let you pay for everything, this was me and Thris's food, I've got it."

"Exactly, it *was* Thris' date, now it's ours, and there is no way I'm letting you have this check."

"So this is a date now?" Aurelia raised a brow. She wondered where this bold side of her had come from.

"Do you want it to be?" Adrian parried back. Aurelia's gaze dipped to his full lips before looking away, hoping the dimness of the candlelight hid her flush.

"Date or not," he crooned, freeing them from the tension of the moment and the question neither was willing to answer first, "you're still not getting this check."

Adrian left a generous pile of coins on the table, far more than the dinner had cost, before rising and holding out his hand to help her stand.

"Let's go."

"Okay but you better use that one last surprise wisely," she said, letting him help her to her feet and following him out into the night.

ADRIAN'S SURPRISE turned out to be a small pastel pink shop two blocks away that was utterly unlike any other Aurelia had seen in the city.

A thick wreath of enchanted pink flowers surrounded the

storefront, their petals coated in shimmery silver flecks. Painted over the glass windows was the name "Blossom Brews" surrounded by falling cherry blossom petals.

Inside, the walls were covered in glossy pink tiles, the floors a dreamy ombre of pink, purple, orange, and yellow. A white counter stretched from one side of the room to the other, and behind it floating shelves were lined with jars of colorful pearls and large glass pitchers of equally colorful drinks. The shop was so small that there were no tables and the line stretched two storefronts away.

"What is this place?" Aurelia asked as they stepped into line, trying to peer down the street for a clue.

"Your surprise." Adrian smirked at her, slipping his hands into the pockets of his high waisted black pants. She glared at him.

"Okay, but what is it? What do they make?"

"Drinks." They shuffled forward, she rolled her eyes and waited for him to say more.

"Alright, alright, I suppose you've had enough uncertainty for one night. What do you like?"

You, she thought, biting her tongue before the word could slip out.

"I like drinks that are creamy, a little sweet, uhm, I'm not sure." They were halfway through the line now.

"Let's try this. What don't you like?"

"Licorice."

"That was fast."

"I feel strongly about it. Let's see, also kiwi, pineapple, definitely melon."

"All melons?"

"I like watermelon."

"Honeydew? Cantaloupe?"

She made a face.

"What if I said honeydew and licorice was my favorite combo?"

"I would have to strongly reconsider this friendship."

Adrian whistled and Aurelia laughed, holding up her hands in innocence. "I might not always know what I like but I certainly know what I don't like."

"Remind me not to get on your bad side."

She elbowed him in response.

"Don't worry," she crossed her arms, "you're solidly in the like category."

He quirked an eyebrow. "Is that so?"

"For now." Who was she tonight?

They had made it close enough to the front of the line to step inside the door. Aurelia expected to see menu cards or a list of flavors somewhere but there was nothing.

"Adrian?" she gulped, getting a little nervous. "Really, what do they serve here?"

"Enchanted teas."

"Enchanted how?"

"Watch." He pointed to the nellin behind the counter who was passing an empty cup to the girl at the front of the line. Swirls of pastel colors flooded from the girl's fingertips wherever they made contact with the cup.

"The cups here have the ability to know exactly what you're in the mood for, even if you don't. Each of the colors represents a different flavor, see how the colors are combining into three shades? It's narrowing down the best possible combination for how that girl is feeling at this moment."

"What if the colors decide I want licorice?" Aurelia joked but she was also a little serious.

"The cups are never wrong." Adrian stepped up, it was their turn.

194

"Welcome, welcome," the nellin said, accepting the coins in Adrian's outstretched hand before passing over a cup to each of them.

Adrian's instantly turned into a medley of hunter green, deep violet, and chalky magenta, the combination so discordant it nearly hurt to look at.

Aurelia eyed Adrian suspiciously, he shrugged, "What? I like unique flavor combinations."

"Do you have any idea what those colors mean?"

"Not a clue," he said with a wide grin.

Aurelia's cup, meanwhile, was a mess of colors, no two stripes the same. She frowned at it, puzzled, and wished it would hurry up so she didn't hold up the line.

As if he could read her mind, Adrian said, "The first time always takes the longest, too many options."

She smiled at him but continued to watch as one band slowly bled into another. After what seemed like ages, her drink finally settled on pale pink, thistle, and plum. She handed it back across the counter quickly before shuffling down to the pickup counter.

When their drinks were ready, all the nellins working behind the counter paused to watch Adrian take his first sip.

"Do you always have such an audience?" Aurelia whispered, unable to help noting how solid his arms felt as she leaned into him.

"The cups are never wrong," he replied, although the attention seemed to make him a little nervous.

"Yes, the cups are never wrong, but perhaps you have some sort of counter enchantment?" one of the nellins asked.

"Nope, I just like to mix it up." He took a sip.

"What is it?"

"Not sure."

"Do you like it?"

"Not sure." Adrian took another sip before continuing to say, "But it's just what I wanted."

The nellins, relieved and definitely confused, returned to work. Aurelia finally picked up her own drink and followed Adrian out of the store.

She took an inquisitive sip. Strawberry, lavender, she couldn't quite place that last flavor but it reminded her of a tea cake.

"What do you think?" Adrian asked as they walked side by side. Aurelia didn't know where they were headed but Adrian seemed to.

"Just right." She flashed him a smile.

"There's a million of these tea shops back home, but this is the only one here in Florevale. My family always loved these because it was the only thing we could all agree on."

"I'm just impressed your parents managed to wrangle that many of you into a shop so tiny."

"Well, it was most often our tutors when they'd had enough of marshaling us in the classroom. Negotiating with an outing for enchanted teas was their final play and it always worked. My siblings and I shared a sweet tooth that was near insatiable."

"Still is by the looks of it," Aurelia nodded to Adrian's empty cup. "Did you ever figure out what the flavors were?"

"Yes, but I don't know if I should tell you."

"No, you have to tell me."

"You'll think it's weird."

"Coming from you that's highly concerning."

Adrian tried to take a sip, the straw making an unhappy gurgling sound in the empty cup.

"Now you're just stalling."

"Mhmm," he said around the straw, tilting the cup. She stopped walking.

"Fine, fine." She started moving again. "It was ube and marshmallow and green apple."

"Green apple?"

"The ube and marshmallow are sweet, the apple adds tartness, this cup was very smart."

"I'll take your word for it." She took another sip of hers. "So, where are we going now?"

"Nowhere." Adrian tossed his empty cup in a trash bin.

"Really?"

"I thought it would be nice to just walk around, this city is so beautiful at night."

Aurelia was surprised she hadn't noticed much of her surroundings yet. She was usually so aware of places, whether she was analyzing a potential situation or appreciating a beautiful moment, but she genuinely couldn't remember anything about where they had been walking the past few minutes. Her entire scope of observations seemed limited to the way Adrian's sleeve kept brushing against her bare shoulder while they walked, the way their steps fell in pace with one another naturally, the way a dimple appeared on his cheek whenever he teased her, and how easy it would be to slip her arm through his.

"It is beautiful," she agreed, if only to have something to say. Now that he mentioned it, though, the city did seem particularly stunning. Warm glowing lights radiated from apartment windows, candles flickered on tables, and night blooming flowers spread their petals wide as they passed by.

"It must be different for you, being here," Adrian observed.

"How so?"

"Living in a city, I mean. The noise and the people."

This was exactly where she did not want the conversation to

go. "I suppose," she replied, her mind scrambling for an escape path away from life before Florevale.

"I haven't spent much time out in the city at night yet," this felt like a good direction. "Most nights I've stayed in, cooked, done some reading and gone to bed."

"I can't blame you with an apartment like that. Hey, has the dragonette come back?"

"A few times."

"A few! And you didn't tell me? Lia, you're holding out on me." He didn't know just how right those words were, but this, at least, she could talk about.

"Its name is Truffi."

"You named it?"

"Her? I think? But yes, Truffi, because she loves truffles."

"How could you possibly know that?"

She tossed out her now empty cup as they walked, rubbing her bare arms. It had been so warm earlier but the tea had left her chilled and the coolness of the night was setting in.

"Truffi and I had a little incident. I was making dinner one night last week," she started to explain as Adrian shrugged out of his button-down and wrapped it over her shoulders. "Oh, thank you, you didn't have to do that, won't you be cold?"

"I'd say don't sweat it but seeing as you're clearly freezing I don't think you could sweat much of anything," he teased, eyes drifting from dress up to her face.

His shirt was warm and soft and smelled like cypress and grapevine and amber. It was woodsy and a little spicy, sweet and fresh, surprising and warm, just like him.

They walked on, Aurelia sharing the antics little Truffi had put her through, Adrian occasionally interjecting with random snippets of dragon and dragonette lore.

Eventually they turned onto Aurelia's street, their pace slowing to a glacial crawl as they approached her building.

Aurelia started shrugging off Adrian's shirt but he reached a hand out, gently holding her arm as he said, "It's fine, you keep it. Wouldn't want you to freeze on that long walk up to the sixth floor."

"I really thought I would be used to the climb by now," she sighed, planning to rip her heels off the moment she stepped through the street door.

They both stood for a moment, not quite sure what came next. Royal etiquette classes didn't teach what to do when a gorgeous guy was standing outside your door, giving you the space to make the next move.

"Well, uhm, thanks for making something beautiful out of this night," she said, noticing that his hand was still lightly resting on hers. Noticing how much she wanted it to stay there.

"You never have to thank me for spending time with you." He reached down, one arm wrapping around her shoulders in a loose hug.

"Besides, tonight was great research for my next Apple Blossom drink, I'm thinking a licorice honeydew spritz?"

"Don't you dare." She laughed against the warmth of his chest before pulling back and opening her door. "Goodnight, Adrian," she said with a little wave.

"Night, Lia," he replied, waving as the door closed behind her.

WEARINESS SET IN ALMOST IMMEDIATELY, which made the climb up to her apartment feel twice as far as usual.

By the time she had reached the top of the stairs, dropped her bag and shoes by the door, and clumsily dragged on her pajamas, she was ready to fall asleep on the couch.

Mustering the last of her energy, she stumbled to her bedroom where a pale pink butterfly was waiting for her.

Aurelia unrolled the petalpaper with sleepy fingers until she saw Adrian's scratchy handwriting inside. There were just three simple words but they set her weary heart racing.

Sweet dreams, Lia.

CHAPTER TWENTY-ONE

E lle, Darya, and Aurelia sat at a wrought iron table beside one of the bubbling fountains in the Square Grand-Glisse the next afternoon.

"Lia, prepare yourself," Elle said, adropping her bag onto the table.

"For what?" Aurelia asked, sitting forward.

"An interrogation, of course," Darya replied. "We need every detail." She arranged her flowy skirt around her as she scooted the chair closer to Aurelia.

"Every detail. Minute by minute." Elle nodded in agreement.

Aurelia decided to have a little fun with her friends.

"Of what?" she asked in her most innocent, confused voice.

"Your date!" Elle and Darya screeched in unison.

"My date?" She wasn't giving in yet.

"You, a tall, muscular, artsy Norwish man, blonde hair, scruffy, any of these ringing a bell?" Elle demanded.

"Oh! My date with Thris, right, I thought you might have meant my other date. Oh, that one was terrible, but the second one was great."

"Wait, wait, wait. Just a minute. What other date?" Elle asked, digging around in her bag for one of her many folders.

"The one after that, with Adrian," Aurelia crooned, looking out to the garden. She knew one look at her friends and all her calm aloofness would disappear in seconds.

Silence.

Aurelia broke first, glancing back to find their mouths were hanging open. Darya dropped the pen she'd been holding, Elle was frozen, one hand still halfway in her satchel. Aurelia blinked at them, failing to hold back a wild grin, and the freeze thawed. Waves of questions and excited squeals poured from her friends.

"Okay, okay, okay. The easiest way to explain what happened is that Thris had some sort of mental breakdown during dinner. I genuinely don't understand what happened, he was funny and charming in the garden but then as soon as we got to the restaurant he started acting so entitled and, and just plain rude."

"So you mean when it was only the two of you he was fine but as soon as other people were around he changed?" Darya asked, rolling her eyes.

"Yes! It was so strange."

"Hun, it's shitty but not strange. He was putting on an act for you but when other people were around he dropped the mask and you could see who he really was." Elle reached over and gave Aurelia's hand a comforting squeeze.

"He made such a scene, not to mention how awful he was to the servers who did nothing wrong. He was abrasive and condescending, demanding they get us new drinks and going on about the faerie server and bartender and their wings."

"Well that tracks," Darya snorted.

"It does?" Aurelia asked, puzzled.

"I think what Darya means," Elle clarified, glaring at her

roommate, "is that some people aren't as appreciative of the diversity of the university. Particularly the diversity of, uhm, species."

"That's just ridiculous, why would anyone come to Florevale if they didn't want to be around all different beings? It's literally why I came here."

"Some people expect the world to bend to their insecurities."

"And we're just supposed to accept that? Be glad he stormed out and move on like it's normal?"

"We can hold people accountable, call it out when we see it, but it's not like we're the queen of Serremont, or something. Big changes take big power." Darya offered with a sympathetic smile.

Elle choked and Aurelia shot her a glare. Darya patted her on the back, "You okay?"

"Yup, I'm fine," she coughed out. "What was that about storming out?"

"Oh!" Aurelia said. "That's where the night got vastly better. Adrian was there and Thris lost what was left of his tiny, obnoxious mind."

She explained how Adrian came to their table to check on her, how Thris unwound like a ball of yarn being chased by a cat. The trees around them shook with laughter as she mimicked Thris throwing his napkin.

"Hold on," Elle stopped her. "Go back, Adrian just happened to be there?"

"Yeah, well, he was at the bar." Aurelia said, unpacking the bread, cheese, and raspberries she had brought for them to snack on.

"Alone?"

"I mean I think so, he sat down with me and didn't mention anyone."

"And you didn't ask?" Darya popped a berry in her mouth.

Aurelia thought back, that *was* odd. Why hadn't she asked?

"I guess I was a little distracted in the moment with Thris and then it just... never came up." She scrunched up her face. "Do you think I should ask?"

"Hunter would have told me if he had a girlfriend, I don't think it's anything like that. If I were you, though, I'd want to know." Elle sliced off a wedge of the aged salty cheese as she spoke.

"I hadn't even thought of that," Aurelia said. "I haven't dated anyone before, not really."

"We can tell," Darya snorted.

Aurelia knew how Elle knew but not Darya. "Is it that obvious?"

"Well you went out with Thris," Darya shrugged.

"So what happened after Adrian stepped in?" Elle asked. Aurelia told them every detail she could remember, the banter, the drinks, the walking around the city. By the time she got to the end her friends were practically climbing over the table.

"In his shirt!" Elle squeaked.

"Did you kiss him or did he kiss you?" Darya asked, waving her iced mocha around.

"No one kissed anyone!" Aurelia cringed, cheeks growing bright red.

"What?" Darya and Elle demanded in unison.

"How do you two keep doing that?"

"Roommates," they answered, still in sync. "Focus."

"I mean we were flirty and it was fun, he's kind and funny and thoughtful."

"All great reasons to kiss him!"

"I don't know," Aurelia huffed. To be fair, she had been wondering this same question all morning.

The moment had been perfect, they could have, she could

have, but Adrian was so trusting and open with her and she never could be like that with him. Being friends, even flirty friends, that was okay. But if they kissed it would mean something more. She had lied to him so many times, she didn't want a relationship founded on deception, a relationship that could never truly go anywhere.

Aurelia looked at Elle, she hated keeping this from Darya but she didn't have a choice. She had to keep her real identity a secret and she didn't know how to explain any of this in a way that wouldn't give it away.

"Alright, alright," Darya said, seeming to sense Aurelia's ambivalence. "You can think about it, but think fast because you and Adrian both practically live in Apple Blossom. You're going to see him and then what?"

"She's right," Elle added. "You're going to see him, a lot, and he clearly wants to be more than friends with you."

"He's nice to everyone, maybe it's just that." Aurelia said, hoping it was more, even if she shouldn't.

"No," Elle replied. "I mean, yes, he is nice to everyone, but you two are more than nice and he's not the type to just flirt for fun. Hunter said he hasn't even talked about a girl in all the time they've been roommates."

"How much do you and Hunter talk about me and Adrian?" Aurelia furrowed her brow.

"Constantly," Elle smirked.

"Elle!" Aurelia yelped and smacked her friend's arm.

"Gossiping is way more fun than color coding schedules."

Aurelia threw a piece of cheese at Elle but Darya caught it mid air and popped it in her mouth.

Silently, Aurelia wondered, what *would* she say to Adrian the next time she saw him? He had said that thing when the bill came about it being their date now, did it really count as a date? Did he want it to be? Did she?

AURELIA DIDN'T HAVE to think about it long. She was studying in Apple Blossom the next afternoon after class with a particularly grumpy Professor Tillegratem when Adrian walked in and right up to her table.

"This seat taken?" he asked in that rich, slightly musical accent of his. He was dressed in a white button down shirt open enough to reveal a slice of his warm skin, the sleeves rolled up to the elbow. He wore a collection of chunky gold rings on his fingers that glinted as he ran a hand through his dark hair. Aurelia swallowed, begging words to form.

"All yours," was the best she could muster but it was enough. He slung a bag off his shoulder and sat, pulling out a thin stack of books and journals.

"You know," she began as he unpacked, "I never had a chance to ask the other night... how did you end up in that restaurant anyway?" She sipped nervously on her honeyed peach chai as she waited for an answer, hoping it wouldn't be to see another girl.

"The bartender Salandria, she was the faerie with the gold streaked wings, was one of my first friends in the city." He took off his glasses, wiping them while he talked.

So it was another girl. Aurelia tried to keep her face perfectly still as disappointment flooded her veins.

"So you and Salandria?"

"Oh, no, nothing like that," he chuckled, pausing to look up at her. His eyes were beautiful with glasses on but without, they were devastating.

"Salandria assists in one of the workshops a few days a week. She's not in my lab now but she ran a tutorial I took last year."

Aurelia would have been relieved if she wasn't still entirely swept away by the brilliant grey blue of his eyes and the brazen way they held each other's gaze.

"Bartending is really just chemistry," Adrian continued, clearing his throat and replacing his glasses on the bridge of his nose.

"Her drinks are always infused with unique faerie essences, so whenever I have a free weekend night I like to visit and see what she's been working on recently."

Aurelia thought back skeptically to the purple iris she couldn't bring herself to drink.

"I know what you're thinking, that you hated the drink you got," Adrian said, pointing the eraser end of his pencil at her as he opened up a notebook.

"Not at all!" How could he possibly have known that?

He cocked an eyebrow at her and she relented. "Okay, fine, yes, how did you know?"

"You're not so hard to read, Lia, if a person knows the right language that is." Now it was her turn to lift an eyebrow at him. "And, no one likes that drink, it's awful, but Chelley's wife came up with the recipe so no one dares take it off the menu."

"That makes far more sense," she laughed, setting her emotional support mug down and picking up her book in its place.

The two settled into a comfortable silence as they each dug into their work. Around them, the sounds of the café blurred into a steady hum.

"Lia? Do plants usually do that around you?" Adrian asked after a while. The mix of his proximity and the complex reading from Fiora had left her entirely distracted. So much so that she hadn't noticed that the potted creeping fig on the table had been turning the pages of her book for her.

"Oh, uhm." What could she even say? To admit she hadn't

noticed would only call further attention to how entirely normal this was for her– and it wasn't remotely normal. But how could she explain it? She was past the point of being able to pretend to be shocked. And if he really could read her, what would he think of such an obvious lie?

"I, uhm, maybe?" She stumbled for an explanation.

"It's fascinating! An Enchanter must have done something to it this morning," he said, leaning forward to get a closer look at the new growth the plant had put out.

"Now if only we could bribe an Enchanter to make it do our laundry too." Adrian laughed and Aurelia joined in. She should have thought of that, maybe it wasn't her at all. The plant, oblivious to their conversation, moved to lift the corner of the next page.

"If only," she said wistfully, thankful for the out he unknowingly gave her.

"Hey, I'm going to go grab a sandwich, do you want anything?" Adrian asked, changing the topic. She could kiss him for that. Among other things.

"Uhm," outside was growing dark and the chai had only reminded Aurelia of how hungry she was. "Hmm, I should probably get something."

He snapped his fingers, "I've got it, you stay put."

Three of his ridiculously long strides took him up to the bar. She watched as he ordered, watched the way he pushed his hair out of his face, the way he leaned on the counter joking with the short haired man gathering their plates. Griffith was his name? Or maybe Greigith? She couldn't remember exactly.

Moments later, Adrian returned, sliding a golden melted-brie and arugula sandwich over to her and dropping a thick smoked-tempeh and tomato sandwich on his own notebook. He doubled back to the counter and returned moments later with two more mismatched floral plates, one filled with pastel sandwich cookies and the other a flower of sliced apples arranged around a small cup of brown butter caramel sauce.

"Thank you!" Aurelia grinned, inhaling the delicious scent of melty cheese. "How did you know?"

"You've been ordering that sandwich for nearly a month, I'd have to be blind to get it wrong" Adrian said. "And everyone loves cookies." He reached out for a purple one and took a satisfied bite.

"Well, thank you, this is exactly what I wanted but it would have taken me another ten minutes to figure that out."

"There you two are," a hawkish voice said from above them. Aurelia swallowed, the bread catching in her throat as she looked up to find Thlynda's piercing gaze trained on her. It was a sight she could go the rest of her life without encountering again. She patted her lips with a napkin and tried not to choke.

"Hi Thlynda," Adrian said, his cheerfulness unaffected by the serpentine way her eyes narrowed on him.

"I'm aware you both are scheduled to work on Friday morning. However, with the Autumnal Equinox celebrations this weekend, I've had to make some schedule changes. Would you be able to switch to work the nine pm shift instead? My Friday night team are apparently setting up some sort of moon festival and have to trade."

"Okay," Aurelia rasped, although she was convinced this was more of a command than a question.

"Sure thing," Adrian said, shooting her a quizzical look and jotting down a note in the corner of his notebook.

"Don't forget," Thlynda commanded, pointing her pen at each of them in turn before turning sharply.

"Please don't tell me that's actually your scheduling system?" Aurelia said, reaching across the table to flip through the messy corners of Adrian's notebook.

"Oh no, that was just to remind me. Are you okay over there?"

"Mhmm, she just surprised me mid bite."

"Ah. And besides, the real system's all up here." Adrian leaned an elbow on the table and pointed to his head.

"Up there?"

"Yeah, once I write it down I remember it."

"And that works for you?"

"Well enough," he shrugged.

"Well enough, huh?"

"I've never actually missed a shift or exam."

"That sounds to me like you've almost missed them."

"Only once or twice."

"A day," Hunter chimed in as he walked up to the table and sat in one of the empty chairs.

"Hey Hunter," Aurelia said, leaning over to give him a quick hug.

"Don't let him fool you, this man forgets appointments left and right, like how we reserved a study room in the library starting about... five minutes ago."

"But now you're here to remind me so I don't miss it!"

Aurelia didn't say anything but smiled as she sipped the last of her chai.

"You'd forget your left shoe if it wasn't for me."

"Hey, that only happened once and it was a very busy morning. And I really didn't forget this time, I just got caught up talking with Thlynda about the weekend."

Hunter shivered. "Whatever it was, I hope you told her yes, I like your insides on your inside."

"She's really not that scary!" Adrian protested, glancing over to check if Thlynda heard them talking. "But yes, she has Lia and I working the Friday night shift."

"And missing the Harvest Moon kickoff? That's just mean."

Aurelia wondered what this Harvest Moon fFestival was. At the palace they always held an Equinox ball and a smaller court dinner the night before, but she suspected here at the university the celebrations would look more than a little different.

"Nah, I think Lia and I will have a great time, especially once everyone starts making their way from the festival over here for a late night milkshake." Adrian turned to Aurelia. "You haven't worked a night shift yet, have you?"

"No, is it different?"

"Only in that all the best stories come from the late night partygoers. Trust me, especially on a Friday night, *especially* on the Harvest Moon Festival weekend, you'll be telling these stories the rest of your life."

"I don't know if I should be scared or excited for this."

"Yes." Adrian laughed.

"Well, I hate to break up the banter," Hunter said, "but those notes aren't going to take themselves, do you want to come to the library with us, Lia?"

"Want to, yes, but I can't. I have an early morning class with Darya tomorrow and if I don't start heading home now I'll never wake up in time."

"Maybe next time," Hunter said, snatching the last cookie from the table as he leaned down to give Aurelia a hug goodbye.

"Thanks for sharing your table with me," Adrian rumbled leaning down for a one arm hug that felt wildly different from Hunter's. But maybe that was just her.

CHAPTER TWENTY-TWO

C lass the next morning was particularly hot and precisely what Aurelia needed to clear her head. Her and Darya both lay sprawled on their mats afterwards, side by side, letting their minds come back to their sweat soaked bodies.

"How can I be so exhausted and yet so energized at the same time?" Aurelia asked, turning her head to the side and blinking the bead of sweat rolling down her forehead out of her eyes.

"You're rinsing all the negative energy out and soaking all the positive energy in." Darya said in her most teacher-like voice before both of them started cracking up.

A man across the room shushed them but their efforts to stop laughing only ended up making them laugh harder.

"Come on," Darya whispered, rising to her feet and reaching a hand down for Aurelia, "let's peel you up."

Aurelia accepted the hand and made some very un-princess-like sounds as her aching core muscles fought to lift her.

The pair cleaned their mats and hung them out to dry in silence, too tired for more talking. Aurelia was glad for it, though. She couldn't stop thinking of how easy it would be to just tell Darya the truth of who she was. The silence gave her space to talk herself out of it.

They grabbed fluffy towels and dragged themselves straight to the showers, there was nothing left to sweat out in the sauna anyway.

As she lathered her hair in the studio's vanilla bean soap, Aurelia tried to think of why she should or shouldn't open up.

Should. Darya was one of the best friends she'd ever had and she hated lying to her.

Should. She knew she could trust Darya.

Shouldn't. No one outside of her immediate circle was supposed to know about her.

Should. How else could she make Darya understand why dating Adrian was not an option?

Shouldn't. If word got out that she was there she'd have to go back to the palace. They'd worked so hard for years to ensure no one knew of Aurelia's powers, it was vital her reputation stayed that way. If people knew she had the depths of the powers she had, the danger of the powers she had, it could cause unrest like Serremont hadn't faced in a thousand years. That wasn't even exaggerating. She rinsed her hair, letting the hot water soothe her aching shoulders a minute longer.

Should. Aurelia was working hard on controlling her powers, her siphoning was going well, maybe she actually would get them under control anyway.

One of the pale pink orchids on the window shelf above the shower head crashed down to her feet.

"Lia? You okay?" Darya called out.

"Fine!" Aurelia shouted back immediately. "Just clumsy!"

She turned the water off, wrapping the towel around herself, and bent to pick up the mess. Thankfully the pot had been enchanted not to shatter, but the orchid had been dislodged and dirt was strewn everywhere.

The plant had two tall stems clipped to thin rods, each full of blooms of soft pink petals with deep red speckled centers. Strangely, the plant had five unsupported stems, each also covered in flowers. The pieces clicked in Aurelia's mind. The orchid had been putting out a new stem with each reason she ticked off, but the weight of the unsupported new growth had tipped the plant over. Aurelia sighed as she gathered up the plant and used the detachable sprayer to clean up the shower.

"I must have knocked the clips off somewhere when I bumped into it," she said as she got out of the shower. Aurelia set the orchid on one of the vanity counters.

"I'm sure you're not the first." Darya laughed lightly, assessing the plant. She fished a few hair clips out of the courtesy jars under the mirror and rigged up a new support system the way only an Enchanter could. Aurelia watched, biting her lip.

"It's okay, see," Darya reassured her. "The plant is fine, the pot is fine, it's all fine." Darya replaced the plant in Aurelia's shower and rubbed Aurelia's shoulder.

"You're right, I was just startled by it I think."

This was definitely a sign, she thought. Maybe when her powers were more under control she could tell Darya, she just... wasn't ready yet.

AURELIA HAD NEVER BEEN MORE eager to get to the workshop than she was that afternoon. The day before had been her weekly check in with Professor Maillie. They talked about how well siphoning was going– and how persistent her overflows had been lately. She had, thankfully, not had any incidents quite so large as the Rose Ramble, as it had become known around campus, but the frequency of smaller overflows was steadily growing. They weren't sure if they were actually happening more or if she was just noticing them more, though.

"Good afternoon, Fiora, Clem," she called as she entered the front door of the cottage, sliding her bag onto the center table.

They stopped talking suddenly and Aurelia looked up to find serious expressions on both their faces. This was standard for Fiora but she couldn't remember ever seeing something so close to a frown on Clem's face.

"Lia, glad you're here, come, let's go sit in the kitchen."

She nodded and followed them, anxious to hear whatever was going on. After yesterday's conversation, she'd hoped today would be something of a turning point.

Lia and Clem sat down at the table, Fiora bustling around to gather tea and a selection of little fruit jellies.

"Fiora, I'm starting to get nervous, should I be?" The faerie was always so calm and straightforward, it was jarring to see the frenetic way she darted around the kitchen.

"Being wrong makes her uncomfortable," Clem whispered, leaning close to Aurelia.

"I'm not wrong, Clementine," Fiora snapped.

"Clementine?" Aurelia mouthed at him. Clem rolled his eyes.

"But there appears to be gaps in my understanding, which, yes, makes me uncomfortable." Fiora spit out the words like it physically pained her to admit such a thing was possible as she set plates of tiny checkerboard cookies and three steaming mugs of tea around the table.

Now Aurelia was truly nervous.

"I'm a bit lost. Yesterday Professor Maillie seemed like he had a moment of inspiration, a new idea. I... I thought that was a good thing?"

"The problem," Fiora grumbled, at last sitting at the table with them, "isn't that. His idea was around a more potent way to weave the enchantment on your binding ring. It would be a way to hold in the overflow incidents more effectively."

"That seems like a great thing?"

"The goal isn't to lock up your powers like a forgotten criminal in a dank dungeon," Fiora shot. "The goal is to establish harmony between you and your abilities. Overflows are merely a symptom, binding them only masks the problem."

Aurelia didn't understand why the two ideas were at odds. Why shouldn't they lock up her powers until she could control them? Wasn't that the safest thing for everyone?

Clem sat silently, spinning a cookie between his spindly fingers. Clem not eating was a bad sign.

"The siphoning has seemed like it's going well," Aurelia ventured, trying to tease out the problem.

"It is, which reveals pent up magic isn't the true issue at hand," Fiora huffed.

Aurelia was still lost, Clem still hadn't eaten the cookie. Very bad indeed.

"Our theory was that the overflows were caused by a buildup of magic and once we released the pressure they would stop. By all our measurements we should have released enough to arrest the overflows, or at the very least substantially limit them."

"But they haven't seemed to stop at all." Aurelia thought about her kitchen plant still making her coffee each morning, the little fig turning pages for her, and about a dozen moments every day she hardly noticed because they were so a part of her life.

"Which means our theory has a flaw. I'm concerned that if we put this never-before-tested binding ring on you, it may have unforeseen consequences."

"Ah," Aurelia murmured, now they were getting somewhere.

"Fiora and I have been working on this all morning," Clem said at last, putting the cookie down. "We think it might be time to start training your magic."

"But that's dangerous, isn't it? When there's still so much to siphon off?"

Every time they'd had her take off her binding ring, power had exploded out of her. Even after two weeks of siphoning it still shot from her in long, nauseating waves.

The faeries looked at each other.

"Just tell me," Aurelia sighed, knowing she wouldn't like what was coming next if what they had said so far was the easy part.

"We're no longer certain the siphoning will work at all."

Aurelia blinked at them, it was all she could do.

"Humans typically have a certain well of power, it might be shallow, like a puddle, it might be deep, like a pool, but no matter how vast, human magic has limits, boundaries if you will. Yours, however, seems more like an ocean – unending."

"Has a human ever had power like that?" Aurelia couldn't believe she was even entertaining this. It seemed preposterous.

"Some, during the first faerie expansion."

"We checked the genealogy records and because you're royalty we were able to trace your lineage all the way back to Ghenevere the First. Without a doubt, you are a descendant of great power. Not that power is strictly hereditary, but it's a factor we have to consider in such an outlying case."

"Uhm." Aurelia froze. She wanted to have a response, but her mind was whirling too far ahead of her tongue. She sipped her coffee, trying to ground herself in normal things.

"It will take Maillie a few weeks to construct this new binding ring. We would like to take that time to attempt to train you in faerie methods of using your magic." Fiora concluded.

"You're asking me?"

The faeries nodded in unison.

"Don't, I mean, I don't understand any of this."

"That's not true," Fiora said sharply, then shook her head and tried again. "You understand more than you think, and more importantly, you have an open mind. You haven't shut down at the thought of it." Aurelia scoffed, Fiora had a much more generous take on her reaction that she did.

"You've been studying and learning, you've been experiencing your magic more than ever before through the siphoning sessions." Fiora continued and Aurelia begrudgingly gave her that.

"What we're asking," Clem chimed in again, "is that after the siphoning sessions, even though we know you're exhausted, you stick around and we attempt to work with the magic. It will be challenging. Siphoning already takes a toll on you, we know, but that is when your magic is at its calmest and the only chance we really have to see what shape you can give it."

Aurelia stood, walking a slow circle around the kitchen to help her think.

"The princess who walked through the front door a month ago was terrified of herself, that you're even considering this is such tremendous progress, Aurelia," Fiora said with more emotional insight than she was usually capable of. "Give yourself a chance."

Aurelia sighed. She already knew her answer was yes. Fiora and Clem had decades of experience to draw from, centuries perhaps. *How old were they anyway?* She pushed the distraction aside.

Knowing that her answer was yes and admitting that her answer was yes were two entirely different things, though, and she wasn't ready for the next step just yet.

"Can I think about it for a few days?" She instantly felt guilty for making them wait.

"Of course," Clem answered before Fiora could push her further. She shot him a grateful look.

"In the meantime, let's continue with siphoning. It does seem to be lessening the magnitude of the overflows," Fiora said, rubbing her temples.

"You mean the destructiveness of them." Aurelia added glumly.

Fiora let out an exasperated sigh. She muttered something about magic being a good thing, not a punishment as she gathered up the untouched cookies and put them back under a dome on the counter.

Clem came over to Aurelia's side, "Let's give her some space to get used to the idea."

"The idea of what?"

He grimaced. "Waiting."

HER ROYAL ADVISOR Josephine was waiting for her when she arrived home that night. Her candles were lit, balcony doors thrown wide, and the most delicious smells were wafting in from the kitchen.

"Aurelia, dear, come in," Josephine called from the other room.

"You know, this *is* my apartment," Aurelia laughed, shrugging off her sweater and dropping her satchel on the couch.

"Yes, yes, and I suppose your city and your kingdom too." Josephine always had a sarcastic sort of humor that Aurelia found refreshing in the sea of compliments and false faces back at court.

Aurelia took a seat at the counter. "Jo, are you... cooking?"

"Heavens, no, I'm reheating."

"That makes far more sense," Aurelia teased.

"Hey! I could absolutely make a–" she hesitated.

Aurelia cocked an brow, "A what?"

"Sandwich." Josephine said with a humph.

Aurelia tilted her head, remembering a very specific kitchen incident that was, for once, not her fault but nearly got them both banned from the bakery stations.

"Fine! I probably couldn't, but I've learned a lot over the past few weeks in your absence, you'd be very impressed."

Aurelia stood, clucking, and took the wooden spoon from Josephine's hand before the good smells turned sour.

"So how's school? How's siphoning? Set any more plants to war?"

Aurelia groaned. "No, no I have not."

"True, I would know if you had." Josephine gathered plates and utensils for them while Aurelia spooned the steaming squash soup into bowls. It was an Autumnal favorite from the palace kitchens, spiced with cinnamon and maple, laden with soft chickpeas and nutty brown rice.

"Speaking of things I know, tell me about this date of yours," Josephine said as they sat around the small dining table in the living room.

Aurelia blanched. "You know about the date?" Had her parents heard? Was the court debating her marriage prospects at this very moment?

"Breathe, Aurelia." Josephine mimed deep breaths. "You mentioned it in your last petalpaper. The court doesn't know. Although most of the nobles expected you to have some level of dalliances in the city."

"Oh, right, what?" Aurelia nearly choked on her soup at the word dalliances, imagining her parents and their round table discussing her late night activities. Not that she had any, or planned to have any, but it was an image she could have lived her whole life without.

She told Josephine about the gardens, the dinner, the way everything changed, Adrian, walking through the city. It was a story she was had down after telling it to Elle and Darya and replaying it at least a hundred times in her own mind. But there was one part that nagged at her that she hadn't mentioned to her friends.

"Jo, do you have any knowledge of the renovations to the grand staircase two years ago?"

"It happened? Why? Is there something specific about it you want to know?"

"Well, Thris mentioned he had gotten one of the internships working on the repairs. He got sick and didn't actually go so it's not like he was in the palace but it just made me a little uneasy." She stirred her soup, looking for the right words between the grains.

"I'll look into it. I'm sure it's nothing, you were at the Summer House that season and it's not as if many people know your face."

"No, you're right." She kept stirring.

"Aurelia–" Josephine started but was interrupted by a candle crashing to the ground and a flap of wings. "Ahhh!"

"Truffi!" Aurelia yelped, leaping up.

"Truffi?"

"Truffi!" She reached out her hands, trying to catch the wild little creature. Truffi evaded her, pouncing onto the table and aggressively sniffing around their soup bowls, whiskers twitching.

"Aurelia!" Josephine gasped.

"Truffi, come here." Aurelia tried to catch her again but the dragonette was too fast, half leaping half flying across the room back towards the couch.

Suddenly the creature stopped to stare at Josephine, mesmerized.

"What?" Aurelia looked between Josephine and the drag-onette, bewildered. Josephine was wiggling a long string of twine back and forth in front of her.

"I always wondered if dragonettes were more dragon or cat." Josephine mused. Truffi hopped, a small pounce but the string flicked out past her paw. "I suppose I have my answer."

Aurelia laughed, looking around at the shattered glass that used to be her candleholder and went to get a hand broom.

"Well, congratulations, Jo, you're the first person besides me Truffi's allowed near."

"I'm honored," Jo gave Truffi a slight bow then looked up to Aurelia. "So you really do have a dragonette," she marveled.

"It would seem so," Aurelia sighed, kneeling to sweep up the broken shards. "That or a very strange cat and a lot of broken antiques."

"Who else knows about her?"

"Elle, Darya, Adrian, Hunter, You, the Royal Librarian, the Royal Kennelmaster, uhm, I think that's it?"

"Let's not tell anyone else until we do a bit more research, shall we? I'll have a talk with Finnigan and Yvette."

"Sure, but, what are you worried about?"

"What am I worried about? Aurelia, I'm worried that the last Queen of Serremont with a dragonette lived a thousand years ago."

"Mhmm." Aurelia sat by Truffi, reaching out to pet her soft head.

"What else happened a thousand years ago?"

Aurelia just looked at her advisor, puzzled.

"Queen Nyamoria? The War of the Lilies?"

"Lilies, right, that was, that was before the Three Kings War?"

"Aurelia, you're going to be queen someday, you of all people should know Serremontian history better than that!"

"I do, I do! It's just a little fuzzy right now."

"Queen Nyamoria, the powerful Enchanter queen who—"

"Weren't all the queens back then powerful?" Aurelia interrupted.

"She was especially powerful, but the legend says she betrayed her dragonette, or maybe her dragonette betrayed her, it's not really clear, but after she lost the throne, the dragonettes retreated to the far north, faded into lore."

"Right," Aurelia nodded, searching her memory for this story and coming up empty. "I remember the War of the Lilies, Queen Nyamoria and something about being overthrown by a handmaiden who was secretly the King's mistress?"

"Yes, yes, and in all that drama, it seems most historians forget about the dragonettes."

"Or maybe they just don't think dragonettes are real?"

"Clearly a myth." Josephine gestured to Truffi who had now moved on from playing with the string to cleaning her terrifyingly sharp claws.

"Right."

"Let's just keep it to the group we have, I think that's enough for now until I do some more digging."

"Sounds good to me," Aurelia yawned.

"Alright, alright, I get the hint, enough history for one night, princess obviously needs her royal beauty rest."

"Ha, ha ha, ha," Aurelia nudged Josephine as they stood, but had to admit to herself, she was more than a bit curious now about why Truffi was there and what it meant for her. A problem for another day, she decided as they washed the dishes and said goodnight.

CHAPTER TWENTY-THREE

Aurelia was eager to get to class the next morning. Wednesdays were her History of the Orendalian Kingdoms seminar and after her discussion with Fiora and Clem, she wanted to spend more time investigating the early history of Orendale.

As usual, she woke early to sit on her balcony watching the sun rise. This weekend marked the official start of the Autumn season and she could feel it as she layered a comfy sweater under her favorite fuzzy blanket.

Poppy– the kitchen pothos that she decided deserved a name after all it did for her– brought out a steaming mug of cardamom coffee while she arranged her journal and pens.

The plant started to slink back to the kitchen when Aurelia held out a hand and said, "Wait."

Poppy halted.

Aurelia cocked her head. "Uhm, I'm not sure how you can hear me seeing as you're..." She paused, feeling a little ridiculous not only for talking to a plant but even more so for trying not to offend it. "Well, a plant. But I think you can and... will you stay out here with me this morning?"

Poppy didn't move and Aurelia rethought her own sanity.

A moment later, to Aurelia's joy and horror, Poppy slithered back to the table, curling around itself a few times beside her book.

"This is new," Aurelia murmured.

As magic-filled as the world was, she had never seen or heard of a sentient plant. Enchanters could charm objects to do tasks independently. If the Enchanter was powerful enough, the object could even be made to carry out a series of tasks. She, however, was not an Enchanter, she had certainly *not* Enchanted Poppy, not meant to at least, and Poppy seemed to be doing more than following a set of commands. Poppy was deciding.

Aurelia needed information, details, answers, and the best place to start was with her history instructor. She opened up her journal to start a list of questions she had about the founding of Orendale and the queen Fiora had mentioned, Ghenevere the First.

The tricky part would be how to ask these questions, of a history professor no less, without sparking a closer look at herself.

She thought back to the last conversation she had with her parents before leaving for Florevale. Their reminders of the consequences of being found out.

Peace among the six kingdoms of Orendale was not easily kept.

Putting aside the internal skirmishes each of the countries faced, every two hundred years or so, there was some king or queen or lord or duke who got in their head that a High Ruler was needed. They were always wrong and the other five kingdoms would quickly remind that one errant noble of their foolishness. But her parents feared that the magnitude of Aurelia's powers might create far bigger problems than the six countries had dealt with in a millennia. Aurelia had no interest whatsoever in being a High Queen, her parents had made sure of that, but their trust in their fellow rulers did not extend half as far as their trust in their daughter.

She would have to start broadly, a gentle curiosity when her true feelings were a raging inferno.

A city bell rang out, her inferno would have to wait.

Inside, Aurelia pulled on a silky cream skirt that fluttered around her ankles and a soft knitted sweater in a pale grey-blue hue. She tucked the sweater into the waist of her skirt and slipped on her comfiest white sneakers.

Even though she knew she needed to hurry to talk to Professor Luciaas before class, she still stopped across the street to pick up a quick fleuret roll from Calyntha. Through some sort of magic, Calyntha seemed to sense she'd be in a rush that morning and had a bag packed and ready to go the moment Aurelia hurried into the bakery. With a quick word of thanks, Aurelia was back on the street and speeding off to class on a community bike.

DESPITE AURELIA'S BEST EFFORTS, Professor Luciaas himself was having a late morning. Aurelia spent a tense ten minutes waiting at her seat in the empty classroom before other students began streaming in. Luciaas didn't arrive at class until three minutes after the lecture's scheduled start time, so Aurelia would have to linger after class long enough to catch him.

Aurelia's luck seemed to be in short supply this day.

After class, another group of students got to Luciaas first. She busied herself shuffling and reshuffling her papers until they left. It was scary enough to be asking such dangerous questions to one person, she didn't want an audience of students wondering at her sudden interest in ancient lore too.

Eventually the other students moved on and Aurelia raced to the front of the classroom.

"Professor?"

"Ah, yes, Lia, I thought I saw you waiting there."

"Yes." She swallowed. All her carefully worded and memorized questions flitted from her brain like petalpaper on a breezy day.

"I had an interesting discussion the other day with someone about the first faerie expansion and the founding of Orendale. It piqued my interest in the topic."

"Well of course it did! It was a fascinating time in our history. Come, walk with me." His wiry beard swayed as he talked.

"Tell me, Lia, what do you know about that time?"

Aurelia reflected. As the future queen, she knew more than most, but that was still embarrassingly little compared to her knowledge of the past five hundred years.

"Not nearly as much as I would like," she said evasively. He laughed heartily at this.

"Good answer! And you are from Serremont, yes?"

She nodded.

"Then I think it best to start your investigation with the alliance of Queen Ghenevere and King Merisyll. I am sure you've heard the children's stories of their marriage, but there are other tales not as often repeated, details not so joyously remembered. Stories of battles and intrigue, friendships broken, secret romances kindled. In fact, if we didn't have primary sources to support our studies, I might think the founding of Orendale was a work of fiction entirely!"

Aurelia hadn't known it was so dramatic or well studied.

Then again, she was talking to a historian, his idea of compelling might not be quite as riveting as most.

"I would love to learn more," she said; even more so, she loved that he had brought up Ghenevere himself so she didn't have to make up excuses.

He paused, pulling a scrap of paper out of his bag. "Here is a set of books to start with, once you've finished these come back and we'll decide what direction to go next. Our Founding Lore Society meets for lunch on Thursdays, you're always welcome to come! The university kitchen prepares a special meal reminiscent of what they would have eaten back then and many of our members like to dress the part. Another Foundie, how exciting!"

"Great," Aurelia replied with as much enthusiasm as she could muster. A room full of eccentric history buffs who knew more about her own lineage than she did sounded like an express ride straight back to the palace.

Luciaas didn't seem to notice any of her hesitation as he wrote title after title. He managed to gush about the parliamentary reenactment the group did last month all the while, pen never slowing until he reached the bottom of the page.

"Here you are. Happy reading Lia, I look forward to guiding you as you embark on a journey through the annals of history!"

"Thank you so much, Professor, and yes, can't wait!"

With a tip of his wide brimmed hat, he was gone, leaving Aurelia wondering what she had gotten herself into here.

AFTER HER TALK with Professor Luciaas, Aurelia decided to set up camp in Apple Blossom. She wanted to get through as much of her work as possible so she could spend the night starting in on her extra history reading.

The morning chill had settled over the day, puffy dark grey clouds promising rain. She ordered a cardamom pumpkin latte and a sweet potato sage scone, fully embracing the early arrival of Fall.

Apparently half the campus agreed with her because as she picked up her drink, she turned to find the café utterly packed.

She scanned the room, pausing when she saw Adrian at a booth in the corner, intently focused on an enormous scroll laid out before him. She debated going over to sit with him, he seemed so busy and she really did need to get her work done, but the options were slim and they were friends, right? *Friends would share a booth, right?*

With a deep breath and a leap of faith, she walked over, careful not to disturb her filled-to-the-brim coffee.

"Hey Adrian."

He looked up, a bit dazed, his hair disheveled in a way that made her want to run her hands through it. Friends was off to a great start.

"Oh, hi Lia," he replied huskily, clearing his throat and smoothing down his hair.

"Is it okay if I sit with you?"

"You never have to ask me that," he grinned, reaching to take her cup so she could slide into the booth across from him.

"Thank you. I didn't want to interrupt, what's all this?"

"Proposed schematics for a new spectrometer we're developing."

"Uh huh," she said, carefully sipping her drink and savoring its spicy warmth.

He chuckled. "It's essentially a way to measure the intensity of light, it'll help us better identify components of a sample and this one is supposed to have special filters to identify specific magical influences."

She nodded as if that made any sense to her. In truth she was far too distracted by how the stubble coating his cheeks accentuated the strong line of his jaw to really focus on his words.

"Have you been here all night?"

"It's not night anymore?" He seemed genuinely unsure.

She laughed and shook her head. "Afraid not. I'm not sure if that means you need a lot more coffee or a whole lot less, though."

He twitched his hands, pretending to have caffeine jitters.

"More, definitely more." Adrian stood, carrying his mug toward the row of self-serve canisters.

Aurelia smiled to herself and unpacked her work, settling into the corner of the bench and pulling her knees up to lean her book on. She glanced up when Adrian returned, taking in his thick white tee shirt and high waisted black slacks. It was such a simple outfit, ruffled from a night of studying, but on him it was utterly ruinous.

They settled into a comfortable silence, the sounds of the bustling café fading as Aurelia focused on her work. Every so often she felt his gaze wander to her. She didn't dare peek over her book in those moments. Every so often she might have snuck a glance at him, wondering if he tapped his pencil against his lip just to draw her attention there, or if when he stretched he held it just a second longer than necessary simply to distract her.

After a while, Aurelia set down her book– Late Renaissance Essays of the Northern Kingdoms– and sighed. She couldn't wait for this introductory unit to be over, if she never had to read another treatise by Whrynspeaire it would be a day too soon. She broke off a bit of scone and let out a decidedly un-princess-like hum at its warm, nutty flavor.

"That good?" Adrian chuckled, finger tracing a line in the schematics.

"Here, you tell me," she said, breaking off another piece and handing it to him. He looked up at her, their fingers brushing as she passed it to him. She grabbed for her coffee mug to hide her blush behind a long sip.

"Mhmm," he groaned. "Okay, you're right, that's an especially good one."

She broke the scone in half, placing one piece on a napkin and setting it next to his coffee.

"Aww, thanks, Lia."

"Booth tax," she shrugged before turning back to her work.

Content as she was, eventually Aurelia had to pack up her bags. Literature of the Etherialis class was calling and it was a call she, unfortunately, had to answer.

Adrian stood as she did, giving her a quick but heart thudding hug goodbye. She had never disliked Whrynspeaire more than she did the moment she had to let go of Adrian to trek across the rainy campus.

CHAPTER TWENTY-FOUR

E quinox preparations had taken over the campus. By Thursday, every garden at the school had sprouted patches of orange, white, tan, and blue pumpkins. Doorways were lined with garlands of leaves, branches, and twinkling lights. Candles sat flickering in every window and vibrant mums lined every pathway. The campus had morphed into an Autumnal wonderland and the transformation showed no signs of slowing.

Elle and Aurelia sat at their favorite covered table outside Apple Blossom, plates of melty apple cheddar grilled cheeses steaming in front of them.

Aurelia sipped her white chocolate pumpkin latte and marveled at how fast both Autumn and its adornments had come.

"Trust me, in Florevale they call it Fall the first day temperatures dip below seventy two." Elle said, pulling her blonde hair back into an effortlessly elegant twist.

"Just wait until the kickoff celebration Friday night. There'll be an enormous bonfire right here in the quad. Each of the schools have their own, but ours is the best. Everyone wears flowy dresses or shirts and weaves flowers in their hair and drinks mulled wine and oh, the music. And all that's just the start of the weekend."

"I actually won't be there," Aurelia confessed, taking a bite of her grilled cheese and closing her eyes in savory delight.

She opened her eyes to find Elle staring at her slackjawed.

"What?" she asked into her sandwich.

"What do you mean not going? You have to go Lia! No way you're missing this!"

"I have to work. Thlynda asked Adrian and I to swap our morning shift for the night shift. I can probably come out before a bit, though. We don't start until nine."

"Okay, there's so much to unpack, I don't even know where to start."

"Start with a bite of your grilled cheese," Aurelia suggested, humming happily to herself as she took another bite.

"This is not a time for grilled cheeses! This is a time for when the heck were you going to tell me you're spending kickoff night with Adrian!"

"First of all, it's always the time for grilled cheeses. And second of all, it slipped my mind, it's been a busy week."

"Uhm, hello, spending the Autumn Equinox, a time of transition and harvest, with your crush who also has a massive crush on you? What could be a bigger deal?"

Aurelia shushed her, unsuccessfully. "We're just friends, it's not like that."

"You literally went on a date last week."

"It wasn't a real date, it was more of a... a rescue, followed by a pity walk."

"Lia, honey, there is absolutely no way it wasn't real for him or for you. And with the Equinox, why don't you *harvest* all those little glances and smiles and arms brushing you think no one notices and *transition* on over from friends to lovers."

Aurelia snorted the most undignified laugh of her life. "I can not believe you just said that."

"You know I'm right."

Aurelia muttered into her sandwich.

"No ma'am, I am not letting you lunch your way out of this, seriously, why not?"

"Because of things..." Aurelia lowered her voice to a nearly inaudible growl, "things I can't really talk about here." She looked around meaningfully at the packed tables surrounding them.

Elle rolled her eyes. "Fine, we can drop it. For now. But as soon as we're done with lunch I'm taking you on a walk of my own because this conversation is not over."

Much to Aurelia's disappointment, Elle was true to her word. The moment she sipped the last dregs of her latté, Elle was on her feet packing their books.

"You're really invested in this," Aurelia grumbled.

"What can I say, I love love, now up. Let's go." She linked arms with Aurelia and marched them out to the workshop paths.

"Love!" Aurelia squeaked.

"Love, heart thundering, palms sweating, googley-eyed love. Now spill."

"Has anyone ever told you that you're a wee bit nosey?" Aurelia teased.

"And you love me for it." Elle replied confidently.

Aurelia sighed. "Okay, okay, you're right. Yes, I do think he's thoughtful and funny and I really like spending time with him."

"Mhmm," Elle nodded.

"And he's smart and kind of gorgeous and there might be something there."

Elle squeaked in excitement.

"But it can't happen."

Elle frowned. "Why not?"

"Because I'm a princess, we went over this. I'm not allowed to date just anyone I want, dating for me is a matter of international politics. If I were to date someone, which is called courting in my station, by the way, that person would need to be *voted on* by parliament. I'm not even exaggerating here."

"But you went out with Thris, and it's not like you're getting married."

"Thris was supposed to be a casual fun night, which it was until he went off the rails. But with Adrian, I just like him too much to mess things up when it could never really work out."

"I'd vote for him," Elle shrugged hopefully.

"It's not just that. It's also that Adrian..." she trailed off, biting her lip in thought. "he just... he deserves better than what I can give him."

"You're a literal princess," Elle scoffed.

"Right, but he doesn't know that. I've lied to him every day since I met him. He doesn't even know my real name. How can I date someone when I know I'm not being honest with them? How can I tell him he can trust me when he can't."

"Hun," Elle sighed but Aurelia had started and she couldn't stop until it was all out there.

"A fun date here and there is fine, but with Adrian it would never be that because you're right, I do really like him, and I think he might really like me too, and it would be so selfish of me to let us start something when it's not real."

Aurelia wiped her eyes, surprised to find tears. The girls walked in silence for a while, trees rustling noisily in the wind overhead. Streetlights glowed along the path, the twinkling lights strung around workshop doors shining bright in the shadows. Up ahead, a small fountain bubbled in a stone circle, six paths sprawling out from it. Little candles floated in the fountain, somehow staying lit despite the patter of the gurgling water. They really don't do anything by half around here, Aurelia thought.

Finally, Elle turned them back towards Aurelia's cottage and started talking again.

"Lia, I understand where you're coming from, and you're not wrong in anything you said. A relationship should be founded on trust and honesty."

"But what you and Adrian feel is real, it's real to everyone who sees the two of you, it's real inside you and it's real inside him. If you had the choice to be honest, would you be?"

"Of course," Aurelia scoffed.

"Then it's not selfish. You don't know what the future holds, you don't know that this can't happen."

"But—" Aurelia started to cut Elle off.

"Uh uhh, wait, I'm not done," Elle said gently. Aurelia waited.

"And if it turns out to be something more, something lasting that has a future, then you'll figure out how to tell him and he'll understand."

"That sounds like a big assumption."

"If that day comes, you'll explain your reasons and he'll find a way to understand or he won't. But don't hold yourself back from something beautiful for the fear of it turning ugly."

Aurelia chewed over these words.

"Think about it," Elle said. "You'll see, I'm always right about these things."

"These things?"

"Loovvveeee things," she sang, stretching the word out in a silly voice.

"I can't with you," Aurelia laughed and rolled her eyes.

"But the most important question is," Elle paused for dramatic emphasis. "What are you going to wear tomorrow?"

CHAPTER TWENTY-FIVE

Even though Aurelia was working Friday night, Darya and Elle convinced her it was still worth it to go to the bonfire lighting ceremony at sundown before heading off to the café. And that they should all get ready together— at Aurelia's place, of course.

Aurelia opened all the windows to let in the cool late afternoon breeze and set out a snack board of cheeses, fruits, and crackers in case they missed dinner.

She was just filing away a petalpaper from her parents when Elle and Darya arrived. The petalpaper was a standard cautionary note: don't let your powers out, be careful with your drink. She had rolled her eyes but knew the reminders came from a place of love, not distrust.

The girls burst through her door, panting from the weight of carrying two obscenely overstuffed tote bags. Aurelia slid her desk drawer closed and rushed to help unload her friends.

"I absolutely need to take another shower after that climb," Elle lamented, dropping her bag and rolling out her shoulder.

A bit confused, Aurelia laughed, "Sure? There's fresh towels on the shelves by the tub."

"Thanks." Elle bounded off as Darya started unpacking piles of clothes.

"Uhm, what is all this?" Aurelia counted at least ten different outfits and nearly as many pairs of shoes.

"Possibilities," Darya said, holding the first dress up to Aurelia before shaking her head. "Immediately no."

"But, I mean, I have clothes."

"Think of the bonfire as more of a costume party. Everyone goes all out trying to look like a woodland nymph the first night." Darya arranged stacks of jewelry onto each outfit option.

"Elle!" Darya called out. "Did you grab the green dress with the corset?"

"Yes, it's under the tan one with the beaded bodice and the feathers" Elle's voice echoed from down the hall.

"Feathers? You two know I have to work tonight, right?" Aurelia retrieved the jug of chilled tea she kept in the coldbox.

"You'll manage," Darya said, accepting a glass from Aurelia and chugging it.

"Right. And what do you think Thlynda will say about feathers?" Aurelia put her hands on her hips, not sure if she was amused or terrified by the idea of showing up in the flowy, feather laden dress Darya was shaking out.

"On second thought, maybe Elle and I should keep to the feathered ones."

Elle appeared, toweling off her sodden hair. "Let's make some magic girls."

Two HOURS LATER, once each of the girls had tried on every dress at least twice, they were nearly ready to go.

Elle had settled on a wispy, nude-toned dress with short, choppy layers of sheer fabric and thin straps.

Darya, meanwhile, was in a long pale yellow dress that just grazed her body and seemed to float while she walked. Elle had insisted Darya wear a tan corset overtop inlaid with panels of tapestry style embroidery.

Aurelia was accustomed to being dressed by attendants and having her outfits chosen for her, but what she witnessed between Darya and Elle was an entirely new level of scrutiny. Dresses she thought were beautiful were utterly wrong, accessories were stacked, layered, stripped apart, and put back together. And she found she actually enjoyed sitting back to let her friends lead the way.

Eventually, Elle and Darya settled on a long cream dress with a built-in corset, flowing skirt, and, much to Aurelia's delight, pockets. Embroidered pink roses and sea green vines had been Enchanted to slowly grow and climb over Aurelia's body, caressing her narrow waist and offsetting her every curve. If Aurelia wasn't already a princess she would have felt like one that night.

They all left their hair down in loose, lived-in curls and wove white, yellow, and pink flowers into their hair.

By the time they had finished primping, the sun was low on the horizon and they knew they would need to hurry along to get to the SAGES quad before the ceremony started.

The city was buzzing as they stepped out onto the street. Candles had been strung on Enchanted strings from balcony to balcony and the sky was a riot of pinks, purples, oranges, and golden rays.

They arrived at the bonfire site just as Chancellor Belthinia was stepping up to the raised platform surrounding an enormous pyre.

The girls snaked their way around the pit to where hot mulled wine was being served in winged mugs.

"They'll fly back to the kitchens once empty," Elle explained. "Helps with the cleanup."

"That's brilliant," Aurelia marveled. "Uhm, how strong is this, though?"

"Not strong at all, the university knows people like to celebrate all night so they keep the drinks light. Kind of like enforced pacing." Darya answered.

Chancellor Belthinia was wrapping up her remarks at this point, keeping them blessedly brief, when Hunter got up beside her.

Darya and Elle started cheering loudly while Aurelia turned, confused, to Elle.

"He's the Equinox chair," Elle shouted over the crowd. "He gets to kick off the celebrations tonight and has a bunch of other responsibilities. We probably won't see much of him until tomorrow."

"Alright, alright, thank you," Hunter said to the crowd, his voice magically amplified.

"And thank you Chancellor for that beautiful and *succinct* history of the Autumnal Equinox." The crowd laughed and the Chancellor nodded.

"Tonight as we light this fire, a fire that will rage throughout the weekend, let us all set aside a moment to reflect on where our journeys have taken us, the roads that have led each of us here to this moment. Let us be grateful for every seed we've planted, flower we've tended, and bush we've pruned. This is a time of metamorphosis, so let's let the old go, it has become something new. And now," he bent, picking up a lit torch from the crowd, "we reap the harvest."

The crowd cheered as he threw the burning torch into the pyre, the entire structure catching at once. The fire flickered through a prism of colors from blue to purple to red to orange and back again.

Silence fell for a brief heartbeat, two, as the crowd took a long drink from their mugs. Then the air filled with the iridescent flapping of mugwings, whoops and joyful cries rising to the sky with them.

Music thrummed jovially through the air, lighthearted melodies winding around each person the way only a Graced musician could play. The entire crowd danced a path around the bonfire like a swirling eddy in a winding river.

Aurelia allowed herself to be swallowed by the crowd, the music, the friendship around her. She had never truly felt lonely at the palace, but now that she was here, now that she knew what community was, she realized how much she had been missing.

Tears shone in her eyes but Elle wiped them away.

They danced nearly a full circle then found themselves back at the bar.

"No more wine for you," Darya said, plucking two full mugs from the counter and handing one over to Elle. "Unless you want to be blubbering all over Thlynda."

Aurelia wiped at her eyes. "One was apparently more than enough."

Darya and Elle tossed back their glasses, their hips never missing a beat of the pulsing melody. The three of them were an island unto themselves, spinning, jumping, arms free, feet in constant motion.

Around them, the world spun. Flashes of shimmering fabric, swaying arms, gemstone jewelry reflecting the light, and at the center of it all, the mountainous blaze.

If the music wasn't so powerful, Aurelia might have entirely lost herself in the leap and twist of the rainbow blaze. Lost herself in the curl of blue fire through waves of golden, the dash of red bounding higher and higher until its embers floated up to the stars. If the music wasn't so powerful, Aurelia might have noticed the eyes that watched her from across the inferno, burning with an entirely different kind of heat.

Eventually, Aurelia had to tear herself away from the music. Elle and Darya both offered to walk her to Apple Blossom but she insisted they stay, that it was just across the quad, they could practically watch her go.

With promises to come visit her later, the girls begrudgingly said goodbye.

Aurelia extracted herself from the circle, dashing between groups of revelers who were oblivious to anything but the music and the flames. She wondered how her little group had managed to dance around the fire with such ease, not noticing anyone else, when it was utterly packed.

With a last duck under the wings of two highly exuberant faeries on the outer edge, she was at last free.

She brushed herself off, her skin covered in swathes of glitter, and looked up to find a pair of laughing gray-blue eyes focused on her. Adrian was there. And it wasn't just the wine or the music, he was beautiful.

He half sat on the arm of a green iron chair, arms crossed over his broad chest. The sleeves of his billowy white linen shirt were rolled to the elbow, as always, and he had left half the shirt's buttons undone. Loose brown pants were belted with brown cord that accentuated his flat waist. The firelight reflected off his tousled black hair and, without his glasses, shadows danced across the planes of his face. Aurelia envied them.

"Glad to see you made it out alive," he taunted.

Aurelia walked over to him, grumbling. "Thanks for the assist."

"You looked like you could handle it."

"I don't understand, why–"

"Was it so hard to get out?" He stood, shaking out his arms before sliding his hands into his pockets. Was he always this distracting?

They started walking side by side, his sleeves just barely whispering across the bare skin of her arm.

"It's a part of the magic, the songs. They draw the better dancers in closer to the fire and keep the less, uhm, graceful dancers to the edges where they're less likely to hurt themselves."

"That's... considerate I suppose?"

"You could take it that way," Adrian chuckled. "I like your outfit, by the way."

Aurelia blushed. "Oh, thank you. It was all Elle and Darya, you should have seen the bags they brought over."

"Well, they did a good job. You look like a woodland nymph princess, Lia." Aurelia did a little twirl, skirts billowing around her.

"Any visits from Truffi while you three were getting ready?"

"You always ask me that," she laughed. "No, she only comes late at night. Usually when I'm about to go to bed or, worse, already in bed. She has a knack for finding the most inconvenient times. I got out of the shower the other night to find her sitting like a cat in front of my cold box."

"That's... quite an image," Adrian choked out.

"If she ever figures out how to open the cold box's door I'm in deep trouble."

"After you," Adrian gestured, opening the door to Apple

Blossom. Aurelia hadn't noticed that they'd already made it across the lawns.

"Thanks," she smiled, Adrian's scent washing over her as she ducked through the door. That was the last time, she admonished herself. They had to work together for the next three hours, she had to stop paying so much attention to him or Thlynda would crucify her.

Only Thlynda wasn't there. In her place was Vaughn, the night shift manager. Right, this was the night shift, things were different.

"Adrian?" Aurelia asked as he walked in behind her.

"Hmm?"

"You've done the night shift before, right?"

"I've got you, Lia," he said, walking behind the counter as he talked. "I had this exact shift all last year, you'll be fine. And besides," he held her gaze, "we make a good team." He bumped his shoulder into hers before walking off to begin the start-of-shift checklist.

While Adrian refilled the self-serve pots, Aurelia replenished the milks in the cold box, falling into the start-of-shift habits as easily as breathing now. Coffees, milks, syrups, dishes, she loved the familiar routine of it all.

While that routine wasn't enough to tear her thoughts from Adrian's words, the flurry of customers was.

The two of them fell into a comfortable rhythm, taking orders, pulling shots, blending up an unreasonable number of milkshakes and strawberry-banana smoothies. Adrian was right, they made an excellent team.

After an hour of nearly nonstop orders, they finally had a break long enough to breathe.

"That was a rush," Aurelia said wearily as she mopped up sticky syrup from the back bar.

"Don't get too comfortable, that was only the first wave." Adrian warned as he cleaned out the blenders.

"The first? Of how many?"

"On a Friday night, a festival Friday night? Hard to say, but you did great." Cleaning done, they leaned back against the counter together, Adrian sipping on some rainbow colored concoction.

"Thanks, you led the charge, though."

He laughed, "Are we at war now?"

"Oh yes, us against the late night munchies."

"Team Liadrian," he high fived her.

"Liadrian?"

"Yeah! Lia and Adrian, Liaidran." It was silly but he said it with the most confident smirk, daring her to challenge him.

"You're ridiculous," she laughed, swatting his arm.

"Now, we need a team mascot."

"Truffi, obviously."

"Good call, good call." Their shoulders were a hair's breath away, so close a sheet of paper wouldn't fit between them. Aurelia felt the space like miles and didn't dare close it.

She was saved by the next rush of customers, these noticeably more intoxicated than the last. A bare-chested boy in a leather vest stumbled up to the counter.

"Hi, what can I get you?" Aurelia stepped up to the register.

"Mmmm," was all she got in response as the boy started picking up everything in sight.

A girl in an outrageously sparkly dress started rifling through the cookies with clumsy fingers. Their friends hung back, laughing and hanging onto one another.

Aurelia glanced over her shoulder for help. Adrian had already come to stand right behind her.

"Are you getting coffee? Or... a milkshake?" He prompted the two.

"I'll just..." the boy slurred, turning his back to them as he picked up a banana and started sliding it into his pants pocket.

"Does he think we can't see him?" Aurelia wondered aloud, leaning into Adrian.

"A banana?" She asked the boy.

"Huh, no, I'll yeah."

Another banana went in.

Aurelia rang up two bananas.

The boy shuffled down the line, looking at the pastries. Adrian followed him sighing, "I've got it," to her.

Aurelia, meanwhile, turned her attention to the girl who had, at this point, gathered up half a dozen cookies in her hands.

"Do you want anything to drink?" she tried to ask, but the girl turned away and called her friends over. They waved her off and climbed over one another to a couch where they fell apart in a fit of giggles.

"So six cookies?" Aurelia asked again.

"Can I have these?"

"Of course!" Relief battled with nerves but then the girl started to walk away.

"Oh, I have to ring you up first."

The girl paid her no mind.

"Um, excuse me? Sparkly girl? You have to pay for those." Frustration mounted in her voice as she called out.

"Huh?" The girl turned back.

"Are you okay?" Aurlia furrowed her brow, trying to get a better look at the girl's face.

"Okay? I'm ammaazhhinnggg." The girl drew the word out in a slow, melodious song. Then, suddenly serious, she grabbed Aurelia's arm and lifted herself halfway over the counter. Cookies smooshed beneath her sequins.

"We slipped quartz caps into our mugs at the fire." The girl giggled. "There's auras everywhere, do you see it? The purple around you?"

Aurelia looked desperately to Adrian, the girl's grip was a vice on her arm. She'd never heard of quartz caps but didn't want to ever try them if this is what it did.

Adrian was around the other side of the bar making the boy unload bananas from his pockets. How big were this kid's pockets? Adrian stacked them on the bar.

Suddenly, the girl let go, dropping the cookies as she fell to the ground. She and her friends found this hilarious.

Aurelia looked for Vaughn to tell her what to do, but he was nowhere to be seen and Adrian...

More bananas? What was even happening? They didn't even stock that many bananas.

The sparkly dress girl leapt up and stumble-ran her way to the bathroom. Aurelia followed across the room but she had locked the door.

Aurelia came back to the counter, writing a quick SOS petalpaper to the campus security and sending it off. She tried to reset the display counter while keeping an eye on the bathroom. Every minute she'd see one of the gaggle of friends run over, the door creek open just enough for them to slip inside then slam shut.

Two campus security officers rushed in. One of them came to speak with her, the other called out "Bayren!"

The banana boy looked up, eyes unfocused as he scanned the room. The officer stormed over. "Not again Bayren, we talked about this last weekend!"

"He took four bananas," Adrian explained to the officer. "But when I started taking them back they just kept coming."

Aurelia wanted to listen more but the first officer was asking her what had happened. She explained about the girl, the symptoms, the quartz caps.

"She's in the bathroom along with I think four other girls, it could be more, though," she finished. "Will she be okay?"

The officer wiped her face with a long sigh. "Yes, they make you act dumb but they're not inherently dangerous, it's more the harm to yourself that's a risk with those. Do you have a key?"

"Oh! Yes," Aurelia handed it over.

The officer took the key and crossed the room while fishing a packet of something brown and sludgey out of her pocket.

Aurelia was still worried but not two minutes later the officer, girl, and all her friends exited. The group slunk back to the bar. All the girls were smacking their lips, brows furrowed in disgust.

"Let's get some water for the ladies," the officer said, motioning for them to sit. Shockingly, they listened and sat quietly.

"Wooly Ear, it zaps the crystal right out of their system but tastes like death's shit."

"Oh." Aurelia didn't know what to say to that but promptly filled five cups with water and handed them over.

"Are they going to be okay?"

"Yes but they'll be tasting that crud for the next two days. Hopefully it knocks some sense into them and, luckily for Lyria, she dropped the cookies before hiding away so no theft charges. Can't say the same for Baylen." They watched as the other officer walked a very confused Baylen out of the café.

"Come on, girls, let's get you home."

The girls nodded, still smacking their lips like they wished they could take their whole tongues out of their mouths.

And then it was over.

Aurelia spun in a circle, her body ready for the next debacle until Adrian caught her shoulders.

"Hey, it's alright, you did good."

She heaved a big sigh then sunk onto one of the little stools they kept under the counter.

"That was..." she didn't have words.

"A lot," Adrian finished, handing her a cup of water.

"To say the least. What happened with you? With the bananas?"

"Don't say that word to me."

"Bananas?"

Adrian pretended to retch. "He had some sort of hydra Enchantment on his pockets. Every time we pulled a real one out it doubled. Except the duplicates were fake. If you tried to peel one you'd find it's, well, I don't actually know what would be inside, depends on the Enchantment. Could be anything from sawdust to glitter, who knows. And since we can't know which are real and which are the Enchantment, they're going to need to burn all the bananas we found along with the pants. There's no undoing it."

"So his pockets would just be fake bananas forever?"

"Fake bananas forever."

They both looked at each other then burst into side splitting laughter. Tears ran down Aurelia's cheeks.

Vaughn walked in carrying a tray of sandwiches, he must have been in the kitchen the whole time.

"I'm back. Anything exciting happen?"

"It was bananas," Adrian said with a wink at Aurelia and they burst into a fit of laughter once again.

CHAPTER TWENTY-SIX

The rest of the shift was busy but nothing else quite so crazy happened. Aurelia started to lag around twelve thirty in the morning and made herself a very large black sunshine— coffee with two shots of espresso and honey cream. It worked but a little too well, and a half hour later she was wide awake.

"Want to play a round of chess?" she asked Adrian as they clocked out. "Or, if you're tired, it's okay."

"Regretting that black sunshine?" he smirked, eyes grazing over her as she bounced on her toes.

Aurelia batted her eyelashes innocently. "Me? Regret drinking a caffeine rocket at almost one in the morning? Never."

He walked over to the game shelves and picked up a marble chess set. "Coming?"

Aurelia smiled and gathered a plate of broken cookies. They were allowed to have as many broken cookies as they wanted during and after a shift, after all. She set the plate down and slid into the booth across from Adrian.

"Good call," he said around a mouthful of brown butter

chocolate chip crumbs. "I think we should make this a bit more interesting, though."

"Oh?" she asked, lining up the white pieces in front of her.

"A question for every piece captured."

Aurelia focused on her pieces. That would be a dangerous game but her caution had fled to the wind about a hundred milkshakes ago.

"Hmm, and what do I get for winning?"

"Well, when *I* win I get to meet Truffi."

It felt like a safe thing to agree to, even though Aurelia never knew when Truffi was or wasn't going to appear.

"Alright. And when I win?" She raised a competitive brow at him.

"What do you want, Lia?" His eyes met hers brazenly, daring her to give him a real answer.

Her stomach did backflips. She wanted to kiss him. She wanted to not be a princess. She wanted a lot of impossible things. "I want to watch the sunrise."

"Done." He reached his hand across the board to shake on it.

"Want me to go easy on you?" she asked genuinely. She had learned to play chess before she'd learned to write.

He looked from her eyes to her lips then back to her eyes again. "Never."

At first, Aurelia thought about playing gently anyway. She opened by advancing her king's pawn two squares. Adrian parried with a counterattack immediately, moving his bishop's pawn to c5. Never it was, then.

Adrian had the first capture a few moves later, taking one of Aurelia's pawns with his own on d4.

"Why a sunrise?" They were jumping right in.

"It's more about the night. I'm an early riser. I watch the sunrise any morning I don't have class at Peace Lily, but I've never stayed up all night to watch it." She took his pawn with her knight. "I imagine it's a different experience. Are you an early riser or a night owl?"

"Definitely night." He moved a knight to f6, coming after another of Aurelia's pawns. "I get up early when I have to, but I would sleep late every day if I could."

"What's the most spontaneous thing you've ever done?"

"I'm not a very spontaneous person," she replied as they traded moves. "Maybe coming here? I don't know if that was spontaneous. I researched and considered it for months, dreamed of it for years, but actually going through with it? Choosing *this* moment to be the time I'd go for my dreams, that could be considered spontaneous in a certain way. Right?"

"Mhmm. Sounds like it was a big deal for you to come here?" He moved his bishop to e7, clearly laying the foundation to castle.

"And that sounds like another question." She prepared for a kingside attack.

"Fair enough, fair enough," he replied, castling just as she had suspected. Aurelia picked up a piece of cookie, held it in front of her lips as she thought about her next series.

"You going to eat that cookie or is it whispering strategy to you?" Adrian asked, watching her. She took a bite, shooting him a smirk and shifted her king to h1. He moved his queen and Aurelia held him off with a pawn to a4.

They traded a quick series of moves, Aurelia bided her time as Adrian built a defense.

She took his g6 pawn. "What's something you've learned the hard way?"

"Sometimes you have to do the wrong thing in the moment to do the right thing in the end." He rubbed the back of his neck with one hand.

"That sounds like a story?"

"Now who's double dipping?" He captured her bishop. "Check."

"Was that your question?" She played her knight to g6, blocking his check while attacking his kingside. She sat back, a smug smile playing over her lips.

"You have absolutely no poker face," Adrian grumbled, looking over the board and moving his king to h8.

"And why should I? A move that good deserves to be celebrated."

"Fine but you owe me a question later."

"Deal," she said, still glowing from a successful attack as she advanced a pawn.

"Honestly, it's a lesson I've had to relearn a few times, it doesn't always seem to stick." She nodded as he spoke, it was a lesson she'd learned young. As a queen she'd have to make hard choices, she'd have to do things that had short term consequences for the ultimate good of her people. She'd spent her whole life hiding her magic for that very reason, no matter how much she wanted to just let it all free.

"But right now, I'm specifically thinking about how I probably should be in the lab tonight, but instead I'm here, with you."

"I'm confused," she glanced up at him. "Which is the right thing and which is the wrong thing?"

"I guess we'll see." He brought his rook to f8, trying to set up a guard. But nothing could slow her now. She had her path, the end was already written.

Moves passed, pieces exchanged, their fingers almost brushed again and again. This was the part that made sure no one ever wanted to play with Lia a second time. Her tutor had nicknamed it her routing posture, when the commander came out and the princess faded away.

Adrian was on the brink of collapse, brow furrowed in

concentration, but Aurelia didn't let up. She relished this one outlet where she was allowed to show no mercy.

"You know, you still owe me a question from earlier, Lia," he said as the inevitable set in.

"Oh?" she asked, moving her rook and taking his last chance for escape along with it.

"Last Friday," Adrian's eyes locked on hers, "was that a date?"

Time slowed, the beats of her heart a ticking clock.

Yes.

But she couldn't say that.

Instead, she moved her rook to e4 and said, "checkmate."

For once she couldn't savor the win, she was too wary of what Adrian would say next. He had known he was going to lose but that didn't make the reality of losing any easier for most of Aurelia's opponents. Was he waiting for her to respond to his question? She couldn't. The sounds of the café around them blended together to a hushed quiet, all she could hear was the thud of her own blood racing through her veins.

She looked up at Adrian, readying herself for the typical responses. Confusion, frustration, anger.

He extended his hand, his smile didn't meet his eyes but his voice wasn't upset. "Good game."

"Good game," she repeated warily. The silence stretched, their hands still clasped over the table. He chuckled, shaking his head slightly and letting go.

"Looks like we have a sunrise to catch," he said, gathering the pieces. Relief swelled in Aurelia but didn't break, not yet.

"It's okay—" she started to say, focusing on her pieces.

"Come on," he interrupted her gently, a more genuine smile passing over his features. "It's only three, we have a few more hours of night to kill."

Something had shifted, Aurelia wasn't sure if it was her win or his question or something else.

"You don't have to." She stretched her arms up as she stood. "It's getting late."

"A promise is a promise." He twisted, cracking his back with a loud pop.

"Adrian, really," she reached a hand out to rest gently on his arm before she could stop herself.

"Lia, really, I want to." His eyes flicked to her hand then back up to her face. "And I know the perfect spot."

THEY WALKED IN A TWILIGHT SILENCE. It wasn't comfortable but it wasn't tense either. Aurelia was keenly aware of exactly where their hands, their feet, their sleeves were, keenly aware of every flex of his fingers, every shift of his gaze.

The quad was covered in a shimmering purple haze, the remnants of so much magical energy gathering in one place.

In the center of the lawn, the bonfire blazed. Small groups of students– humans and faeries and every other sort of creature– sat on the grass talking, laughing, and watching the twisting flames.

"Let's sit," Aurelia suggested.

"We'll miss the sunrise if we do. It's Enchanted fire, once it catches your attention it's nearly impossible to break free until the sun rises."

"Oh," was all she said back. That was puzzling.

"It's a safety precaution, if you're looking at it you can't run through it." Adrian led them towards the Enchanters building. "This way."

"Why would anyone run through it?" Aurelia asked, even more confused.

"It used to be a hazing thing for one of the legacy groups on campus; drove the administration nuts so hypnosis was their solution."

"That's crazy, did someone try to get you to do it?"

"No," he laughed, "it was years ago, before my time, but one my lab partners a while back did, told me all about it. He seems to miss the 'glory days' as he calls them."

"Nothing says glory like running through a blazing inferno." Aurelia shook her head at the stupidity.

"While wearing feathers."

"While what?" Aurelia shook her head at the madness. "Did anyone get hurt?"

"Yes, but not seriously."

They walked side by side down the hallway now, only the occasional candle and the light of the bonfire through the wall of windows showing them the way.

Aurelia thought about those students, what could they have been thinking or feeling that was strong enough to overcome their innate fear of running through the fire. Maybe it was just peer pressure, the situation, everyone cheering and laughing, not wanting to let them all down. But at the same time, maybe there was a sort of exhilaration, a joy to it? Letting go to the moment and just hoping for the best on the other side? If no one got seriously physically hurt, then maybe the real risk was the brief spark of time when you stared danger in the face and claimed yourself as your own.

You must really be tired, she thought to herself, if you're suddenly sympathizing with drunk students running through a forty foot tall bonfire.

"You're quiet?" Adrian coaxed.

"Mhmm." She weighed her words.

She could feign sleepiness, even though she was wide awake, or she could tell him the truth. Elle's words came back to her – if she had the choice to be truthful with him, would she be?

"I know it's not sleepiness, even I don't mess with those black sunshines after midnight. What is it?" He bumped her elbow, the contact electric.

"Okay," she laughed, tucking a strand of hair behind her ear. "But you're going to think I'm crazy."

"I swear to you, if it's nuts I'll blame it on the Equinox."

"I was just trying to understand what could make someone run through a fire like that. I mean, yeah, all your friends doing it, I'm sure there was a lot of following the crowd. But, ugh, I can't believe I'm saying this. Maybe there's something sort of... freeing?"

"About running through fire?"

"Letting go. Knowing it's not the best idea, okay maybe it's actually the worst possible idea. But, I don't know, maybe the experience in that moment with those people would somehow be worth it?"

He stared at her, eyes running over her face.

"Nevermind, I'm talking crazy." She tried to laugh it off.

"I mean I could go start a fire out by my workshop," Adrian offered with an annoying smirk.

"No! I don't mean I want to."

"It wouldn't be quite as large," he continued, counting out the idea on his fingers. "I would need some logs, tinder, it would have to be more of a hop than a run but if you want fire, Lia, I'll bring you fire." His glanced at her and she thought she could almost see the reflection of the bonfire in his eyes, shining in the dark.

"Although you might need a change of clothes after," he continued, "that skirt looks quite flammable." He inspected her dress, taking his time as his gaze trailed from her neckline down to her ankles and back up again.

"Stop it! That's not what I meant."

"If you say so, Sparks." He slipped his hands into his pockets, obviously pleased with himself.

They approached a grand staircase, grand even by Aurelia's royal standards.

It was made entirely of stone with balusters intricately carved into the shapes of flowers. The bottom steps curved broadly around the lower newels while the entire structure narrowed as it rose to the first landing before splitting off to reach the balcony on the second floor. It wasn't so much the size of the staircase that awed Aurelia, though, but rather the way the stone flowers seemed to peel open and zip shut in a slow, silent wave.

"How do the pillars even hold it up if they're moving?" Aurelia asked softly, as if her words could spook the stones.

"That's Enchanters for you. Don't get me wrong, they create amazing devices, but sometimes their ideas are a little, how shall I put this? Unpredictable?"

They climbed the stairs, Aurelia sliding her hand gently over the railing, the stoney flowers perhaps the only she had ever encountered that didn't have some small reaction to her presence. She found a kind of emptiness in that, but quickly pushed the thought away as Adrian led them across the second floor landing to another beautiful stone staircase.

They climbed until they reached the fourth floor in relative silence. Adrian apologized for how high up they had to go but promised it would be worth it.

Aurelia told herself the thud of her heart was because of the climb, but if she was honest with herself, this was nothing compared to the creaky six floors she scaled to her apartment every day.

"Where are we going?"

"I love that you ask me that at the top of the stairs and not the bottom," Adrian replied, leading her down a series of smaller, door lined hallways. It was darker here in the interior of the building but he walked with purpose.

She waited.

"You'll see," he assured her, making another turn. She had long since lost track of where they were.

"You really like surprises, don't you?"

"I suppose." He stopped them outside a door, entering a four digit code on a pad outside the room.

"Growing up with so many siblings, it was hard to keep a secret, there was always someone else around." He pushed open the door and led them into the dark classroom.

"So when I could pull off a surprise or someone could pull one off on me, it was a hard won victory."

They walked to the back of the room where two sets of double doors stood closed, blinds drawn.

He tried the handle, but it was locked.

"Uh, Adrian?"

Undeterred, he went to the next set and found them open.

"This way."

She followed him through the dark.

Beyond the doors was a rooftop patio. It had stone pavers with manicured grass set between the squares and a long stone railing overlooking the tree lined paths of the workshops. There were a few benches set along the wall and oversized pots filled with climbing clematis. Silver moonlight washed over the space, mixing with the occasional golden embers drifting on the breeze.

Aurelia walked to the balcony looking out at the view while Adrian took a seat behind her.

She turned. "Where are we?"

"The Royal University of Florevale," he said with a yawn and stretched.

"You can be a real scutch, you know that?"

"Only when I'm tired." He rested one arm over the bench. She walked over and took a seat on the other side of him, mindful of his long legs. The clematis sent a curious tendril across the back of the bench, tickling her shoulder.

"I mean it, what is this place?"

"It's an observation deck. I took an elective course in the Enchanter's college last year in this room and we sometimes came out here. It's supposed to be for demonstrations or lessons where one might need open air, but really, I think the professor just liked being outside."

"That sounds like fun, why did you take a course here? I didn't even know we could do that."

"Some people at this school think magic isn't quite so tightly restrained between the three arts."

Aurelia remembered what Fiora told her about how humans had categorized magic to make it easier to understand but it wasn't inherently tied to one particular nature. She wished she could tell Adrian but then she'd have to explain who Fiora was, what Aurelia was doing with Fiora and a whole cascade of questions she could absolutely not let loose. She plucked a star shaped flower, running her finger along the soft velvet of its petals.

"That's an interesting idea." She dared a look over to him, gaze tracing the sharp line of his jaw as he looked out on the campus, the thick eyebrows above his black glasses.

Adrian took off the glasses, as if he noticed her looking at them, and cleaned them with the hem of his shirt as he continued answering.

"I've always wondered where the boundaries of the three arts came from, and since there were no rules against cross-selecting courses, I decided why not take an intro level in another specialty? The students were a little surprised to see me but the professor was more than happy to alter the syllabus so I could follow along without trained Enchanter magic."

"That was very kind of them," Aurelia watched the sweep of his fingers over the glass with rapt attention.

"Professor Sherby's a good one. I've come back to consult with him so many times, it's actually been really helpful to have another perspective to run my research past outside of the Summoners..." he drifted off. Aurelia looked up to realize she had been staring at his hands and blushed, looking out in the other direction to hide her nerves.

Adrian replaced the glasses and sat up straighter, pulling his feet in so one crossed just in front of Aurelia's foot. She could feel the air between them, a wall of sand, solid yet so delicate. Just the slightest graze and the whole thing would come down and their legs would be pressed together.

Had Adrian even noticed where he'd placed his foot? Was she losing her mind to the last vestiges of the night?

"When do you think the sun will come up?"

"Maybe another hour?" Adrian looked at his watch and then up to the sky. Aurelia looked up too. It was still dark but there was a tinge of grey to the black. Puffy clouds crossed the moon.

"I can't believe we're still awake. Maybe we should have brought snacks."

Adrian pulled a bag of cookie pieces out of the pouch at his waist and held them out to her.

"What? I couldn't let perfectly good treats go to the cookie graveyard."

"The cookie graveyard?"

"You know, where uneaten cookies go," he leaned over to her. "The trash," he whispered in horror.

She took out a piece, her knuckles grazing his she reached into the bag. He cleared his throat, taking a piece of his own and holding it out.

"Cheers," he said.

"What are we toasting to?"

"Sunrises, bananas, and daring to jump through the flames." He caught her eye at that, tapping his cookie to hers.

"Cheers," she repeated with as much bravado as she could muster.

They sat watching the clouds drift by, passing the bag back and forth as threads of crimson, violet, and magenta ever so slowly unfurled across the horizon.

Aurelia stood, careful not to step on the curious clematis that had nearly encircled her feet. "Let's watch from up here."

She walked up to the balcony, forearms resting on the stone. A light breeze rippled the hem of her dress against her legs.

She heard the creak of the bench amid the first chirps of the morning city birds she knew so well. She heard the slow pad of his steps coming closer, closer. The trees below reached their branches towards her. And then his warm body was next to hers, his arm was hovered behind her, his hand was on the stone beside her own.

He wasn't touching her, not a hair on his arm, not a whisper of his skin, but he was all around her. If she took so much as a deep breath her back would be pressed against his shoulder.

She closed her eyes, trying to shut out all the voices in her head trying to tell her what to do next.

The voice telling her to lean into him, to rest her head against his chest.

The voice telling her to step away, create space.

The voice telling her to make a joke, to speak, to break the silence.

She shut them all out, let go of trying to figure out what

would come next, focused entirely on preparing herself to find out. There was no way back to the bench now. Behind them, clematis flowers unfurled in purple and pink waves across the brick faster and faster. But they weren't looking behind, only forward.

"I think the sun will come up any moment now," Adrian murmured as more riotous light spilled over the horizon. The coming sun infused the greys and blues of the sky with rays of gold and soft peach.

"I wonder what makes a sunrise pink or purple or orange." Aurelia mused absently, waiting.

"It has to do with the qualities of the air, what elements make it up and how much of those elements are present," Adrian said softly, his breath so close to Aurelia's face, she could imagine the shape his lips made around the words.

She shifted her hand, the smallest movement, but enough to intertwine one of her fingers with his. His breath hitched, hers stopped entirely. Even the breeze in the trees paused to watch.

He wrapped his long fingers around hers.

They stayed like that, bodies perfectly still, hearts racing into the blazing fire before them.

Time stretched, wider than the bands of radiant color traversing the sky.

And then it snapped.

She turned her head to Adrian, he was already gazing at her. The sun crossed the horizon just as he leaned down so slow, so fast, all at once.

His right hand tilted her chin up with the faintest touch. Her eyes drifted shut.

She took one last inhale and...

THEIR LIPS MET.

CHAPTER TWENTY-SEVEN

Aurelia had been kissed by three men, boys really, before Adrian.

The first taught her to guard her heart. The second taught her to guard her heart when that first lesson didn't stick. The third, perhaps the most painful of all, tried to teach her to guard her heart one last time. But as it turned out, by then, she didn't have much of a heart left to guard at all.

When Adrian kissed her on the rooftop, as the morning birds sang and the dawn colors rang across the sky, Aurelia learned that she did, indeed, still have a heart to protect. And yet, once again, she couldn't bear to hide it.

CHAPTER TWENTY-EIGHT

Adrian kissed Aurelia until the pinks and purples and golds melted to blue. His strong hands held fast to her waist, his soft lips learned the shape and movement and rhythm of hers. Gold and crimson and taupe leaves swirled around them in invisible eddies as trees across the campus waved in delight.

Aurelia kissed Adrian until the sounds of the sleepy city rose to their balcony. Her curious fingers swept through his hair and ran along his exposed collarbone. The soft ruffles of her dress fluttered around his legs as they leaned against the stone, her back arched, melting their bodies together. Climbing ivy and roses raced up the building, covering the railing in leafy green.

They kissed until the sunrise came and went and morning began until at last Aurelia pulled back.

"I think we might have missed the sunrise," she whispered against his lips.

"We'll have to try again," Adrian replied in a husky voice, arms still encircling her waist. Aurelia laughed again, leaning her forehead against the hard muscle of his chest.

"Come on," Adrian said, stepping back, sliding a palm down her arm to take hold of her hand.

"Come on where?" They paused, a thick web of clematis covered the wall, completely obscuring the door.

"Breakfast. I think they can hear your stomach rumbling all the way across campus." He didn't comment on how their balcony had become a flowering jungle and Aurelia was too kiss-drunk, or perhaps simply too sleep-deprived, to be afraid.

"Adrian? Is that you?"

"What?" His smile dropped in sudden concern as he found the doorknob.

"Telling me where we're going? Not just saying it's a surprise."

Relief washed over him as they climbed through the net of vines, neither willing to comment on the sudden growth. "Listen, Sparks, if everything's a surprise then nothing will be."

"You're not going to let me live that bonfire comment down, are you?"

"Not a chance," he said with a wink that would have utterly ruined her if she wasn't already ten feet deep without a ladder in sight.

THE WORLD HAD TAKEN on an opalescent shimmer as they walked out of the Enchanter's building. Maybe it was just the remnants of last night's magic or her own sleeplessness or the way Adrian squeezed her hand every time they turned a corner. Maybe it was all three, Aurelia wasn't sure.

She leaned in closer to Adrian as they walked, goosebumps pebbling her arms in the early morning cool. He draped his arm around her shoulders, rubbing warmth back into her skin. Little white flowers leapt from the ground as they passed by.

A windy route through the main college had them off campus in half the time.

"You really know your way around here, first the Enchanter's school and now," she looked around, momentarily blanching at the path of daisies left in their wake, "how did we get here so fast?"

"Knowing the back roads comes in handy. Besides, you haven't met a shortcut until you see what I can do back in Waldon."

"You'll just have to take me sometime," she hummed, turning her attention away from the flowers.

"Deal," he grinned.

Now Aurelia was really getting herself into trouble. Visiting a foreign court? A princess couldn't just walk in unannounced. There would have to be arrangements, announcements, introductions, not to mention how would she explain all of that? But for right now, she pushed those thoughts aside and reminded herself of the fire. The dream would have to be enough.

Adrian led them to a café close to her apartment, one she had walked past dozens of times but hadn't yet tried.

It had a light green and white striped awning and white faux-marble tables, each set with a dainty group of pale yellow zinnias. Green rattan chairs that perfectly matched the awning were all around and at the tables closest to the street, the chairs were lined up side by side for perfect people watching.

Adrian chose a middle table so they could sit across from

one another. A grey-furred nellin dropped two thin menus with a smile and not a word.

The breakfast offerings were simple, a hot drink and pastry or a hot drink, pastry, and eggs. They both opted for the eggs; Aurelia's soft with chives and Adrian's fried with cheese.

Two steaming mugs of hot chocolate appeared along with an old silver dish piled high with freshly made whipped cream.

"You would think after the night we had we'd be going straight for coffee," Aurelia said as she scooped cream into her mug.

"We need to sleep someday, Sparks," Adrian replied, ladling easily twice as much into his own chocolate.

"Sleep? Who's she? Never met her." Aurelia pretended to dust off her shoulders but was interrupted with an irrepressible yawn.

Adrian laughed and bumped his knee into hers. The zinnias twirled unnoticed in a phantom breeze. It was amazing to Aurelia how in just a few hours, the space between them had transformed from so precise and immovable to so comfortable and warm. She bumped her knee back against his, just because she could.

As she took her first sip of hot chocolate, the nellin reappeared with their plates and a bowl of strawberries.

"For fixing our percolator last week." The creature was gone before Adrian could reply.

"So do you know everyone in Florevale or just almost everyone?" Aurelia asked, spearing a fork full of the fluffy golden eggs.

"Just the Shrubs," he shrugged, raising a cocky eyebrow.

"Is that so?"

She savored the buttery, salty, perfectly herby bite.

"Okay, fine, you caught me. I actually can't cook, not at all, it's terrible and mortifying, trust me. So rather than eat burnt

rubbery plain pasta every night, I got to know the neigh-
borhood."

"But you're so good at making coffee, I don't understand."

"Not all of us were gifted with a chef's thumb."

"A chef's thumb?" If Julietta could see her now, elbows on
the table, eggs still in her mouth as she talked to a suitor...
Aurelia would be sitting with dowels in her dress for a month.
Suitor? No, Aurelia wouldn't go there. *Friend.* More than a
friend but... not a suitor.

"You know, like a green thumb is someone really good at
gardening, a chef's thumb would be someone really good at
cooking."

"I don't think that's a thing," she said, swiping a strawberry
through their still very full bowl of cream as she tried to burn
the s-word out of her mind.

A petalpaper landed in Aurelia's lap with a flutter of iridescent blue wings.

Aurelia set down her fork with a sigh, she didn't want
anything to come between her and another bite of breakfast.

"Everything okay?" Adrian's brows knitted together, Aurelia
could get lost in how it made his eyes shine.

"It's from Darya, she wants to make sure I got home safely
last night."

"How is that girl possibly awake right now?"

"Try having early morning exercise classes with her. She
goes from asleep to giving a hundred percent in an instant."

Adrian took another bite of his eggs, and fished a pen out of
his satchel. "Here, I have a pen."

"Are you always this prepared?"

"Not a chance, but these little bags are actually coming in
quite handy, I wonder why they fell out of fashion."

Aurelia looked over his outfit, the deep V of exposed chest

and peeking curl of ink under his collarbones. The cord wrapped around his waist where two small bags were secured.

"You know, I honestly couldn't tell you, I think it looks great on you."

He gave her a cheeky smile. "Glad you think so."

They were quiet a moment after that. Adrian plucked a still slowly spinning zinnia from the jar, a row of petals popping out to wrap around his fingertips. Aurelia focused all her attention on jotting out a quick 'all good' to Darya then set the petalpaper loose to fly away.

Adrian replaced the flower, watching the butterfly swoop and climb before asking, "So, what did you tell her? About last night?" He tried to make the question seem casual but it was a flimsy attempt. There was nothing casual about Adrian's questions when he looked at her like that.

"I said I had a good time and am excited to see her tonight. Both true."

"So then, no details?"

"Nope." She couldn't meet his gaze. Suitor. Suitor. Suitor. That horrible word was back and with it the perky zinnias on their table shook all their petals loose.

Adrian looked from the naked flower up to her then back down again but said nothing. Neither did she.

Aurelia picked up her hot chocolate, hoping she could hide the embarrassment written all over her face behind the mug.

"Do," he cleared his throat, "do you want to tell them about last night? About," his eye contact was devastating, Aurelia fought to avoid it and lost. "This morning?"

"Do you?"

He laughed but it wasn't funny. "Fair enough."

She sighed. "Yes."

"Yes?" His whole face changed. She bit her lip, what had he thought she would say?

"Yes, but..."

"Yes, but?"

She bumped his knee again and tried for a reassuring smile. "Yes, but maybe not tonight? I... I want to talk to Elle first. She's been saying how we should have done this weeks ago and I think I just need to talk things through before, you know..." It was a funny thing to say since she didn't actually know how to finish that sentence. Maybe with a few hours of sleep she'd figure it out.

"So, what I'm hearing is that you and Elle have been talking about me?" Adrian asked with a self satisfied smirk.

"No comment," she replied, returning to her eggs and waiting for him to say more.

"That's fine with me, and I understand. But just so you know, Lia," he leaned forward, tan forearms resting on the table, thighs squeezing her knee between his own, "the moment you're ready, I'm all in."

She thought she knew what blushing was before, but the color her cheeks must have turned in that moment, the reddest rose couldn't compare.

"You have to stop saying things like that," she mumbled with a giddy smile.

"Things like what?"

"Saying you're all in?"

"But I am, Lia. You can have all the time you need, we can have all the time you need, because when you're ready to have me, I'm yours."

Aurelia wished so fervently that he was right that she nearly believed it was true.

She waved her fork at him accusingly, "You." She was out of words.

"Me?" he replied with all the innocence of a young pup right after it chews up a pair of brand new slippers.

"You," she said more firmly, deciding one word was plenty.

Aurelia reached for a croissant and ripped it in half. How could she be so much more nervous now than before the kiss? But Adrian only smiled and leaned back, playing with the open collar of his shirt.

"How about after breakfast we get changed into more... modern attire and go for a walk?"

"That sounds perfect, I actually wanted to stop by the produce market to pick up some things for the week, want to come with me?"

"As long as you don't expect me to know what to do with any of it."

"Wouldn't dream of it."

CHAPTER TWENTY-NINE

Adrian walked Aurelia around the corner to her apartment, sweeping her up in a kiss that made her want to entirely rewrite their plans for the afternoon. But as fast as it started, it was over and she was opening the door and he was waving goodbye.

Tiredness weighed her feet down like thousand pound stones growing heavier with each stair. But when she at last trudged into her apartment, she was rewarded with a pale pink petalpaper waiting for her at the window. Inside was a note from Adrian.

Just in case you think it was all a dream,
here's a note to remind you it wasn't.
See you soon, Sparks.

Aurelia raced to her closet, her feet alight with sudden energy. She replaced her flowy festival dress with a pair of high waisted brown shorts and a floral tank. She took one look out the window and ripped them both off to try again.

Three discarded outfits later, she turned to find Poppy's leafy arms curling around a short, pleated, brown-tartan skirt and a butter soft cream sweater. It was perfect.

She slipped them both on then added knee high socks and supple black leather boots. Poppy returned with a matching silk bow for her hair and, at this point, Aurelia figured who was she to question Poppy's fashion sense.

There was a knock at her door just as she was grabbing a netted shopping bag. She opened it to find Adrian leaning against her doorway. He had changed into a pair of black jeans with a light blue tee that made his eyes sparkle and a short black jacket.

"Oh, hi, you didn't have to come all the way up here. Do you want to come in?"

Adrian took his time looking her up and down, eyes lingering on the hem of her skirt before looking up to her eyes.

"We should go." He leaned in close, his breath tickling her ear. "If I come in I doubt we'll ever leave." He said it with such cool Aurelia thought she would ignite on the spot.

"Sure, right..." she sputtered. "Okay, yes." She needed to pull it together.

Adrian laughed then grabbed her hand and pulled her in for a kiss. She leaned her back against the doorway and he lifted one hand to rest on the wood over her head. His other hand drifted from the side of her face down to her waist, squeezing for just a moment before breaking away.

"Let's go or the markets will close."

"Alright, alright, but promise you'll do that again when we get back?"

He looked straight into her eyes as he purred, "Promise," and Lia knew she was well and truly in too deep.

THEY RETURNED from the market towards the end of the morning, Adrian carting Lia's haul with ease. As promised, the moment she unlocked the door he was over her again, one hand reaching above her, the other firmly pulling her waist against him. Her arms twined around his neck, savoring the feel of his hard chest against her, but this time, it was she who broke away first.

"Come on, we don't want that quad-cream brie to melt." She walked inside with a little extra swoosh of her hips.

"Not the brie," he teased, following her to the kitchen where the groceries were swiftly dropped once again.

They kissed, hands roaming, until Adrian accidentally stepped on a banana of all things, prompting a fit of side splitting laughter from Aurelia.

"Am I ever going to be free of these retched fruits?" Adrian growled as he pulled off his shoe and started to clean up the mess.

Aurelia put the milk, vegetables, and bulk sundries away then started slicing cheeses. She assembled the pieces on a tray with some of the rosemary sourdough crackers and lemon brined olives they had bought at the market.

Adrian sat on a stool, watching her work, occasionally reaching for a nibble of cheese only to have his hand hastily swatted away.

Poppy stealthily deposited a few golden pansies from the balcony garden onto the board while Aurelia's back was turned, unbothered by Adrian's studying gaze.

"Lia?"

"Mhmm?" she dropped almonds onto the last sliver of exposed board and looked up.

Adrian pushed his hair off his forehead and adjusted his glasses. "Nevermind."

"No, what is it?" She picked up the completed board.

"Just," he paused, eyes shifting to the window then back to her. "Uhm, here, let me take that from you."

She passed it over to him with a curious look but let it go.

Lunch ended up lasting most of the afternoon in their sleep-deprived delirium. At last, they finally had to admit it was time for a nap and came inside.

"Go sit, I'll be right there," Adrian said as he carried the board to the kitchen.

Aurelia wandered over to the couch, trying desperately not to fall asleep, when she felt a soft breath on her cheek. Her eyes fluttered open to find Adrian's scruffy cheek against hers.

"Sorry, I didn't mean to wake you," Adrian whispered, brushing the hair out of her face from where he was kneeling beside the couch.

She gave him a sleepy smile and scooted back into the pillows to make room for him.

He nestled himself onto the couch beside her, arms wrapped around her body, legs tangled. Her head fit perfectly into the crook of his shoulder.

She was asleep again before she could even reply.

THEY WOKE A FEW HOURS LATER, just as the sun was starting to dip. Adrian tilted her face up to his and kissed her with sleepy softness. She ran her hand across his chest before pulling back and murmuring, "I suppose we should get up now."

"We should," Adrian's voice was a rumble she could feel in his chest.

"What are we supposed to wear tonight?"

"The second night is much more casual, although as much as I like this skirt you'll probably want something warmer." His fingers trailed lower down her waist towards her hips as he spoke.

He kissed her again, lingering, before pushing himself to standing then reached a hand down to help her up. She stretched then took his hand and headed to her closet.

Aurelia swapped out her skirt for a pair of fitted medium wash jeans. In the bathroom, she fluffed her hair and added a touch of liner to her eyes.

When she came back, she found Adrian at the sink, cleaning off the board and cutlery they had used earlier.

"Thank you, you didn't have to do that," she said, drying the dishes as he washed them and putting them away.

"It was such a nice board, I wouldn't want to break it."

"Break it?"

He dried his hands then, in a whoosh, picked her up by the waist and set her on the counter.

She let out a soft yelp that was hastily cut short by the crush of his lips against hers. In a moment it was over and she was landing shakily down on her feet. Adrian held onto her until she righted herself.

Laughing, she asked, "What was that?"

He shrugged. "I needed one more kiss before we go since I won't be able to kiss you once we get there."

"In that case," she said, rising onto her tip toes to reach him, "do it again."

As THE SKY crept closer and closer to darkness, Adrian and Aurelia finally headed out to the bonfire. Adrian kept his arm around her until they reached campus then slipped his hands into his pockets. Aurelia desperately wanted to tell him to forget the whole waiting thing, to scoop her up and kiss her in front of the whole school. But that word wouldn't leave her brain. *Suitor. Suitor. Suitor.*

They arrived at the bonfire together, spotting Elle, Darya, and Hunter almost immediately.

"The late-nighters!" Hunter called out, seeing them before the girls did.

"Hey!" Adrian waved. The girls squealed and ran up to Aurelia.

"What happened last night! Tell us everything!"

"Later!" Aurelia shushed, hoping they wouldn't press. Both girls looked back and forth between her and Adrian as if the story of their night might be written on their foreheads.

"We're going to go get drinks, wait here," Adrian said with a smirk. *Suitor. Suitor. Suitor.*

"Lia, dish! We've been waiting all day!"

The music swelled, saving Aurelia from further explanation. She called out, "Later! When I can hear you!" They must have gotten the gist because they both rolled their eyes in defeat.

Aurelia felt a whisper of a hand across her hip as Adrian appeared to her right.

"Here, Lia," he said, their fingers lingering for just a moment as he passed over the mug.

And then the spell was broken. "Elle, here's one for you," he tore his gaze away, "and Darya, one for you."

They stood in a small circle, Lia, Adrian, Hunter, Elle, and Darya. Hunter tried to say something but his words were lost to the celebration. They all clinked glasses in the middle anyway and called out "cheers!" as they started to sway to the music.

Aurelia wished she could dance with Adrian, but this wasn't the kind of music two people danced to, anyway. It wasn't a court waltz or a romantic ballad, it was more primal, terrestrial, thrumming. A melody sung by the ground and the trees. Their bodies swayed and turned.

Every so often, though, Adrian's hand would graze Aurelia's, her hair would caress his arm, their shoulders would press together and their eyes would sink into each other's.

They would have time to dance together the way Aurelia wanted. They may not have all the time Adrian had claimed they'd have, but they had right now, and she was jumping through the fire because these moments were worth any burn.

CHAPTER THIRTY

E lle met Aurelia downstairs the next afternoon for a little outing to her favorite park, the Garden Luillersyne. It was on the border of the Shrubs and Trellis districts so with their bags full of books, they opted for bikes.

The Garden Luillersyne was a large, open space with broad grassy lawns and wide white-pebbled pathways. The lawns were more for appreciating than sitting on, though, and were blocked by a tiny rope fence. Just inside the fence, each was bordered with artistically arranged beds that mixed annual and perennial plants so masterfully, they looked like florist-designed bouquets.

Around the lawns were dozens upon dozens of green iron chairs, some upright, some more reclined, some with little tables or foot rests.

They dragged two of the reclined chairs with foot rests under a shaded row of pleached oak trees.

"So Hunter had to carry Darya up the stairs," Elle was chattering as Aurelia unpacked books, notepads, a bag of freshly baked serrequettes, and two bottles of fresh orange juice.

"Wait, wait, I'm still so confused, why didn't she just take the shoes off?" Aurelia had clearly missed something important in this story.

"They were Enchanted, although cursed would be more accurate." Elle unpacked her own wad of disheveled papers, weighing them down with her caramelized pear mocha.

Aurelia eyed the precarious stack.

"What? I live on the edge."

Aurelia laughed. "That you do. So, um... shoes?"

"You didn't hear a word I said did you?"

"I definitely heard... some of it!"

"Okay, whatever happened Friday night clearly has your mind in a tailspin." Elle picked up her coffee, Aurelia slammed one of her heavy books on top of Elle's papers. Maybe Elle wasn't worried about them blowing away but Aurelia had no interest in chasing them down the paths.

Her mind raced, how could she even start to explain this? All the flowers in front of them swiveled their heads to listen.

"Wow, it really has you going" Elle said, a crease of worry wrinkling her freckled forehead. "Just start at the beginning."

"The beginning, okay, I can do that. So Adrian found me at the edge of the bonfire." Elle squealed at that.

"You're not ready, that wasn't even the tip of the iceberg of this night, that was like, a singular snowflake in a blizzard."

"I'm from Lownden, I've never seen a blizzard, but sure, go ahead."

"Elle, do you want to tell this story or should I?"

"Alright, alright, I won't interrupt."

Aurelia waited a moment, Elle made a zipping motion over her lips.

"So Adrian found me at the bonfire and we walked over to Apple Blossom together." She told Elle about the shift, about the girls who were drunk on quartz caps and the security officer and her wooly ears.

Elle had apparently been given wooly ears last year and shuttered at the story. "Ugh, my tongue was absolutely trauma-tized by that stuff, even now I feel like I can still taste it."

"And the whole time Adrian was dealing with the banana thief and his hydra Enchantment."

Elle gasped at this, apparently hydra Enchantments were sometimes done as a prank, usually only by delirious first-years who didn't realize how permanent it would be.

Aurelia continued with how the rest of the shift passed by without incident but how, by the end of it, she wasn't ready to go home.

When she got to the part about the game of truth or chess, Elle cheered but held in further commentary.

She told Elle about how Adrian asked if the previous week had been a date and about how she avoided the question. She described how they walked around the quad for what must have been at least an hour before he led them to the roof of the Enchanter's Hall. She explained how she couldn't stop thinking about the Enchanted bonfire and how when they sat on the bench, Adrian's leg had crossed over hers.

Elle was practically crawling out of her chair by the time Aurelia got to Adrian's arm around her at the balcony and she let out a glare-inducing whoop when Aurelia finally made it to the part where they'd kissed.

"So what do I do now?" Aurelia moaned, dropping her face into her hands.

"Do now? Uhm, jump for joy? Be that obnoxious couple that's always together? Invite him back to your apartment every night because trust me theirs is not even worth looking at."

"Ughhh," was all Aurelia replied.

"Okay, what am I missing here? You two have been dancing around this from day one, you've obviously liked each other, and now you're together?"

"But I can't be!"

"You're not going to be..." Elle looked around then mouthed the word, "queen" before continuing "for a very long time."

"First of all, we need a code word." Aurelia sighed, sitting back in her chair.

"Agreed, how about..." Elle's eyes darted around the garden, "head gardener?"

"Fine," Aurelia rolled her eyes but went along with it.

"I know I won't be... head gardener... for years but as... apprentice gardener... I still have a responsibility to the... garden?"

"So?"

"So, if it was just casual I could probably get away with it, but with Adrian, it could never be casual." Her cheeks flamed at his name and Elle grinned like it proved her point.

"The night was too perfect. The sunrise and the breakfast and the kissing. But no matter how hard I tried, I couldn't get the word suitor out of my head."

"Hmm." Elle rested her head on her hand thoughtfully.

"I've been taught since I knew what a spouse was that mine would probably be arranged for political gains, or at the very least whoever it was would have to go through a strict vetting process. A process that, no matter how much I wanted it to work out, might not go my way."

"That's a lot to put on your shoulders."

"I'm not trying to complain, I've been born into so much privilege, I came to terms with the costs of that privilege long ago."

"Yeah, but you still deserve to love and be loved."

"My people deserve a ruler who puts their interests first."

"But you're still a citizen of Serremont too, you deserve love, Lia. And I'm not saying you are going to marry Adrian, we're literally talking about dating right now, but don't speak for him.

If that day comes, maybe he'll want to go through the process, and I think if he knew the reason for your hesitation, he would still want to take that risk. Experiencing love is worth the possibility of losing it."

"You sound like a greeting card," Aurelia mumbled.

"I sound right," Elle retorted.

"Okay, fine, maybe he should get to decide for himself. I don't know if I believe that he would choose me, choose all the battleships worth of baggage I come with, but even if he did that's the other thing. He doesn't know and I can't tell him."

"I think you're a better judge of character than that, Lia, and you trust him."

"I think my date with Thris would beg to differ."

"That was just a momentary bout of hot-guy-induced psychosis. Doesn't count." Elle dismissed with a flippant wave of her hand. Aurelia started to protest but she continued. "Seriously, one mistake doesn't mean your lifetime of good decision making is thrown out the window. You were raised to understand people and their motives, you just lost your head for a second."

"And you don't think I'm losing my head with Adrian?" Something like hope flared in her heart.

"Not a chance." Elle rested a reassuring hand on Aurelia's arm.

"Maybe you're right, but I'm just... not ready to tell him."

"That's fine, though. Trust him to be there when you're ready. Didn't he tell you to take all the time you need?"

"Yes, but that was to hold hands in public, not admit I'm secretly the princess... the assistant gardener of Serremont destined to be... head gardener? And that whoever I marry will become a... gardener too."

Laughter fought through her pressed lips, strange gurgling

noises escaping from them both. She dropped her head, wiping her eyes with her palms.

"I just hate being dishonest with him," she sighed. "I don't want the foundation of our relationship to be a lie."

"It's not, Lia."

"My name isn't even Lia."

"Remember what I said two weeks ago?"

"To never let you drink coffee while wearing white again?" Aurelia looked meaningfully at the splotch of tan on Elle's bone white trouser leg.

"Aghhh!" Elle jumped, dabbing at the spot with a napkin for a moment before throwing her hands up in defeat.

"Besides that." She pulled the edge of her beige trench coat over the stain. "You're not pretending to be someone else you're just being a different side of you"

"Oh, right, that."

"Well it's true. You *are* Aurelia and you *are* Lia. He doesn't know all of you– yet– and you don't know all of him yet either. That's okay."

Aurelia looked out and realized the flowers were nodding their faces in a distinctly up and down motion. Were they... agreeing with Elle? No. Maybe? Why were so many plants *listening* to her these days? They didn't even have ears, what was going on? Aurelia made a mental note to tell Fiora and Professor Maillie, see what they thought of it.

"Just think about it, alright?" Elle was saying. "Don't close any doors just yet."

"I'll give myself some time to try to get used to the idea, okay?"

"Yes!" Elle yelped, more glares spinning their way.

"I said *try*!"

"I heard you," Elle preened in a way that said she had absolute certainty she had won over Aurelia's fears. Aurelia shook her head but smiled, maybe, just maybe, she had.

ADRIAN WAS WAITING for Aurelia outside her building Monday morning. He took a long, slow look down and then back up again as she stepped through the doorway and whistled.

"Hi there," she laughed, turning pink.

"Let's see, do a spin." A lopsided grin brought out his dimples.

She did a little twirl, her long patchwork skirt floating around her calves. Aurelia was fully in her Autumn wardrobe now and had paired the pastel orange, tan, and brown skirt with a sleeveless button down denim vest and a chunky, mauve, knitted cardigan. Her hair was loosely braided down her back with peachy verbena blossoms woven in.

"Stunning," he said, resting a hand on the crook of her neck as he leaned in for a soft kiss.

She pulled back. "Okay, okay, your turn."

"My turn?"

"Mhmm, a twirl, go ahead."

He dropped his shoulder bag and stepped back, adjusting the rolled cuff of his light blue linen button down with a wink. He did a spin, the hem of his wide leg trousers flaring just a bit, then ran a hand through his perfectly tousled hair as he stepped towards her.

Aurelia's happiness turned into breathless anticipation. They stood so close it was a wonder they weren't touching. He leaned down to pick up his bag at her feet. Rising, he lowered his lips to hover just over hers then, quick as lightning, planted a kiss on her cheek.

She let out a small, frustrated sigh, to which he said, "Wouldn't want to make you late to class, Sparks."

"You owe me one later."

He took her bag off her shoulder, slinging it over his, and led them across the street.

"Done."

They entered Calyntha's shop where the nellin fully paused, scanning them from joined hands down to their feet then finally up to their faces. Aurelia had never seen Calyntha so still.

Calyntha let out a little "humph" then proceeded to open the paper bag on the counter and slip two more fleuret rolls into the bag.

"Good morning Calyntha, this is Adrian. Adrian, this is Calyntha, she's the most talented baker in the city."

"Nice to meet you, Calyntha," Adrian said with his easy charm. It didn't work.

"Hmm," the nellin replied, rolling up the paper bag of goodies.

"Thank you," Adrian reached to take it from her.

Calyntha didn't let go of the bag right away, squinting her furry eyelids. "I know every baker in Florevale. Hurt her and expect nothing but burnt ends the rest of your days."

"Wouldn't dream of it," Adrian swore, a smile tugging at his lips. Aurelia dropped her face into her hands in a mixture of embarrassment and affection for her furry, motherly friend.

"Alright then. In that case, here." She unwound the paper, tucking a spiral of soft bread and gooey cheese into the already stuffed bag and handed it over.

"Thank you." Aurelia tried to infuse the simple words with all the warmth and gratitude she felt for this small but utterly fearsome being.

Adrian walked Aurelia to her workshop, both of them dropping flaky crumbs like a trail leading from Calyntha's straight to her doorstep.

"You know, one of these days you're going to have to tell me how you managed a workshop like this in your first year." Adrian whistled, admiring a gathering of taupe nightingales perched on the roof.

Aurelia choked on her fleuret roll.

"Are you okay?"

"Oh, mhmm," she coughed, eyes watering. "I'm great."

Adrian eyed her skeptically.

"Hey Lia, you okay?" Clem popped up out of seemingly nowhere, his iridescent wings raised.

"Just choking on chocolate, I'm fine" she rasped, wanting this interaction to be over immediately.

Clem and Adrian watched her suspiciously. Clem's long arms crossed in consternation while Adrian rubbed soothing circles on her back.

"I'm just going to go get some water, thank you for..." she coughed again, "for walking me." She waved and headed inside, hoping Clem would follow quickly.

"I've got her, don't worry," Clem reassured Adrian. "I'm Clem by the way."

Not quickly enough, Aurelia thought. She let out another bout of coughs trying to will Clem's mouth shut.

"Adrian," he replied, shaking hands with the faerie. "Thanks."

"I'll see you later, Lia," Adrian called out. He stood there a moment longer before begrudgingly walking deeper into the forest towards his own workshop.

By the time Clem was inside, Fiora had already handed Aurelia a glass of water which she was downing greedily.

"So, Adrian?" Clem asked with a cocky smile.

"He's a friend." She walked the empty glass into the kitchen as the faeries trailed behind.

"A friend?" Clem repeated suggestively.

"Maybe more than a friend, but he doesn't know who I am."

"Ah," he replied, helping himself to the plate of scones on the counter.

"Anyway," Aurelia was more than eager to switch topics, "I wanted to talk through some things with you both." Fiora held herself with that peculiar stillness, Clem slid onto a stool.

"I noticed some things about my magic over the weekend that, well now they seem obvious but we've never discussed the implications of it before. Is Professor Maillie about? He should probably be here for this too."

Fiora sighed. "Professor Maillie went to the libraries of Sunsykett just before the Equinox, apparently found more than he bargained for. He won't be back until closer to the winter holiday."

"Oh." Aurelia stared at her hands. She hadn't ever thought about Professor Maillie working on other projects but she had to admit that had been a glaring oversight. Of course he had more going on, she was going to be at Florevale for years. This felt so urgent to her but to someone with as long and important of a career as Maillie, of course the scope of his work was bigger than just her.

"But you are in the very best hands with us," Clem reassured her, perhaps seeing the way her face dropped.

"I actually think it's a good thing," Fiora added, sitting down with them. "It gives us more time to prove my theories before that insane rebinding nonsense."

Aurelia gave a half hearted smile. "Sure."

"So, what is it you wanted to tell us?" Fiora said, flipping her notebook open to a fresh page.

She explained how plants seemed to be listening to her now, responding to her words, actions, and even thoughts. Before coming to Florevale, her overflows had been centered around plants flowering, growing, dropping petals or shooting up limbs. She had never experienced her magic making plants act beyond their nature before arriving in the city.

Fiora and Clem agreed this was odd and said they would set up testing for early next week to see if Aurelia's interpretation had merit. If it did, Fiora said, she had an idea of what was happening, but she wanted to wait for the test results less her musings skew the outcomes.

Aurelia spent the rest of the morning reading and studying in the library. She curled up with her books, sheer pens, and a mug of steaming pumpkin, clove, and blackberry tea. Someone, probably Fiora, had lit the fireplace, and from her perch under the large windows, Aurelia could hear Clem and the birds humming an endless song together.

CHAPTER THIRTY-ONE

"Lia, would you stick around after class for a moment?" Professor Luciaas said as she walked into class Wednesday morning.

"Sure, Professor," she replied, trying unsuccessfully to not worry. Despite her love for this class, she spent most of the next hour and a half lecture imagining that he had discovered her identity, or, worse, that the entire Founding Lore Society had uncovered it.

She took her time packing up her notebook and pens, as if maybe delaying their talk would stop whatever horror he was about to unleash.

"Ah, Lia, come, walk with me," Professor Luciaas said eventually. Apparently she wasn't getting out of this.

"You wanted to see me, Professor?"

"Yes, I was talking to my colleague over at the Royal Libraries in Jardeisailles."

She might actually throw up, right here on the marble floors of the lecture cottage.

"Oh?" She aimed for casual, it came out more strangled.

"Yes, dear Finnigan, the Royal Librarian, is an old friend of mine." Aurelia wished her doom would come just a little faster and perhaps with a bit less pep.

"And I was telling him-"

"I can explain," she interrupted. He didn't notice.

"About a student of mine—"

"Maybe we should go to the chancellor's office?" She tried again.

"Hmm? Oh, no, no need to involve the Chancellor, I exchange petalpapers with Finny, that's my nickname for Finnigan, all the time! Anyway, I was telling him I had a student interested in the alliance of Queen Ghenevere and King Merisyll and *he* said he would send over copies of their journals!"

"What?" Aurelia was dumbfounded.

"You can't expect them to send out the originals, those are, well I do believe some may be over two thousand years old."

"Copies?" Aurelia was so focused on willing her heart to start beating again that she hardly processed with Luciaas was trying to tell her.

"Yes, lucky for us they have copies of all the originals that *can* be loaned out. If one has the right connections that is, and it just so happens," he leaned in conspiratorially, "I do."

"That's wonderful news," Aurelia said, not talking about the journal at all but rather that her identity was still intact.

"Indeed, indeed," he replied merrily, "I expect they will be here in the next, oh say, two to three weeks. It takes some time to go through all the proper channels and whatnot. I will let you know the moment they arrive, perhaps we can arrange for some theatrical readings for the Foundy lunches!"

"Wonderful." Her vocabulary had evidently withered up in her terror.

"Yes, yes, and the invitation still stands, every Thursday!"

"Yes, right, I... I can't this week but perhaps next?" Her ability to focus was slowly returning.

"Excellent, excellent, we shall be ready! Good day, Lia!" He tipped his hat and strode down the path toward the library.

Aurelia stood for a long moment then sank onto a bench trying to remember how to breathe.

AURELIA COULDN'T TAKE her eyes off Adrian for most of her bonus afternoon shift on Thursday. She normally only worked Tuesday afternoons and Friday mornings but had picked up an extra session to clear her head.

Adrian had met her every morning for breakfast on the way to campus and every night to take her to a different sidewalk café. When he worked on Wednesday afternoon, she had sat in a booth and pretended to read the entire time. Now he was sitting at a table in the center of the room, strands of hair falling over his face as he copied numbers from one page to the next. This was her payback, she supposed, as she found herself so thoroughly distracted that even Thlynda's razor-edged glare couldn't make her focus.

"You okay?" Bette had asked finally when Aurelia scorched a pot of milk for the second time. She had to pull herself together.

"I'm great," Aurelia said over her shoulder.

"Here, I've got the steamer, you take the next... oh, hi Adrian." Aurelia turned so fast she splashed the almost-boiling milk onto her hand.

"Ow, ow-ow-ow, ow."

"Run it under cool water," Adrian soothed, a mix of concern and amusement in his voice.

"It was just a drop, I'm fine," she insisted, taking his advice nonetheless.

"You okay?" He asked, leaning forward over the counter to take a look. She made the mistake of looking up, making eye contact, getting lost.

"Go, make your own drink, Adrian," Thlynda's thin voice snapped Aurelia back to her senses. Thlynda looked Aurelia up and down slowly, a fox assessing a wounded rabbit.

"Lia, why don't you restock the milks in the cold box."

"Milk, got it," Aurelia nodded.

Thlynda was right, a minute of shuffling around the various milks under the counter cleared her head.

She was so deliriously happy with Adrian and so danger-ously close to agreeing to be with him truly, publicly. Her heart was steadily overtaking her common sense, and apparently her sense had taken all her concentration with it on the way out.

She stood, finding Adrian right behind her, brows knitted as he fiddled with the espresso machine.

"Ooh, a new drink?" She adjusted the string of her embroi-dered lace-up top.

Adrian did a double take, glancing at her, his drink, her fingers, then back to his drink.

"Mhmm," he replied thickly.

"Can I try it?" She leaned forward trying to sniff out what-ever it was he was concocting.

"Ah ah ah, not until it's done." She pouted, and he dropped his voice low. "Maybe if you're very good and *don't* burn your-self again I'll give you a taste tomorrow."

Her eyes went wide, her cheeks scarlett. "Adrian!" She swatted at his arm.

"Yes, Lia?" He was utterly, infuriatingly calm.

She thought she'd melt, actually turn into a puddle right there in the middle of Apple Blossom.

"You can't just say things like that," she hissed, turning to rest her back against the syrup counter.

"Things like seasonal coffee drinks?" He flashed her a wicked grin.

"You know exactly what I mean."

"Do I?"

"Go back to your booth, it's not even your shift."

"Ooh, bossy, I like it."

"Go!"

She laughed as he turned, wiping her hands on a towel for something to do with her body. Then she noticed Darya and Elle at the register.

"Oh, hi!" she said brightly, walking over to them. Like cats hunting a cricket, their eyes flicked between her, Adrian, and each other.

"Someone has a *lot* of catching me up to do," Darya scowled.

Aurelia debated, how much had they heard? Could she deny it? Did she even want to? She bit her lip as a smile crept across her face, Darya and Elle squealed.

"Shhh!" Aurelia admonished them.

"Tell me everything!" Darya demanded, half climbing over the counter in excitement.

"Okay, okay, I'm done in an hour, come over and I'll make us dinner."

"And?" Darya asked expectantly.

"And, I'll tell you, you know," she trailed off. The three of them looked to Adrian who was, much to Aurelia's embarrassment, watching every word with the satisfied, feline smirk of his own.

"Alright, alright, are you two getting coffee or just trying to get me in trouble with Thlynda?"

Darya and Elle looked at each other and replied in unison, "Both."

ELLE AND DARYA took mercy on Aurelia, waiting until dinner was served before launching their inquisition.

Leaning into the season, Aurelia made ravioli stuffed with a cheesy pumpkin filling. She topped it with a thyme-infused brown butter and toasted crushed up hazelnuts that had her friends drooling.

Elle tried to help, but after bursting four of the little pumpkin-shaped packages, Aurelia relegated her to spreading whipped ricotta and figs over toasted slices of bread.

Darya, meanwhile, worked her magic on the balcony table. She gathered up candles and lit them on every surface she could find so the whole space glowed. Then she set out a blanket on the back of each chair and Enchanted Aurelia's plates with motifs of pumpkin vines and fall leaves.

In the center of the table, she gathered petite arrangements of flowers– sourced from Aurelia's blooming balcony– and little terracotta pots of herbs. Ducking outside, Aurelia thought for a moment that she had stepped into an entirely different world.

"This can't be my balcony," she half-asked half-shrieked at Darya.

"Oh, it was just a little of this, a little of that."

"How did I end up with the most talented, beautiful, generous friends on the planet?" Elle cooed, slinging her arms around both girls' shoulders.

"By being our eternal sunshine," Aurelia replied, leaning her head against Elle's.

"Okay, okay, let's eat before we all start crying," Elle said, pawing at her shining eyes.

"So about last Saturday," Aurelia began. She didn't let on that Elle had already heard most of this, and Elle, for her part, replied with just as much surprise, enthusiasm, and encouragement as she had the first time through.

"So you two are dating now?" Darya asked around a mouthful of pasta.

"Not exactly," Aurelia trailed off, scooping some of the strawberry, goat cheese, spinach salad onto her plate.

"Why for goodness's sake not?" Darya replied, spearing another ravioli and waving it around.

Aurelia took a big bite of salad.

"Nope, nope, nope. This dinner is delicious but you're not getting out of that one," Elle chided.

Aurelia swallowed and took a long sip of her sparkling cider. Her friends waited impatiently.

"I... I don't really know."

"Ah-hah!" Darya howled, shooting up to her feet then sitting again.

Aurelia sighed. "I had reasons, good reasons," she glanced over to Elle. "But the more time I spend with Adrian–"

"She means kissing Adrian," Elle teased with a wink.

"That too," Aurelia blushed. "The more time we spend together, the less those reasons seem to matter."

"Mhmm," her friends said, not letting their excitement slow down their forks.

"The reasons aren't, I mean, they haven't changed, they're not going to change. But maybe... I don't know... maybe since they're not going anywhere, I can be with Adrian for now?"

"That's what we've been saying," both girls nearly shouted.

"Okay, that whole saying the same thing at the same time thing is starting to get weird."

Darya and Elle looked at each other then looked back at Aurelia. "Lia has a boyfriend, Lia has a boyfriend," they sang with perfect synchronicity.

"Stop it!" Aurelia insisted, "I'm so serious!"

But they only got louder.

"You two!"

Aurelia tried to quiet them but was giggling so hard she tipped her chair, landing squarely on her butt. There was a brief pause as the girls peered around the table to make sure she was okay before the three were overtaken by side splitting, tear inducing laughter. Aurelia didn't even bother getting back in her chair, instead picking up her plate and settling herself on the floor.

Elle and Darya joined her, the three reclining against the iron balcony under flowering sweet peas and night blooming jasmine.

"I'm really doing this," Aurelia said at last, gazing up at the stars. A little sweet pea vine crawled down over her shoulder.

The three girls exchanged a look then let out a squeal of joy together.

CHAPTER THIRTY-TWO

The next morning, Aurelia, Darya, and Elle all woke early to go to Peace Lily together. They had stayed up so late into the night talking and laughing on the balcony that, by the time they cleaned up and headed inside, it made more sense for them to just stay the night.

"I can't believe you do this twice a week," Elle yawned as they filled their water bottles and slipped on shoes.

"You get used to it," Darya said as if it was midmorning and not still technically night.

"Mmm," was all Aurelia could manage.

It was a chilly morning but the studio was deliciously warm. The girls spread their mats out beside one another while the instructor lit amber and sandalwood incense sticks.

At the end of class, all three lay drenched in sweat, breathing deeply while the room picked up around them. Elle rolled to her side, whispering, "So when are you going to tell him?"

"Tell him?" Aurelia laid still, turning her head slightly to crack an eye open towards Elle.

"That you want to make it official." Darya said, rolling into a squat on her toes then lifting herself in an intricate hand balance they had worked on during class.

Aurelia pressed up to her elbows. "I think..." she started to whisper back before being met with a chorus of shushes from the other corner of the room.

"I'll tell you later," she mouthed to Elle as they pulled themselves up to standing.

Aurelia would never be over how blissful the Peace Lily showers were. The owners had stocked each stall with apple clove shower steamers, marshmallow pumpkin sugar scrubs, and moisturizing cardamom vanilla hair masks. She gleefully took advantage of all three while she gathered her thoughts.

The girls emerged from Peace Lily in an Autumnal daze.

"Okay, now I get why you two get up so early to come here. I could eat my own arm that scrub made me smell so good!" Elle joked.

"Easy there, little cannibal," Darya said, clutching onto Elle's arm.

"So I was thinking," Aurelia started.

"She's coming to us with details?" Elle asked in shock. "Are we taking the right girl home? What did you do with Lia?"

"Ha ha ha," Aurelia said, drawing out the words. "Do you want to hear or not?"

Elle flung her hands over her mouth.

"I'm going to tell him... that... that I... want to..."

Aurelia took a deep breath and rolled back her shoulders. She could do this.

"I'm going to tell him that I want to make it, us... official."

Darya let out a whoop but Elle was not so easily appeased.

"When?" Elle prompted.

"When?" Aurelia repeated. Why was this so hard, she wasn't even saying it to Adrian yet.

"Yes, when? On the way to campus? At work? Next week?"

"Oh, that's right, you two have a shift together this morning." Darya added. "I have class but maybe I can skip it. What about you, Elle? To watch? I mean... to support Lia?"

"Not at work!" Aurelia squeaked. "Um, I think... after our shift." The words felt branded into her skin, unshakable, permanent.

"That's good," Elle said.

"Good, that's good," Darya echoed.

"You think?"

"You'll have some time to relax, get some nerves out. He's waited this long, he can wait a few more hours."

Aurelia briefly wondered what Elle meant by Adrian waiting but the thought was quickly lost to a mixture of giddiness and terror. Not for Adrian, she knew he'd be happy, but for what it would mean for herself. We're jumping into the fire, she reminded herself. Jumping. Into. The fire.

"Good morning, Sparks," Adrian crooned as she opened the front door of her building. He leaned in the doorway, as he did every morning. Her heart managed to skip a beat each and every time.

"You know, if you're not going to let that go, I'm going to have to come up with a name for you." She gave him a long once over, taking her time as she drank in every detail of him. Her eyes danced from his wind-tousled hair, to the rings he wore on his fingers, to the way the sweater he wore stretched around his biceps. He gave her a feline smirk as she did.

"Peels?"

"Peels?" he asked as if he didn't understand, brows furrowed in that way that made the blue of his eyes shine.

"You know, banana, peel, banana peels."

"Uh huh, keep working on it, Sparks." He took her bag and then her hand, leading her across the street.

"Oh, I will," she promised with a slightly giddy laugh.

They were just stepping onto the opposite curb when he tugged on her hand, throwing her off balance. His free hand pressed into the small of her back, pulling her body tight against his as she let out a little yelp at losing her balance. He held her firm and dipped his head close.

"I look forward to it, beautiful," he whispered against her lips.

Her knees turned to jelly but he kept her upright as he pressed a slow, luxurious kiss to her mouth. The kind of kiss Princess Aurelia could never indulge in publicly but Lia, Lia could bask in moments like this.

With a smile she pulled back. "Breakfast first, then flattery."

"Flattery," Adrian gasped, one hand to his heart, "I was just stating the obvious, you can't blame me for having eyeballs. Have you seen yourself in a mirror today? You're..." he paused to drape an arm around her shoulder as they walked, "glowing."

"It's just the after burn from Peace Lily, today's class was hot" she said as they entered Calyntha's shop.

"Calyntha, doesn't sweet Lia here look beautiful today?"

"Stop!" Aurelia giggled.

Calyntha studied Aurelia then narrowed her furry-lidded eyes at Adrian. "Are you saying she doesn't look beautiful everyday?" She snapped her tongs in Adrian's direction.

"No... no, ma'am" Adrian stumbled. Calyntha winked at Aurelia.

On their way out of the shop, Calyntha leaned over the bar towards Aurelia, dropping her voice low, "Have to keep them on their toes, Lia, especially the pretty ones."

"Calyntha!" Aurelia gasped in her most scandalized voice.

Calyntha only snapped her tongs at them and returned to her work.

Adrian kept one arm slung over her shoulders all the way to campus. Once they crossed onto the main quad, though, he gave her temple a kiss then dropped his arm.

"You can... it's.." Aurelia started to say, but Adrian cut her off.

"It's okay, Lia, I'm in no rush."

"Thank you." Their eyes met, and she could tell he meant it.

She looped an arm through his, it wasn't as intimate as before, but she hoped he would know it meant something. Something good and new and hopeful.

He glanced down at their interlaced arms then gave her a quizzical look.

"After our shift, okay?" She tried to infuse her voice with all the happiness she felt, all the promise and excitement she had felt just an hour ago with Elle and Darya.

He nodded and squeezed her arm in reply. And as they walked, Aurelia didn't mind the little white daisies that sprung up in their wake.

THE SHIFT STARTED out as it always did, inventory checks, instructions from Thlynda, a rush of customers at ten to nine as everyone stopped by on their way to class.

Aurelia and Adrian made a dynamic team. Gone was all her distractedness from the day before. They sailed around each other like hummingbirds. Swooping and diving, pausing and twisting. It was so intoxicating, the way they flowed around and together and apart that when the first rush was over, she was actually a bit sad.

"That was fun," she grinned at Adrian. He leaned next to her, their shoulders pressed together.

He smiled down at her, "It's always fun working with you, Lia."

She bit her lip so the butterflies in her stomach couldn't escape. She wanted to tell him now. The words were on the tip of her tongue, but a customer approached the register before she could let them out.

Adrian stepped up to help them. *Good*, Aurelia thought, stick to the plan.

"So when do I get to try your super secret new drink?" she asked as he worked.

"Hmm, soon," he replied.

"Soon like now?" She leaned towards him.

"I suppose soon could be now, but I'm not telling you what it is until you try it. I need an unbiased test set to see if I hit the mark."

He called out, "White pumpkin mocha!" and placed the cup on the counter. Aurelia was momentarily dazed by the strong line of his shoulder as he reached forward. The customer came to collect their drink while Adrian started gathering supplies.

"So about before, can we go on a walk after this shift?" Aurelia asked, allowing the edge of her pinky finger to just graze his from where he worked beside her.

"A walk hmm?" He might have said more but Thlynda approached the counter.

"Adrian." I need you to go to the supply closet and get the bag of raw sugar from the upper shelf, it's too heavy for me to get something so high up. One day soon we're going to need to reorganize that closet."

"Sure thing, Thlynda."

She nodded and turned back to her booth, re-straightening a few already perfectly aligned cookies on her way.

"Hold that thought, I'll make this as soon as I get back." He let a slow smile cross his lips then ducked into the hallway towards the supply closet.

Aurelia watched him go, stepping forward to the middle of the service counter to look out over the café. Her café.

"Oh, Lia," a voice she recognized called, dragging out the last syllable like nails on a chalkboard.

Aurelia whipped her head around to see Thris leaning on the other end of the counter. How long had he been standing there?

"Come closer, Little Dove," Thris taunted. "I don't think you want your boy over there to hear after all." He nodded to where Adrian had been just moments before.

Against her better judgement, she obeyed.

Aurelia was a storm, emotions volatile and wild, every plant in the room seemed to feel it, swinging their faces, vines, leaves towards her, reaching out for her. Outside, thorny canes of trel-lised roses rattled in warning, fighting against their protective Enchantments to reach her. But Aurelia didn't notice anything beyond the boom of her heart and the hideous smirk widening across Thris's face.

He crooked a finger at her and she stepped closer, not wanting anyone to overhear whatever vile thing was about to spew from his stretched lips. He leaned in so far across the counter that she could feel the scratch of his beard on her cheek.

"Or perhaps I should call you..." he trailed off, drawing the moment out with excruciating slowness.

Aurelia's heart thundered, knowing yet unwilling to accept what he was about to say.

. . .

"Princess Aurelia?"

ACKNOWLEDGMENTS

In true Swiftie fashion, I have to start by thanking every person who's made it this far. Thank you for picking up this book, thank you for reading it, thank you for for laughing with me, for crying with me, for hoping with me, and for walking with me in Florevale.

Next, I have to thank my daughter Madelyn, the best of all the early readers who's always happy to listen to more of Mommy's "princess with too much magic" book. You inspire me with your kindness, empathy, and love every single day.

David, my best friend, my partner, my heart, and my toughest editor, this whole thing is really for you. I hope you read these words and know how much I love you. Always and forever.

To my family, Dad, Mom, Pop, Anna, Molly, thank you for the unending support, for being the best cheerleaders, first readers, and inspiration I could ask for.

Joey and Kili, my fur babies, thanks for sitting on my shoulder these last six months and making sure this story came out right. I know deep down, you're both truly dragonettes.

Thank you to all of my wonderful beta readers. Grace, Jennifer, Chelsea, Madeline, Sam, Jade, Grady, this book is only what it is because of your feedback, thank you for so much love and encouragement and for finding so many places to add a bit more magic.

To Amy, the most talented, kindhearted, incredible artist and cover designer, I don't even know how to put into words my gratitude for your time, artistry, and care. I will genuinely treasure each piece you created for these covers for the rest of my life and I can not wait to dive into writing book two just so we can continue dreaming together.

Most of all, I have to thank my savior Jesus Christ, without whom none of these stories would be possible. You're the love that fills me every day.

And one last acknowledgement...

To David (yes, again), thanks for taking me to watch the sunrise from the Dana rooftop at Bucknell. We might not have had all the colors of Lia and Adrian's morning but I wouldn't trade these past thirteen years for anything.

ABOUT THE AUTHOR

KATIE TRAUFFER

Author, Wedding Photographer, Dreamer

As a destination film wedding photographer, Katie considers herself an expert in love stories.

She wrote her first in third grade (during a unit on Greek mythology, her heroine "Tornada" scoured the Earth to find a lost love), and grew up on a steady diet of Lord of the Rings, Ralph Waldo Emerson, and, of course, Disney princesses. Today she lives in Maryland with her college sweetheart David and their beautiful daughter Madelyn.

When she's not traveling the world photographing love, tending her ever-expanding heirloom rose garden, baking "rainbow unicorn" cookies, or savoring gluten-free treats in a garden in Paris, you can usually find her curled up with her cats, an iced latte, and a great book.